A Boston Homecoming

Ron Iannone

Destination Press
Morgantown, West Virginia

ISBN: 978-0998202013

To Mary
for being
Mary

If I stoop
Into a dark tremendous sea of cloud,
It is but for a time;
I press God's lamp to my breast;
Its splendor, soon or late,
Will pierce the gloom;

I shall emerge one day.

—*from* Robert Browning's *Paracelsus*

1

It was late afternoon, and I was sitting at my desk correcting papers. Outside, freezing rain was falling on the campus of Wheeling State University. It was the winter of 1971.

I was getting frustrated because so many students were failing the exam I had given them. In a little while, I shoved all the papers to one side, turned in my chair, away from the desk, and stood up.

In the distance, the trees looked like they were being skillfully sculpted by a master glass blower. Directly in front of me, the cars moved slowly up the glassy blacktopped road. Along its sides, brand new gray rectangular buildings stood. Some ten stories high. The result of the recent coal boom, I thought. The administrators wanted Wheeling State to get all they missed out on during the last twenty or thirty years. They were yearning to be a first-rate university like Ohio State, Penn State and others. Old buildings were being torn down, new ones were being built, and more professors were being hired. Last year, they finished building a twenty-five-million-dollar football stadium. Everyone now expected that respectability would be achieved very soon.

A bus carrying students between classes stopped, and then slouching, long-haired, gray-faced students quickly filed out with their umbrellas popped up and collars pulled tightly around their necks. Behind, moving too fast for this kind of day, I saw a blue university maintenance truck slam on its brakes as it approached the rear of the bus. Swerving from one side to the other on the slick road, the bus in front took off just in time. After this, the truck slid out of control making a half circle, turning wildly, and then stopped abruptly in the middle of the ice-covered lawn. Two stocky men, wearing blue and yellow parkas, quickly jumped out, stared at the front of the truck for a while, shook their heads, got back in and slowly drove off the lawn onto the road, leaving behind two deep ruts. I wondered if the ruts would still be there come spring.

Nothing ever heals completely, nothing.

The phone rang. Startled, I jerked back toward the desk.

Finally, I went over and picked up the receiver. "Yes," I mumbled, barely getting out the word.

"It's your wife, Chris. She says it's important," Fay, my secretary, said in an uneasy voice. Fay was twenty-two but looked sixteen. Freckled, light-ivory face. Sandy brown hair. No chest. Young, but she was efficient and motherly. Before Fay, I had had six secretaries who were either too lazy, too stupid, or too concerned with reaching age twenty without a husband.

"I hope nothing is wrong," Fay now said with deep concern.

"I do too," I said, carefully forming my words.

"She's on 61," she said. Then she hung up.

I pushed in the 61 extension button.

"Yes," I answered.

"Vinnie?" Her tone was hurried.

"What's wrong?" I asked, expecting her to tell me that she was taking the kids bowling after school, paying an overdue bill, making arrangements for a get-together or asking me to stop at the grocery store after work for some milk. These were normal important things she called about.

"Your mother called," she said, "and said that Uncle Louie died last night. They think it was his heart."

"Oh, that poor son of a bitch," I said, shaking my head.

"Vinnie!" she said in an accusing tone of voice. She hated swearing.

"Your mother wants you to fly home for the funeral. She said Aunt Concetta is expecting you."

I said nothing.

"I'll start packing some of your clothes now. Okay, Hon?" her voice was more gentle.

Thanks, I love you Chris. Always so thoughtful. I don't deserve you.

"Okay, dear, I'll see you in a little while."

"Bye," she said.

"Bye, dear, thanks," I said. I hung up as I tried to concentrate on what Uncle Louie looked like. But I couldn't. I was worried about facing my father again. Eight years was a long time. I felt sweat underneath my arms.

I went over and sat down at my desk. I picked up some papers from the in-basket and tried to read them. I couldn't. I thought about some one-liners I had written. *Beneath the subtle murmurs of the sea. I hear someone playing a song for me. I struggle daily to understand my strangeness and to keep myself from anonymity.*

The Pittsburgh International Airport terminal came into sight. The stark nakedness, the rawness of the cement, glass and steel was now in front of me as I drove the car around a traffic circle, and without much trouble found a place in a huge parking lot. Wheeling had an airport, but it could only accommodate small aircraft.

I felt good. Now I liked the whole idea of getting away for a while. Lately, I thought, I've been drinking entirely too much wine at night in order to block out boredom.

After picking up my ticket at the Appalachian Airlines counter, I went down an escalator and through the security's x-ray machine. They confirmed my suspicions that I was not a hijacker carrying a huge bomb. I then walked toward Gate 20 where my flight was to board.

The red carpeted boarding gates of Appalachian Airlines were arranged in a circle. It reminded me of one of those sparkling new cinema lobbies that house three or four movie theatres. In a sense, I thought, both are temporary holding places for people who hope to fulfill fantasies beyond some doors, or in this case, beyond some gate.

I was checked in by a wise-cracking, blond, curly-haired counter attendant who was trying to impress a doll-faced stewardess standing next to him. I wondered how long it would be before both of them were in bed together.

I found an empty seat near a back wall. Then I surveyed the room. To my left, a stocky, middle-aged man with sad eyes was standing alone reading a *Playboy*. He closed it. His multicolored, silk shirt was unbuttoned at the collar so that his grayish-black, pubic-like chest hair peeked through. To my right, a young girl wearing an oversized blue sweatshirt and faded blue jeans kept staring at the paperback in front of her as if she was looking at it but really not reading it. Her long brown hair, which hung below her slouching shoulders, needed to be combed. Her face was narrow and triangular shaped. Once I caught her looking at me, but she quickly looked away.

I saw an elegant-looking lady standing near one of the long, narrow, silty windows that dotted this part of the terminal. She was staring out. Then she glanced over her shoulder and quickly back again. Her whole manner seemed cultured. She looked like Jacqueline Kennedy, tall, with lion's mane black hair falling over her square shoulders. She was wearing a smartly tailored green pantsuit.

The call to board came. The stewardess with short, peach-colored hair greeted everyone with computer-like politeness. "Hi." "Hello." "Welcome." "Hi." Pure phoniness. Enough to drive one mad.

I slowly moved down the aisle. Passengers in front of me were putting things in the overhead rack. On my left, I caught sight of the Jacqueline Kennedy look-alike. There was my seat, next to her. I quickly slid into the vacant seat. She was sitting next to the window. She turned and smiled. I smiled back.

I thought how I had always loved to watch Jacqueline Kennedy on TV during the Sixties because of the mysterious, sensuous, foreign look about her. Spanish more than anything else. Her wide-open, dark eyes and that crescent moon grin of hers always warmed me.

After a few minutes we were flying above the thick cotton clouds. Nothing below us was visible. The sky was clear and blue. A bright sun shined. It looked warm.

"Going to Boston?" I asked, leaning back against the seat and partly turning my head toward her.

She turned and nodded. "Yes."

"Are you from Boston?" I asked.

"No," she said. "I'm going to a conference. It's being held at the Sheraton-Boston." Her voice was friendly but her face was too serious.

"That's a nice place, you'll enjoy it," I said.

"That's what I hear. Have you been there?" she asked.

"Not lately," I said, trying to sound casual while also quickly deciding to keep the conversation centered on her. That memory was still there—the nightly search for whores, and I didn't want to take a chance of spoiling this situation by her asking why not lately. "Are you from Pittsburgh?"

"Yes," she said. "I used to live in Fox Hill. But now I live in the city and I'm enjoying every minute of it," she emphasized. "How about you?"

"I teach math at Wheeling State and live just outside of Wheeling in Baywood."

"Oh, you teach, huh?" she asked smiling. "How do you like it?"

"Some days are better than others."

"I know what you mean," she said. "I just started teaching again and have had the same feeling. I love them some days and hate them others. I used to teach high school. Now I teach English Composition at Carnegie Mellon; the college student is so different. Of course, I haven't taught in fifteen years. Thank God I have an eighteen-year-old daughter who's a freshman there. She's just been wonderful in helping me understand students today."

I shook my head. "God, you don't look like a woman who has an eighteen-year-old daughter."

She smiled, hesitating. "I was married for twenty years but got a divorce last year."

"Look," I said quickly, "I know sometimes people have things to do and don't want to be bothered on a plane. So please feel free to stop. Really, I don't want to interrupt anything you had planned."

I felt embarrassed because I was getting too personal. Even though her being divorced made her all the more alluring.

"No, you're not," she said. "I'm enjoying your company."

"Well, I'm Vinnie Serrano," I said, sticking out my hand.

She reached over and with a strong, warm grip shook it. "I'm Angie Castro."

"You're Italian?" I asked, feeling great now for at least we would have something in common to talk about if everything else failed.

"Yes. My married name was Peters. Angie Peters. How's that for a good American name?"

"Pretty good," I said, laughing. "Have many people told you that you looked like Jacqueline Kennedy?"

She blushed. "Yes, a few."

I had a feeling she didn't want to talk about it. And yet I had another feeling that made me think that she really liked the comparison.

The stewardess broke in and took our order for drinks. She ordered a screwdriver, and I ordered a Scotch on the rocks. I was surprised at what she ordered. A martini would seem to be more her style.

Both of us took huge gulps after they were placed in front of us.

"Was the divorce hard on you?" I then asked.

"At first it was," she said, "but it was all worth the initial pain. The freedom and happiness that followed was wonderful. The biggest decisions I had to make before the divorce were like, what country club we would have lunch at, what style for my new tennis outfit, what to serve for a party, where would we go for our vacation, France, the Caribbean or Switzerland. Then, one day, I saw that all of that was attached to my husband's life, the three-hundred-thousand-dollar home, country clubs and all. I had no life except what belonged to him." She quickly glanced out the window and then back again.

I thought perhaps it was still painful for her. "What did your daughter think about all of this?" I now asked.

"I think she thought it was best for both of us," she said in a sincere tone of voice. "She's happier now. I just couldn't be like some of the other wives of my husband's friends who complained day after day about their depressing lives but never did anything about it. Sure, some ran to therapy groups, psychiatrists, consciousness raising groups, but it never got any better for them. They're unwilling to give up their opulence and material comforts. They're sucked in too far just like their robot-like husbands. One night I heard a professor from the Yale Divinity School speak at the University of Pittsburgh. He said people like my husband are caught up with themselves and the gospel of self-fulfillment. Always looking for big and bigger Big Macs for themselves. But the more they have the less secure they become. They could not stand being needy. He said people don't know how to live with needs or with neediness. I think that's the word he used. He said in turn they preach the gospel of self-fulfillment to people around them. They want the other people to be like them and then they won't feel guilty." She stopped for a moment and took a sip from her drink. She, like me, seemed more relaxed.

I couldn't believe a woman as beautiful as her was telling me her whole life story. I had never been unfaithful to Chris, even though I had thought of it. My darkened past and Catholic upbringing had kept me from doing what many other married men were doing all the time.

"After I went home that night," she continued, "I told my husband what I heard at the lecture. I asked him to just take a minute to look at our lives outside of accumulating material possessions. He wouldn't do it. He said I was just getting carried away with the Women's Libbers. Hell, it wasn't just a women's thing, it was for all human beings. That's when I told him that our life was going nowhere. It was also going nowhere sexually. It was cold and mechanical like the computer he worked with. You know, I used to wish he was impotent so he would stop trying. Can you understand how I felt?"

I flinched and felt weak. I had never talked to a woman about what actually happens in sex. Chris and I only talked about the right time, the God Almighty right time, and that was the extent of our sex talk. *Saints don't talk about those things. It's dirty.*

"Yes," I finally said, quietly.

"It was amazing, just amazing," she said, "how people could be so insensitive. What used to really burn me was when he would come home at night and tell me about the great conversation he was having with some female at the office. 'It was very stimulating,' was always the remark he made. Of course, our conversations were not stimulating, even though he used a lot of my ideas. I was nothing. Finally one day, I told him I was leaving him and I wanted a divorce. He didn't fight it and I wasn't surprised. I had a feeling at the time he was having an affair with one of his secretaries. The funny thing was that he thought I should go to a therapist. He had been going to one for the last ten years and I guess he thought I was crazy too. Anyway, I moved out with my daughter and for the first time in my life I started to feel happy about myself as a woman and as a human being. I know, I know, you're thinking to yourself that sounds like corny Women's Liberation rhetoric. But it's real for me. It is! I now have a future to look forward to. Most of all, I got me and...."

A lackadaisical voice suddenly started speaking over the plane's public address system. It was the pilot telling us that because of a problem with an air pressure gauge we had to land in Rochester, New York, for some repairs. He assured us that it was no big problem and that it should only take about an hour to fix.

"Good ole Trepidation Airlines," she said sarcastically.

"Yeah, that's about it," I laughed halfheartedly.

We sat in silence now. She seemed suddenly shy, maybe because she had exposed too much of herself.

When I heard the plane's wheels skidding and thumping underneath, I turned and asked, "What are you going to do?"

"I guess I'll walk around the airport for a while," she said.

"Would you like to get a drink?"

"Sure, I'd love to," she said, touching my arm.

In a few minutes the plane stopped. We got up. As I let her go ahead of me, she brushed against my body. Immediately I felt my face get hot, and soon I was trembling with desire for her.

The airport lounge was dark. Almost too dark to see. Dark barnwood paneling covered the walls. Two men who looked like salesmen sat at one end of a long, circular bar.

We took a seat in a booth, near one corner of the bar, facing the entrance. A tired-looking waitress came over and took our order. After the waitress left, Angie said, "I hope you're a great drinker. Appalachian Airlines is well known for turning one-hour delays into ten-hour delays."

"I am," I lied.

She studied me for a second and said, "You don't look it."

"My looks are deceiving," I said. "I'm really sixty years old and have been drinking a quart of Scotch since I was twelve."

She laughed and then started talking about a book she was reading. She said the author, a woman, used a character by the name of Theresa to really express her own insecurities about sex. "It was quite evident," she said, "because no woman could write about those sexual experiences she wrote about without experiencing them firsthand."

I felt myself blushing.

"Do you write?" she asked.

"Y... yes," I stammered.

"What kinds of things do you write?"

The waitress now brought our drinks, and I quickly took a sip of my drink before I answered. "Up to this point, just pure mathematical stuff, but now I'm getting ready to write something I think is very significant."

"A novel?"

"Oh no," I said quickly. "It's more philosophical than anything else."

"Hey, don't tell me you're one of those intellectual tweedy types," she said, smiling.

"No, just a hard-working Italian who's trying to express what he feels inside."

"Good for you," she said. "There are still too many male writers writing about how the man always conquers the woman. Pure macho crap, you know!"

"You're right," I said. "I have always felt the deep mysteries that lie behind the male's ego are seldom written about. What if I told you I was a virgin when I got married?"

"I wouldn't believe you," she said, suddenly serious and hard. "Sometimes people live in a fantasy world and won't accept their own truth."

"See, maybe what you just said explains it all," I said firmly.

"Nothing," she said, "ever explains it all. I just know too many men and that's why I find it hard to believe you."

"But that sort of contradicts what you said earlier about male writers always writing about men conquering women. Don't you think?"

"No, I don't believe so," she said, her voice rising. "I was just saying that I'm sick and tired of male writers dumping on females by constantly telling the world how great they are in bed."

"Okay, I can accept that," I said in a friendlier tone of voice. I was no longer bothered by her refusal to believe me because it was such a little thing to get worked up about. Especially, I thought, since I was really enjoying myself. So I decided to change the subject by asking her if she wanted another drink. "How about another drink?"

"Sure," she said quickly.

I felt she understood what I was trying to do because soon the serious expression on her face was gone and she was smiling again.

With the mood now back to where it was when we were on the plane, we started to get pleasantly drunk together.

I was feeling loose, very loose. Then a comforting, sexy female voice came over the public address system and announced that due to a Nor'easter moving over Boston, our flight was now canceled and we were grounded in Rochester for the night. She also went on to say that Appalachian Airlines had put our luggage on buses and that the buses were now waiting to take us to the Mount Hope Inn in Rochester.

"I bet," Angie laughed, "that Trepidation Airlines bribed Mother Nature so that they wouldn't be hassled for being delayed."

"A good point," I laughed too.

The bus was almost filled up with passengers when we arrived. We couldn't sit with each other, but when the bus stopped in front of the Mount Hope Inn, I went up front to where she was sitting and asked, "How about dinner tonight?"

"Excellent idea," she said, "but give me an hour or so. I want to take a shower and clean up a bit."

"Okay, then stop by my room when you're ready, and we'll have a drink before we go to dinner."

"Vinnie, are you trying to seduce me?" she asked, laughing.

"No," I lied. "Really I..."

"That's okay," she said, "don't say any more. I'll be there in an hour." I dropped off my bags in my room and left immediately to find a liquor store and drugstore. I wanted to buy an expensive bottle of white wine and some condoms.

I asked a skinny, very pale-faced clerk at the front desk where I could find a drugstore. He told me there was one in a shopping center two blocks up the street. When I reached the drugstore, I was trembling. I stood outside for a long time staring at a cosmetics display. I couldn't believe it; here I was thirty-two years old and scared shitless of buying rubbers. *This is ridiculous, Vinnie, hell they're being sold like cigarettes now. Everyone uses them. Even nuns and priests.*

Finally, I went in. I looked and looked all over the drugstore but no rubbers. *Damn, damn, damn, Vinnie, just your damn luck, of all the drugstores in Rochester, this one doesn't sell them.*

I looked at my watch. I was wasting time. Quickly I went over to a female, pimple-faced clerk who looked about fourteen, and asked in a deep Southern accent where she kept lotions for vaginal diseases. I figured they had to be in the same area. She told me with no expression on her face, Aisle 3B. But she didn't fool me. *Horny son of a bitch, was really what she thought.*

I found the condoms, picked up a pack of Trojans, paid the clerk, and rushed out. I veered right and walked until I came to a liquor store where I bought a bottle of white wine.

When I got back to the Inn, I felt like I'd start climbing the walls. I didn't know what to do until she would come. I couldn't wait. I looked at my watch and saw that I had a half hour to waste. I prayed that it would go by quickly. I opened the wine and poured myself a glass. It helped.

Then I remembered the condoms. I wanted to place them in a convenient place so when the time came they would be accessible. I opened the box, took out one of the foil wrapped packages, tore it open, and nervously slid out this slimy-feeling thing. Goddamn, it was greasy. It was disgusting.

My stomach started to tighten. Other thoughts penetrated my mind. *What if she gets pregnant, wants to keep the baby, causes trouble, goes to the university, Chris finds out, then the kids... hell, it's not worth it, I bet once we get started, I won't even know it's on right.* Now concentrate on where to put it so that it will be easily accessible to you. Okay. I thought about placing it under the pillow, but no, it might fall on the floor if our sexual gymnastics got hot and heavy. I looked around the room as I slid it back into the opened package. I smiled to myself as I then thought about placing it in the Gideon Bible, which was lying on the bedside table. I could see myself pulling it out while at the same time citing a particular lurid chapter and verse. *Come on, Vinnie, get serious now.*

Finally I decided to place it underneath the left side of the bed. Then I lay down on the bed and with my left hand I tried to reach down and grab it quickly. It didn't work. My left arm felt too cramped. *Shit.* So I tried the same thing on the right side. *Fine. Perfect.*

I looked at my watch. Still time for a shower, I thought. I took a real hot one.

Afterwards I slapped cologne all over my body, and half-dressed I jumped on the bed and practiced a couple more times reaching down and grabbing the condoms from underneath the bed. *Still perfect.*

I got up and slid on my midnight-blue, button-down shirt. I remembered Chris getting mad at me because I always wore, she said, dark mourning clothes. I didn't care. With my shirt still unbuttoned, I looked at myself in the mirror and patted my stomach with short, quick slaps. Not bad for a thirty-two-year-old, I thought, but still too much loose skin around the waist. I must go on a diet. Then slowly I ran my hands over my bare chest. Smooth and not too hairy. However, I wished I was taller and not so round-shouldered. Next, I looked at my face. Kinda ugly, I thought. My nose was too beaked, and my brown eyes always seemed tired.

After I finished buttoning my shirt, I looked at my watch. It was almost time. Tension started to creep into my body. My armpits were wet. *Another problem, Vinnie Serrano, you sweat too much.* I tried reading a real estate brochure. But I couldn't. Then I turned on the TV. Nothing on. I switched to the FM radio channel. Soft, soothing music was playing.

I looked at my watch again. She was late. I started to get upset. *Here I am going through all this shit and she's probably out trying to seduce someone else, damn nymphomaniac.* I felt miserable now. My head started to throb near the temples. I took a large gulp of wine. It didn't help.

Please God, if she comes, I'll go to daily mass and communion for two weeks. Please don't let me down now.

An hour later, I called her room. She answered on the first ring. "Hello."

"Angie?"

"Yes! Vinnie?" Her voice was tense. "God, I was worried, I called to find out what room you were in and they said you weren't registered."

"I can't believe it."

"I know I couldn't either. They kept insisting they didn't have any Vinnie Serrano registered here."

"Well, good thing I called.

"Yes, good thing. I've been sitting here for the last hour wondering what to do."

"It's okay now, we still got the whole night. I'm really looking forward to seeing you, dear." *Why did I say that "dear."*

"So am I," she laughed. "Dear." She laughed again.

"See you in a little while."

"Vinnie," she interrupted anxiously. The intake of breath got louder over the receiver, "the room number."

"Sorry," I said, shaking my head. "Almost blew it again. It's 1137."

"Thanks, I'll be there in a few minutes."

"Okay, bye." I hung up.

Right after, I called the desk clerk and asked him if he remembered being asked for Vinnie Serrano's room. He said he did. Then I asked him in a nasty tone of voice, "Who do you have registered in Room 1137?" Politely he said, "I can't seem to make out the name, sir. It looks like Vannie Semono, or Vanna Seumano... something like that."

Then in an apologetic tone of voice, I spelled out my name for him. Slowly and clearly. I remembered what a nun once told me. "Vincent, your handwriting reminds me of a crazy boy I once knew."

I heard her two weak knocks at the door. I gave the room a quick going over. I just hope I'm able to get to that condom in time.

As I hurried over to the door, I turned off all the lights except for one small lamp near the TV. Now everything was set. I opened the door.

"Hi," she said. Smiled shyly.

"Hi," I said.

Now with my hand sweeping back, I motioned for her to come in. As she did, she brushed by me, electrifying me. I followed her in and closed the door.

She looked more elegant and more beautiful than earlier today. She wore a light-green jersey dress that gently curved around her firm breasts. Her lovely black hair looked fluffy and washed. The dim yellow light made her olive face more shadowy, more mysterious, and even more alluring.

She stopped in front of the mirror and carefully rubbed her hand over the Mediterranean-styled desk.

"Oh, how nice," she laughed, "just like mine."

"Yes, uniformity holds America and hotels together," I said.

She laughed, turned around, and scanned the room.

"How about a glass of white wine?" I asked.

"I'd love it," she replied quickly. I hope, I thought, she doesn't spot the condoms under the bed.

There was a long period of silence as I handed her a glass of wine. Perhaps she was thinking, like me, about being in a hotel room with a person you hardly knew while at the same time realizing what the consequences could be later on.

I poured myself some wine and led her to the edge of the bed. We sat down. An instrumental arrangement was playing on the FM station.

"Where's your family from in Italy?" I asked.

I wondered when I was going to make my move. How long would it take to get the wine glass out of her hand, undress her, get on top of her, slip the condom on, and make love.

She slid back onto the bed, kicked off her shoes and leaned back against the headboard. She dropped her long and slender legs over one another. Her stony face was turned on again. Serious and very little expression.

"Both my father and mother came from a small island near Venice. They were married there when they were about sixteen. Then my father came over here with my mother in order to join his brother who was working in a coal mine near Uniontown, Pennsylvania. He got my father a job. And for eight years my father worked as a coal miner. But he couldn't stand it. He hated bosses. He wanted to be his own boss. He then tried carpentry but failed miserably. Finally, another brother who lived in Pittsburgh got him started in the grocery store business. And for the last thirty years that's what he's been doing until last year when he retired."

She took a long, silent sip of wine, looked at me obliquely and continued with her story. "I feel sorry for him now. These days all he talks about is going back to the old country. I don't blame him. Both he and my mother worked their asses off for my three brothers and me. Two are MDs and one is a screwed-up musician who lives in New Orleans. They were always worrying whether or not America would accept their children. If I couldn't please people then I wasn't a good American. And for a long while I had a hell of a lot of guilt because of being raised this way. I think it was also harder on the females in the Italian American families. I was taught that the place of an Italian girl in America was to be quiet, find a nice boy, get married, have kids, and, oh, of course, don't bother anyone. Keep your mouth shut was my mother's motto. Sacrifice." She shook her head and peered into her glass. "How about you?"

"I can't remember too much of my growing up time," I lied.

"You're lucky," she nodded, "I remember my mother running our house with a nonstop yell. In a way I couldn't blame her. During the day she worked her fingers off, wrapping shoe boxes in a shoe factory, and at night she had to feed all of us, even though at times I helped. Then, after supper, she would start cleaning the house. She was almost obsessed with cleanliness. She wouldn't let me help because she said I had to study. Over and over again, she told me she wanted me to go to college so I could meet a smart lawyer, doctor, or engineer, then get married and not end up like her."

"My mother was also a clean nut. She had foil on all the handles in the kitchen."

"Well, it must be a common characteristic of all Italian families," she said. "My mother also treated sex this way. Everything about it, for her, was dirty. To this day I haven't lost all the shame and guilt she taught me. Pleasure was always bad. Once when I was sixteen I told her about a dream I had about a boy in my class. Before I knew what was happening, she had me kneeling next to her on the floor, saying the rosary and praying for forgiveness to the Virgin Mary."

"Thank God, we can forget those days," I lied.

"I wish I could," she said. "During the first two years of college, I was always running to a priest after a boy tried to kiss or feel me. That was until a young priest tried to lay me in the confessional. Still, when I first got married I used to shake if I had to talk to men other than my husband. And if I found myself in such a situation at a party, shivers used to run down my body and eventually I would get sick to my stomach. Even with all my reading in literature, I didn't know it was normal to have sexual feelings about other men. I was very naïve."

I bet she would die if she knew I've never been to a pornographic movie or even read a pornographic book.

I heard her say "...but once I realized how my husband was using my naïveté, I started to despise him. And it was after this realization that I started to read books not for English class per se, but for personal meaning. That really helped. My friends also really helped me at this time to work through a lot of what Ed was doing to me. I told Ed that something was going on inside of me and I wanted to share it with him. But all he could say was that therapy would help me." Her voice quavered a bit. "Did I tell you that's what he said when I asked him for a divorce?"

"Yes," I lied, I couldn't remember if she did or didn't.

"Also, did I tell you about my family's reaction to the divorce?" she asked. Her face was quite serious now.

"I don't think so," I said.

"Well they thought I was crazy," she said, as her face blushed red. "I know my mother thought I was going directly to Satan. The evening I told them, they said I would suffer the rest of my life, and my daughter would grow up to be a whore because of not having a father. That was a laugh. Living the way we were, it was the only choice for her. It would be the only way for her to block out the crap she saw around her, from drunken cocktail parties, to drug parties, to wife swapping parties. It was around us, even though we never did any such thing.

I should say *I* didn't.... Well, after about a year my parents started to talk to me. It's still hard for them to accept the divorce. I guess, realizing their background, I understand now and perhaps I would've reacted the same way. I just don't know." Her eyes were welling up and her slender legs were slightly opening up.

"I'm glad you're making it," I said. "In a way, I'm envious." I gently took her half-finished glass of wine from her hand and along with mine placed it on the floor. We kissed. Softly at first. Then harder. Her mouth opened wide, she moved her watery lips around, around, and around on mine. Then her tongue licked my lips, teeth, and for a while stayed twisted around mine. We stopped, got up, and got undressed. She got in bed first, cuddling under the covers. I followed, reaching down for the condom. It worked. My hand fell right on it as I picked it up with only my thumb and forefinger.

"How do I get this on?" I asked seriously. I took it out of the foil package, held it in front of me, hoping that maybe she could see it.

She turned over and stared at the thing between my fingers for a long moment as if she was trying to focus on it in the dim light.

"What the hell... how?" she chuckled. "That's your business, I don't know anything about them."

Finally, somehow, I slipped it on and then I turned over and placed my arms down on each side of her head. And we did it.

I loved it, but I also hated it because of my insecurities and thoughts of Chris. Now I wanted out, and quickly. We finished, but she must have been satisfied, as she drifted into a deep sleep in my arms. I was wide awake so I got up, walked over to the window. Snowflakes, illuminated by the Inn's parking lot lights leisurely fell on the already snow-covered ground.

I felt depressed as I thought about Chris. God, she would kill herself if she ever knew. And the children. I could see Paulie's and Linda's eyes staring at me with pity and abandonment.

Feeling terribly guilty now, I got dressed. Put on my watch, and went out, closing the door quietly behind.

I started to walk along a four-lane highway, which was separated by an island that had thick shrubs and small fruit-like trees peeking through from underneath large banks of recently plowed and old-piled snow. The world seemed to have no edges tonight. It was white and smooth like the shining moon above. Only a few whipped snowdrifts here and there spoiled the scene.

I remembered the time when our friend Wanda Stone asked me if I had ever fooled around with other women. I said no. She didn't believe me. She said all men fooled around, they can't see girls as friends and only as lovers. I disagreed. Then one night after one of Chris's get-togethers, Chris asked me to walk Wanda home because Frank, her husband, never showed up. When we reached her door, she turned and kissed me on the lips, and embarrassingly I held on to her as she broke away. "I understand, Vinnie," she laughed smartly, then turned and walked in. I avoided talking to her for weeks afterwards, angry because she knew the truth. She was beautiful and I would've given anything to have her for a night.

Ahead, in the white speckled distance, I saw a figure approaching. It looked like a dark, moving branch with a very thin layer of snow. I was scared for a moment. As the figure got closer, I could see that it was a man; his face was buried in a thick, fur coat-collar.

After he passed me, I stopped, turned and looked at the man fading into the dark shadows of the night. I imagined that it was an old part of me fading away while another part of me was being reawakened after being suppressed for so long. Then I wondered if tonight would reawaken other things, which I doubted now I was ready for.

Stop it, Vinnie.

Later, after walking a couple more blocks, I found a McDonald's open. I went in, ordered a Big Mac and a large orange Crush. After my order arrived, I sat down in the rear and ate like someone who hadn't eaten in days. As I drank my Crush, I looked around the restaurant. Near the entrance sat a man with a puffy face, he sipped at his cup every so often. He glanced over at me. Quickly I lowered my head and looked into my half-finished drink.

After a while I looked up again. The man with the puffy face was gone. Just three clerks remained behind the counter. Two were young girls. One had a plump figure with baby blue eyes; the other had a tight ass with long blond hair falling like silk against the middle of her back. Standing next to the tight-ass girl was a tall dark-haired boy. I doubted any one of them was over eighteen. The two girls were now giggling at something the dark-haired boy was showing them.

How I wish, I thought, I was young like them.

After I finished eating, I got up, walked over to a trash container, threw my Big Mac wrapper and the empty drink cup in, and then smiled at the tight-ass girl who was smiling at me. I wondered if my first affair would've been easier with a girl like her than an experienced divorcée like Angie.

As I walked to the Inn, I decided that I couldn't go back to the room. I wanted to stay away as long as possible, hoping, praying, that she would go back to her room.

When I reached the Inn, I went directly to the lounge area, which was to one side of the main desk. The pale-faced clerk was still working. He looked at me suspiciously as I sat down in a large overstuffed chair. Then I leaned back, closed my eyes, and waited for sleep to come.

2

At first I didn't know where I was when I heard loud talking in the background. Then I opened my eyes and saw three sharply dressed men checking out at the hotel counter. I looked at my watch. It was nearly seven thirty. I wondered if Angie was still in my room.

The door was open as I slowly walked in, cautiously. All the lights were turned on. I sniffed. Traces of that smell still remained. I glanced over to the bed. It was empty. Thank God, only the twisted covers at the foot of the bed reminded me of last night.

I walked to the bathroom.

The phone began to ring, and I hurried out of the bathroom to answer it. A female voice on the other end said that my flight to Boston would leave at nine thirty. Also she said that the airline would reimburse me for the taxi ride to the airport; the buses were not available.

As I hung up, I sighed with relief. I couldn't wait to leave this room. I called a taxi, packed, washed, and left the room where I lost my fidelity to Chris and the kids.

Ahead, in the parking lot, I saw the green and white cab waiting with its engine running. As I reached it, I saw the figures of a man and woman sitting in the back. A heavy-set taxi driver with dark rings under bloodshot eyes got out, took my suitcase, and asked, "Going to the airport?"

"Yes."

"Okay," he said. "The other two are also going."

"Fine," I lied. I was in no mood to share the cab.

I opened the front door and nodded politely to the couple in the back.

The woman smelled strongly of a perfume that made me grimace. She smiled. She did not look more than thirty. Her long platinum hair fell over the shoulders of a white fur coat, and her lips were unusually wide, smeared here and there with dark rose lipstick. In her hand she clutched a small pearl-studded, black purse. I thought she was rather attractive in a lustful kind of way. The man, gray-haired and dressed in a gray tweed overcoat with an expensive-looking shirt and tie, was sitting next to her, a *New York Times* lying on his lap. I figured he was somewhere in his mid-forties or older.

I got in beside the driver and closed the door. I stared straight ahead as the cab drove off. We sat in silence until from behind my left ear a voice asked, "Were you on the grounded flight to Boston?" She sounded like a New York waitress imitating a Southern belle. She failed miserably.

"Yes," I said as unfriendly as I could. The woman was already bothering me. I turned around and watched her more intently.

"So were we," she said flirtatiously.

"That's nice," I said.

"The weather is supposed to be clear today in Boston," she said. "Isn't that right, Hon? Didn't they say that on the news this morning?"

The man yawned, "Yes," cupping his hand over his mouth. Then he started to read the *New York Times* with a sleepy expression on his face. He looked bored with the world. His hands were fine boned and manicured like a woman's.

"I'm glad," I said. I turned around and looked straight ahead at the partially snow-covered road. I thought perhaps when I got to the airport I should go back to West Virginia instead of Boston.

"Well, we're looking forward to the trip to Boston," she said, "My husband is presenting a paper at Harvard. He's an engineer at Kodak, you know."

"Is that right?" I asked, trying to sound impressed. The man still stared at the front page of the *Times*.

"I hope to do a lot of shopping at Harvard Square. Last year I spent over five hundred dollars there. But I loved every minute of it. Have you been there?"

"No," I lied.

"Oh, you should go sometime."

"I plan to," I said.

"Good."

The rest of the trip to the airport she talked about her travels to New York, Paris, and some other places I've forgotten about.

At the airport, as the taxi driver took out our suitcases from the trunk, she invited me to come over and visit them at the Holiday Inn in Cambridge. I said I would. I left them without finding out their names.

As I checked in at the Appalachian Airlines ticket counter, I decided I had to keep out of sight until my flight was ready to leave. I didn't want to run into Angie.

I bought a *Time* magazine and went to the men's room. I sat in one of the stalls and tried to read an article about oil companies bribing politicians. Very little sank in.

At nine twenty-five, I left the men's room, checked a TV monitor for my boarding gate and hurried in that direction.

When I got there, the gate area was almost empty except for a couple of passengers rushing to get into the plane. A fleshy-faced clerk smiled as he handed me my boarding pass. "Don't worry, sir," he said, "they'll wait."

"Thank you," I said as I swiftly turned and walked toward the gangway door.

A black stewardess with large blue eyes forced a smile as I handed her my ticket. With my head lowered, I moved quickly down the aisle. I could feel someone's eyes on me. Angie, I thought.

At the back of the plane, I found two empty seats next to each other. I sat in the one nearest the window.

Once the plane took off, and the fluffy white clouds appeared underneath, I closed my eyes, hoping that deep sleep would finally come. But all I could think about was Angie and how warm her skin felt.

I was in a half-awake state when I felt the presence of a lightly scented body sitting next to me. I opened my eyes and turned around. Angie's well-shaped body was leaning toward me. Her dark eyes looked affectionately at me as she flashed a smile. For a fleeting moment I wanted to reach over and touch her.

"How are you feeling?" she asked, pushing her hair back from her eyes in a sexy, feminine way. I could hear the plane's engines humming loudly.

"Okay," I said, feeling hot and trembling inside. "I felt a little sick last night so I took a walk in the fresh air. I was sorry to see that you had left when I came back."

"Well, when I woke up and saw you missing," she said, "I thought maybe I did something wrong." She touched my shoulder lightly and then took her hand away slowly.

"No, it was precious, a moment to remember," I said. I thought about a song with a similar line.

"Yeah," she said, as if she didn't believe me.

"It was, I really feel that way," I insisted.

"Well, all I know," her voice was soft, "you were great."

"It was my first time since I was married."

"I know."

"Was I that naïve?" I asked.

"No, oh, no, I just could sense it."

"Thanks for being so understanding then."

"I wasn't. I was just being selfish," she said. "Being Italian I have a special proclivity for beautiful dark handsome men."

I blushed, "Come on, now!"

"Well, it's true. However, I felt last night you were feeling guilty about it. You should think of it as a growing experience, Vinnie."

"I will."

"And don't worry, I'm not the type that calls men at home or chases them."

"I know," I lied.

She leaned over, kissed me quickly on the cheek. "Here is my address and phone," she said as she handed me a small folded piece of paper. "If you want to see me again, I'm available."

"Thanks, I would like very much to see you again," I said honestly.

She got up, smiled warmly, touched my shoulder, and left. I looked at her as she moved slowly down the aisle. Her ass bounced to and fro as she wiggled back to her seat.

I unfolded the small piece of paper and read

Angie Castro
40th Street
Pittsburgh, PA
412-518-2614.

After a while I asked the black stewardess for some Alka-Seltzer. My stomach was sour and twisting. In a few minutes the stewardess came back with the bubbling liquid.

"I hope nothing is wrong?" she asked.

"No, just too much spaghetti," I laughed.

She left. I gulped down the whole glass, grimacing at the bitter taste in my mouth. It didn't help.

I leaned back against the seat and closed my eyes. I saw my father approaching; behind him the kitchen light bounced off the floor of my bedroom. The room filled with a strong smell of stale wine. He moved closer, closer, and closer. He said nothing. Then I felt pain from the razor-strap... *I hate you....*

3

I was jolted awake by the abrupt thump of the plane's tires on the tarmac. Three good jerky bounces, one loud tire-screech, and the always scary sound of the reversing jet engines—that was enough to bring me to full consciousness. We taxied to our gate.

I looked out the window and saw the silver buildings of Boston, standing like icicles against a clear blue sky. The sun was shining brightly. I looked at my watch. It was eleven thirty.

After we came to our stop, I stood up and followed the single file of passengers leaving the plane. Outside, it was cold and crisp. But the bright sun felt warm against my face as I walked down the plane's narrow steps. I thought I saw Angie entering the terminal. I slowed down, hoping that we wouldn't run into each other again while we picked up our baggage.

Inside the terminal, standing just outside the enclosed gate area, were my cousins Patsy and Jimmy. Patsy waved. I waved back. Jimmy smiled weakly as if he wanted me to know that he was going out of his way to meet me.

I was shocked how they'd changed in eight years. Before, Patsy's jet black hair was always cut in a crew cut but now it was frizzed and curled like an Afro. He wore a wrinkled, bone-colored raincoat like the detective Columbo on TV. In fact, to come to think of it, he also had the same kind of squint as Columbo.

"Hi, Patsy," I said, hugging him. We both knew that age had worked against us all.

"Hi, Jimmy," I said now, as I turned to hug him, and met his piercing eyes. He embraced me strongly. The lines on his face were also showing the wear of age. He was my age, whereas Patsy was three years older. Before, I always thought he was the perfect model of what I wanted to look like. Handsome. Dark. Strongly built. And very masculine.

But now his face looked gaunt, his once shining olive skin was dull and pale, his teeth were yellow and capped in the front, and his long, windblown black hair seemed to be thinning on the top. Probably dyed, I thought. However, his chest, although not as erect or full as before, looked to be in fairly good shape. The muscles still flexed powerfully underneath a black turtleneck sweater that he wore under his open sheepskin coat.

We stood silent for a few moments. Hell, I thought to myself, what do you say to each other when you haven't seen each other in years, and now the death of their father has brought you together?

We started to walk down the long corridor at Logan toward the baggage area. Patsy walked beside me leaning in a sort of ten after six position. Jimmy was a few steps behind.

"Vinnie, Mother is really grateful that you came," Patsy said. "When your mother called to tell us you were coming, we had to call the airport afterwards and find out when your plane was getting in. But the storm screwed everything all up. They said you were grounded in Rochester. Is that right?"

"Yes, a lovely town, I guess, but I never saw it. I slept and left first thing this morning." I thought quickly about Angie.

"Fucking planes," he said.

Jimmy was still trailing behind, trying to look important and hoping someone would recognize him from his acting roles on TV. Nobody ever did, because he was no more than a small bit actor all these years.

I turned and shouted back, "Jimmy, how you doing?" I stopped and waited for him to catch up. Patsy continued to walk toward the baggage area, which was a few feet in front of us.

"Living a good clean life," he winked as he reached me.

"I bet Hollywood has cleaned you up," I said, disbelieving. Then I walked over to the baggage area and found my suitcase on the floor beside a wide, empty running conveyor belt. I looked around, Angie wasn't there.

We headed to the parking garage that looked like a huge space-ship that had landed. Jimmy started to tell me about his most recent visit to Italy, where he'd just finished making a movie with Clint Eastwood. I noticed that his voice was clearer and deeper. Even so, his Italian American–Boston dialect was still evident, regardless of his efforts to hide it. Someone once said, this was the reason he couldn't make it big as an actor.

Jimmy shifted the subject of the conversation back to me. I had forgotten how skillful he was in doing this. So I decided that I would have to concentrate harder on what he was saying.

"How about you, how many books did you write?" he asked in a serious tone of voice.

"Just mathematical stuff. However, I'm working on a very important one now."

"Jesus, every time I think of you, Vinnie, I shake my head in wonderment," he said as he shook his head, of course, in wonderment. "I still remember the little shy kid who was scared of his own shadow. And now you're a famous mathematician. You son of a bitch," he joshed, fondly.

I blushed. "Right."

"I'm serious, you amaze me. You would screw up words in a sentence like saying you neither was to suppose to do it. You son of a bitch, I'm proud of you," he said as we reached Patsy's car now. I got in the back, and Jimmy slid in up front with his brother.

Patsy revved the engine for a while and then drove off, screeching the tires as he turned with entirely too much speed around the corners of the parking garage.

On the expressway to Boston, I started to relax a bit and began to listen more closely to what Jimmy was saying about me. "Hell, it was all our mother would talk about when I was growing up, how smart you were, and how every time she saw you, you had your head in a book, 'just like Abe Lincoln.'"

I smiled with embarrassment.

"When's the funeral?" I asked, hoping to change the subject. I wondered why I couldn't get myself to say I was sorry about their father's death.

"Monday morning," Patsy said.

"Who's taking care of it?" I asked.

"Longo!" He said with disgust in his voice. "Old man Longo died last year, and his crazy son Butch has taken over the business. Do you remember him, Vinnie?"

"I think so."

For the next few minutes, we drove in silence. I thought about Jimmy's life. Over the years he had flunked out of six colleges. He had gone through two wives and seven kids. All, he claimed, to be the occupational hazards of pursuing a career in acting. My mother's letters had kept me updated on his activities. According to her, in the last few years, he had gotten some bit parts on TV and in the movies. None of the parts, my mother said, lasted more than five minutes. I had only seen one of these parts, and it only lasted ninety seconds. He had played a prisoner who got in a fight with the star of the movie. Once, it was rumored, he was a bodyguard for a famous Mafia boss in New York City. Another time, there was a warrant out for his arrest in Nevada for supposedly selling hot jewelry. It was also said that big stars, like Clint Eastwood, Al Pacino, Robert Redford, all worshiped him. I often wondered why, when my mother wrote about Jimmy visiting a big star, why they never gave him a big break. Plain and simple, I think his acting was stiff and mechanical.

"The whole funeral scene bothers me, Vinnie," Jimmy's icy words broke through my thoughts about him. He was turned around in the front seat. He looked tense and frustrated. "They're all a bunch of frauds, shaking hands, hugging and kissing each other. All of them, pretending that they loved him. Christ, they hated him, like I did..."

"That's a lie, and you know it," Patsy shot back at him with a trembling voice. "I didn't understand his world and his ways, but I still loved him. He was very proud of his heritage and who he was. And I respected him for that. I know I made fun of him at times. But he had something. And that's more than I could say for you."

"Shit, what the hell do you know?" Jimmy frowned sarcastically. "All you know about is doing nothing."

"Oh, piss," Patsy said defeatedly, "one can't talk to you."

"Bullshit," Jimmy snapped. "The truth hurts."

Patsy said nothing.

In a few minutes the car stopped in front of the East House Hotel on Tremont Street. I'd wondered a while back when we came out of the Callahan Tunnel, why Patsy hadn't turned into the North End.

Jimmy opened the door, got out, leaned in and said, "Come on up for a drink, Vinnie, I want you to meet someone."

"Well," I hesitated, "okay."

I got out on the sidewalk. Jimmy was standing there, waiting for me. Patsy rolled down the window. "Listen, Vinnie, don't listen to any of his shit," he said coldly.

"I won't," I smiled weakly.

"I'll be at Longo's until ten if you need a ride, and I'll drop your stuff off at your parents'," he said in a warmer tone of voice.

"Okay, thanks," I said.

"Sorry, my love," Jimmy said, reaching in and patting him on the shoulder.

"Fuck off," Patsy angrily pulled his shoulder away and quickly rolled up the window, almost catching Jimmy's hand.

"Asshole," Jimmy laughed, as he watched Patsy accelerate his car and quickly disappear in traffic.

I followed Jimmy into the East House, and we took the elevator to his room. On the way up, he told me about his former two wives and kids. He said he was still good friends with one of the wives and loved all his kids. He had a nine-year-old boy who was captain of a little league team in Los Angeles. He talked about how the alimony payments were draining him. He said it left very little money for himself. His children had everything, he said, private schools, expensive clothes, large suburban houses, good teeth, guitars, mini-bikes, and more. He felt he was running himself ragged, trying to get enough jobs to meet all their needs. A great gift, he went on to say, was the money he got for helping out his mother in her work. He loved the work. Whatever it was, he didn't say.

As we got off the elevator, he took out his wallet and showed me a photograph of his three sons from his first wife. They were beautiful. Strongly built like him, with huge black eyes and silky smooth skin. They ranged in age from seven to eleven. He didn't have a picture of his other four kids who lived in North Carolina with their mother. She hated him, he said, and wouldn't let him visit the kids or have them write to him.

When we got to Jimmy's room, he opened the door with his key. As I walked ahead of him, I heard the shower running. There were two double beds in the room separated by a bedside table with a large lamp on top of it. The room looked like it had been recently spruced up with a loud orange carpet on the floor, two gray cushioned chairs, a small coffee table, and a dark maple desk-dresser combination with a large mirror above.

From behind me, Jimmy asked, "Scotch or bourbon?"

"Scotch on the rocks will be fine," I said. I went over and sat on the edge of the double bed nearest the door. He brought the drinks over, and sat directly across from me on the other double bed. The sounds of the running shower were coming from the wall behind him. He went on to tell me that he was hoping to make a good chunk of money from a movie he was making with Al Pacino. He was playing his double in fights and car-chase scenes. I could see a resemblance in his eyes. The kind, you knew, that kept secrets that go back centuries.

He drank his drink in one gulp, stood up, and poured himself another. As he sat down again he said, "I needed that, having a fag for a brother is hard to accept."

"I don't believe it," I said, shaking my head.

"Well, I know it's true," he said, with hard eyes peering fiercely into mine.

I said nothing as I sipped my drink. I was too tired to argue.

"I wish I never came back," he said in a melancholy tone of voice. "The only reason I'm here is because of money. I'm doing some more work for my mother. One of my kids is going to a psychiatrist. Twelve years old. Unbelievable. I feel terribly guilty about it. His mother won't even let me talk to him on the phone.

Now on top of all of this, that son of a bitch had to die. I'll be damned if I go to his wake and funeral. Not after all he did to me. My mother says it doesn't look right. I don't care. So what. But I think she understands. That's why I agreed to go with Patsy to the airport to pick you up. She needs a lot of help. Patsy is useless and my sister Rose is no better. Another drink?" he asked as he stood up and waved his empty glass in front of me.

"No, I'm doing fine," I said. He will be drunk in no time, I thought to myself. That's what the glamorous life of Hollywood does to you.

He poured himself another, and this time he staggered a bit as he sat back down on the bed. The shower was still running. I wondered what kind of beauty would come walking out.

He kicked off his shoes, crossed his legs under him, and after a few moments, surprisingly, he seemed to be getting sober. His face took on a serious expression as he spoke to me in a professorial tone of voice.

"You know, Vinnie, like I said before, I was always jealous of you. I just wish I was able to discipline myself like you did. You seemed to enjoy studying and reading. I hated it all. Females were my problem. I have to fuck every minute of the day. That's what ruined my marriages. Now, at least, I'm able to concentrate on things other than fucking."

"Good," I said, praying that he would stop this type of talk.

"You know, Vinnie," Jimmy went on, "Movie people are the dumbest people in the world. All they want to talk about is who's screwing whom, the new Mercedes they bought, their tennis game, their meditation highs, their guilt-ridden liberal causes... I don't have anyone to discuss with me the important questions of life. So, lately I've buried myself into books on all sorts of subjects. My mother has helped me there. I especially enjoy reading macabre things. I don't know why. It may be because I keep thinking, there might be a candle hidden in one of those weird stories—a candle that might light the world. Sorry for that shitty line." He seemed completely sober now as he peered at me with confident eyes.

"That's okay," I said.

"Even though I can't stand the majority of people I work with," he said, "the thing I do love about my job now, is the traveling and all the free time I have for some serious reading, between endless takes. You know you may have a PhD in mathematics but I'm getting a PhD in life. I read things, and then I see them actually working in reality. You know what's in now?"

"No."

"Noses."

"Noses!" I laughed.

"Yes, my dear cousin, noses," he said paternally. "Don't laugh until you hear what I have to say.

"Okay," I muffled another laugh. His eyes were full of childish glee. He was really excited about noses. I was certain now that the drink had affected his brain.

He jumped up, poured himself another drink, frowned seriously, then slowly paced back and forth, gradually getting faster. His eyes looked like that of a man who was possessed by something. "Well, I found out from reading an unpublished manuscript that my mother gave me, that a nose is not only an organ that can smell. This Matt Ziegler, who wrote the manuscript, says that it has the ability to taste and even see in certain cases. Also it's a highly sensitive sexual organ, if stroked properly. In addition, Ziegler says if it's pinched just right the pinch could knock a person unconscious. Also you can kill someone by taking a small peashooter and blowing a little piece of meat or a pea, just something small, into the nostril, and they're done. It brings on a heart attack or a stroke. The perfect murder. Think of the lives that could be saved, Vinnie, if armies fought their battles with their noses and peashooters! I love it. Christ! It would also be a great way to fuck—with our noses. No more population explosion. And all the third-world countries of the world could be taught this new technique of birth control. Really, it could be considered a new type of art-form."

"I can't believe you're really serious about this," I said, laughing.

He stopped his pacing and looked at me with a hurtful expression.

"I am, I am, Vinnie," he said, almost pleading with me to believe him. He gulped his drink down and then rolled the empty glass between the palms of his hands. Dreamily, he said, "Hell, Vinnie, if I had the money now, I would quit everything and go study Eskimos. They have many secrets about noses they haven't revealed to us yet. I think they may have a clue to the mysteries of our existence. You know, it may be that the only true ideas lie in the form of a nose. Language today means nothing. Nobody knows who controls it, so nobody listens anymore. We've know that for a hell of a long time in film. The dialogue is the most insignificant part of the film. Visual imagery is the most important, and all the words used in film are really useless, like they are in society. But if my theory is right, the language of the nose could be just what we need in this country. The Theory of Nosetivity, as Ziegler calls it, could create a new world language. The nose doesn't lie. Hmm, I like that line. Don't you?"

"Yeah, I do," I said. It's a line that would come from a crazy man's mouth, I thought to myself.

Suddenly, from behind him, the bathroom door opened, and out walked a very thin girl, with long, silky black hair cascading down over a large man's white terry-cloth bathrobe. She had warm, sad brown eyes. It was not the kind of girl I would expect Jimmy to go to bed with. I saw no breasts.

"Vinnie, this is Sharon Kelly, a friend," he winked.

She nodded shyly in my direction and then walked over and sat down next to Jimmy on the bed. He reached over and gently stroked her hair near the nape of her neck, and with his other free hand he stroked her nose a couple of times. She blushed.

"Vinnie is a cousin of mine who teaches mathematics at a university in West Virginia, Shar," he said with a queer grin on his face. We haven't seen each other in years."

She smiled politely at me and then lowered her eyes, as he kept stroking her long black hair.

If his fellow students only knew how naïve Vinnie was when he was growing up. Now I understood his queerish grin. He was getting ready to dump on me. There was no way to fight it. It was a skill he had perfected when we were kids. His dark, beautiful eyes jerked from me to her. "Ole Vinnie would have to go to bed at seven each night, while the rest of us guys played baseball or chased girls. His mother was always scared he was going to get hurt. She was kinda nervous, right, Vinnie?"

"I guess," I said. It was true.

"Everyone thought that he was going to become a priest because he served mass every morning and hated to hear talk about fucking and things like that."

She didn't flinch, as he laughed stupidly.

"Jimmy, I think I better go," I said as I stood up.

"You're not mad are you?" he asked, echoing concern.

"Oh, no," I said honestly. "I feel kinda beat from all the trouble with the delayed flight and all. Also I should visit our cousin Candy while I'm in the area."

"Listen, Vinnie," he said, as he stood up and came over to me, "if you need anything while you're here in Boston, please let me know." He wrapped his arm around my shoulder, as he walked me to the door.

"Okay."

Near the door, he leaned over, looking back at Sharon, and whispered in my ear, "She doesn't look like much, but she's the best fuck I ever had."

I blushed.

"Oh, before I forget," he said, "Sharon's throwing a party here tonight." Then he cupped his hand over one side of his mouth, leaned closer and said, "Shit, most of them are complete assholes. Please come, I need help."

"I'll see," I said, as I went to the door.

"Good," he said, pulling my body toward him in a friendly gesture. "Hey, I just hope you have better luck with Candy than I did. I met her the other night at Charlie's, a singles bar. I think she was spaced out on something."

Shaking my head, "she's had a lot of problems of late. Anyway, thanks for telling me, perhaps I'll see you later."

"Okay."

I opened the door and left.

4

Outside, in the brisk cold air, I took a long deep breath and looked at my watch. It was nearly five. At this time of day the people who passed me looked healthy. Their usually pale, ashen faces of morning were now brushed with ruby warmth. For a moment, I was glad I was back in Boston. It felt good to be away from the almost endless bulges and bulges of West Virginia mountains that surrounded me wherever I turned. Many times I felt as though I was confined in something like a seawalled canyon. Especially in the winter, people, scenery, and feelings all seemed to mirror the hueless and changeless existence that enclosed them.

I walked until I found a phone booth. Then I checked the directory for Candy's address on Beacon Street. I stared at it for a long while. I now wondered if it was a good idea to go visit her after all. I thought about those desperate phone calls late at night. But then I thought about the time when I was growing up; she was always good to me, and I respected and loved her like a sister. Even though she was part of that past I wanted to forget, she was my cousin, and I had a duty to her.

It wasn't hard for me to be kind to Candy. Her mother, my mother, and Jimmy's mother were sisters. They were born to Vito and Rose Cassallano who later prearranged their marriages to the three Serrano brothers. Her mother, Margaret, died from breast cancer, and her father, Emilio, died from a pulmonary embolism. This happened when she was in college. Since then, she seemed to be a lost soul. But I loved her. She was six years older than me and used to babysit me when my mother was helping out Aunt Concetta with the antiques store. I remembered her as treating me very warmly and lovely even when I disobeyed her. She had a way with me, always so understanding, like a mother should be. As she got older, she became like the sister I never had; likewise, I became like a brother to her. She very rarely saw her older, actual brother. Supposedly he worked for the Mafia in Arizona. Sometimes, she used to take me along on her dates to drive-in movies, miniature golf courses, and hockey games. Once, in a pizza place, both of us got terribly silly after we each got gum stuck on our face and fingers; the more we tried to get it unstuck, the more it pulled and stretched. We laughed hysterically; and when her date left us, we laughed even more wildly until tears came to our eyes, until finally we were asked to leave. She didn't care. She was carefree, naïve, and childlike then. By the time I started college, she had married a textbook salesman, was settled down, and was happy. I thought.

About three years ago, out of nowhere, late at night, she started calling me occasionally, and then, more frequently, every few months. At first, she asked advice on her recent divorce; then, after a while, she sought help on problems that ranged from psychological to missing her periods. For some reason, she thought because I had a PhD, I knew everything. That was Candy's logic. Simple and ordered. So, I didn't disappoint her. I played whatever role she was expecting of me on the night she called.

On a narrow street off busy Beacon Street, the cobblestones looked as if they had just been recently plowed or swept clean. I walked toward Candy's red-bricked apartment house, which looked brilliantly aflame in the twilight. The uniform alignment of the other houses with their stoops and their black wrought-iron banisters made it seem like each apartment house was part of a large coke furnace, carefully fed and banked by black stokers that stood on each side. The high polished windows, most of them covered by fresh linen curtains, gave me a feeling of the gentility that once existed here.

I rang the doorbell to Candy's apartment. No answer. I rang again. Still no answer. Then I tried the doorknob. The door was open. So I walked in. I heard kids running around and screaming at each other, somewhere in the back of the apartment. I shouted in a loud voice, "Anyone home?"

The screaming continued.

I looked around the room. GI Joes, Barbie dolls and Tinker Toys were scattered here and there on the floor. Black bikini panties and a bra were hanging over a Boston rocker, and a pair of panty hose was draped over a screen that was in front of a blocked-up fireplace. On a deeply scratched maple end-table that stood near the entrance of the room was a stack of unread *Boston Globes*. In the middle of the room, there was a high-backed, threadbare, lumpy green sofa, and in front of it was a glass-topped coffee table with *Time, Newsweek, Better Homes and Gardens, Cosmopolitan*, and other magazines with some of their front covers torn off.

Suddenly, from the rear of the apartment, I saw Candy excitedly ambling in, with sluggish hips tightly packed into her faded blue jeans. Her graying black hair was pulled back in a bun. Her face, with her thick, pursed lips, large brown eyes, and her fat, bold nose, still bore scars from a bad case of acne in adolescence. The most sensuous part of Candy was where her unscarred neck curved and met her body. Her loosely fitting blue sweatshirt, with "Harvard" written on the front, made her neck look lovelier than ever.

"Vinnie," she exclaimed in a high-strung voice, "I didn't expect to see you until the wake. God, am I glad to see you!"

She came over and kissed me tightly on the lips. "After all my stupid phone calls to you," she said, "we're finally getting a chance to talk face to face." She led me to the sofa where she leaned over and brushed aside some Barbie doll clothes. "Kids," she sighed. We sat down, her leg touching mine. "I feel so guilty about those calls," she added. "I bet your wife thinks I'm just awful."

"Oh, no, she's not like that," I said, thinking, I'm sure the saint loves to hear about your suffering. It's an honor, she always says, to suffer for Jesus.

"Well, I don't believe you," she said, "you're just being nice, like you always are." She looked at me with affection. "Vinnie, you look pale. Are you all right? Look at those dark rings under your eyes."

"My flight to Boston got grounded in Rochester last night and I didn't sleep very good."

"I wanted to call you earlier this week to talk about some things that I couldn't hold from you any longer," she said. "You have a right to know."

"What things?"

"I can't now with the kids around. Anyway, did I tell you that Michael now lives up the street with the woman he was seeing while we were married?"

"No."

"And now he's got his lawyer trying to bring me to court in order to get custody of the kids. He's trying to prove that I'm incompetent as a mother."

"When did this happen?"

"About a month ago, just after the last time I talked to you," she said.

"Oh."

"Hey, how about something to drink?" she asked. "I think I have some wine."

"No, not now, later maybe," I said. "Tell me, how have you been feeling?"

"Well, I don't know," she said. "I still hate getting dressed in the morning. It seems like I can't wait until the day goes by so I can go back to sleep again. That's the only time I have peace. And my leg doesn't shake then, either. You know about that."

"Yes," I said, "how's it doing?"

"It either shakes all the time or it feels numb, like it was paralyzed or something," she said. "The other day I was in a coffee shop by myself, and it started to shake so much that I had to leave."

"How about now?" I asked.

"Numb!" she replied. "The pills my therapist gave me don't seem to help the shaking, they only make me dizzy and more tired. It seems I'm always too tired to do anything. The therapist says my shaking is caused by a fear I have hidden deep in my subconscious. He says once I identify it, the shaking would go away."

"He might be right," I said, "he just might be."

Impulsively, she leaped up. "I doubt it," she said. "God, look at this house."

Then, like a diving loon, she bent over with quick, jerky motions, and picked up some of the toys that were scattered about. Blushing red now, she moved quickly toward the Boston rocker, grabbed the black bikini panties and bra from it and threw them into a dark wooded chest near one end of the sofa. Suddenly she stopped her nervous jumping around and stared blankly into the space in front of her. Then she shook her head and let the toys she had in her hands drop to the floor. Slowly she walked over and sat down on the sofa again.

She turned to me with sad-looking eyes and said, "Vinnie, I must stop doing that—my therapist says the only reason I want a clean house is because I want to please my mother. And, he says, deep down I've come to hate her for that. I think he's right. Last week I told her to get out of my house because of her screaming about cleaning. She said Michael left me because of my cleaning and the clothes I wear."

"Hell, Candy, you're growing," I said, hoping she would see I was pleased. "A few years ago you would have never done that. That shows me that you are gaining a sense of who you are."

"I just don't know," she said, shaking her head. "I'm saying things now and doing things that even confuse me more."

"Like what?"

"Well, like the outbreak with my mother," she said. "Or another time when I was over to my friend's house, and she started up on this advice kick about what I should do with my life. It seems in the last three years every girl my mother or Aunt Concetta knows in the North End, who's had a problem with her husband, has called me. Well, this one day I was fed up with it all. So I got up and told my friend I was going out for a walk because it was a beautiful wintry day. Vinnie, you should've seen how she looked at me, like I was some kind of nut. I got so mad that I called her a 'stupid guinea asshole.' Jesus. Vinnie, do you believe simple Candy Serrano said that?"

I thought about Angie and how her parents wouldn't speak to her because of the divorce. I wished now I knew where she was staying in Boston for she'd really be the kind of person Candy needed to talk to.

"No, I don't believe it," I said, "but it's good you're doing things like that now. I met a woman on the plane who, just like you, had an Italian mother always screaming about cleaning. Last year, she also got a divorce and she says it was the best thing that ever happened to her."

"I don't know, Vinnie," she said, shaking her head again, "I just don't know. I'm really scared of this new part of me."

"Everyone is when they start pulling it together," I said.

"I hope so," she trailed off. "God, I'm glad you're here. I am feeling better already."

"So am I."

"Vinnie, what were you planning to do right now? Want to take a drive? How about Wollaston Beach? We can talk there. I love the sea in the winter. I just love to stand near it and to be taken up in its wildness. I've been doing that a lot since my problems started."

"I would love to. The later I get to the wake, the better," I said.

She got up from the sofa. Looking down, she said, "Vinnie, I'll tell Michael Junior we're going out. He's so good. I just don't know what I would've done without him. Especially this past year."

While she drove us toward Wollaston Beach, darkness squeezed in, like from a toothpaste tube, into the corners of Boston. In the distance, the lights of Boston looked like blurs of chalk suspended in infinite black space. I looked at my watch. It was nearly eight.

Before we left, Candy had picked up a bottle of wine and a large hunk of sharp cheddar cheese. I poured each of us some wine into the paper cups Candy had brought along, as she drove south on Route 3 toward Wollaston. Candy looked as if she was in deep concentration as I handed her the drink. What conversation we did have after this was only small talk, the kind that gives one a chance to think about other things.

As we approached the large seawall that fronts Wollaston Beach, I could see in the distance the rhythmic signals of the lighthouses that guarded Boston Harbor. I remembered one night, so many summers ago, sitting on the wall and staring at them for hours. I imagined putting the rhythmic signals of the lighthouses to music and when finished I would call it the "Concerto of Lights." Tonight, I saw one lighthouse sending out one long beam of light, followed by five short beams; it repeated the cycle every ten seconds. I wished I had learned the names and positions of the lighthouses in school, so I could identify this particular one.

Candy now parked the car, facing the seawall. The engine idled, while hot heat rushed in from underneath the dashboard. It was too hot. I wiped some of the condensation from the side window and saw no other cars parked. It was still too early for the neckers, I thought. On many nights, especially in the summer, I remembered the hundreds of cars stacked in one after another; heads bobbed up and down, like a string of buoys marking off a swimming area in a stewing sea.

While I sipped at my wine, Candy was fussing about with her coat; eventually she took it off, keeping it draped over her shoulders. The coat was black and paper thin. She then leaned back against the door and asked for some more wine.

"I saw Nicky Ziggeralli the other day," she said, warmly and sisterly. I poured some more wine in her near-empty cup.

"I think she still has a crush on you," she added.

I smiled, embarrassed, and said nothing.

"She married some Irish guy from Roxbury," she said. "I think he's kinda screwed up."

I tried hard to remember what Nicky looked like. I couldn't. The only thing I could remember was being on top of her on the back steps of Saint Anthony's.

"I met him at a party Nicky had. Gee, I don't know how Nicky does it. His hands were all over every woman he talked to."

"Do they have any kids?" I asked.

"Yes, two. Basically, Nicky said, he's a good father. But listen to this—I don't think I'll ever understand people—Nicky also admitted to me that another reason why she stays with him is because of their home in Cohasset. You should see it. Really beautiful! All I could think of when I first saw it was the house I saw in the picture *The Great Gatsby*. Nicky said if she left him he would immediately sell it, and she just couldn't stand that. Now that's the part I don't understand. She said she has too much of herself invested in getting the house the way she always wanted it. A pretty weird trade-off, don't you think? Her life for a house, gee."

"Yes."

Candy had two more glasses to my one while she went on to tell me about some of her other friends from the North End. Freddie Rossi, who was a priest in East Boston for a while, was now quitting and marrying an ex-nun. Anthony Aliotti, who was a lawyer, was now running for a state legislative position. Tony Fantini, who was an old boyfriend, was now a disc jockey in Florida. And finally, Pete Baroni, who took orders for advertisements in the Boston phone directory, got fired because a rumor got started he was stealing money from the company. "It's terrible what people's talk will do," she said, slurring her words. "He's married and has four kids too."

"I'm sorry to hear that," I said. "Wouldn't it be wonderful if people knew how to talk and also be honest at the same time."

"Never happen," she said, her voice suddenly sounding sober. "There are just too many dishonest people in the world."

"I've often thought," I said, "what the world would be like if talking was forbidden and only feelings could be expressed. Look at the deaf-mutes. I heard one time that no other group of people is as honest as they are with each other."

"Then let's join the deaf-mutes, Vinnie," she said half kidding. "Okay?"

"Okay."

Suddenly her face grew grimmer as she now changed the subject: "Vinnie, did your mother or father ever tell you they loved you?"

I felt my body go numb. Thank God she didn't wait for my answer.

"You know, I couldn't answer that question when my therapist first asked me. I was too ashamed to tell him that my mother never did. All she was good for was to criticize me for how I dressed, talked, and walked. Anything but 'I love you'..." Her voice trailed off.

"I ca... can't remember, Candy," I stuttered, moving closer to my side of the car, "if th... they ever said anything like that."

Suddenly I felt tears in my eyes.

"Vinnie, I understand," Candy said, as she reached over and cupped my face in her warm hands.

"I wish you did," I said, trying to get my voice to sound normal.

Then she lifted her head and gently kissed me on the cheek. At the same time, I felt her hand unfastening the buttons on my coat. I felt her stroke my chest gently through the fabric of my shirt. It made me feel a little bit better. Finally I started to relax, but I now felt myself feeling something else for her. Almost instinctively I pulled back.

"No, Candy," I said, trembling. "God, no."

"What's wrong?" she asked, her voice shaking.

"You."

"I thought, Vinnie, we could have fun like we used to. Remember those hot summer days, when we played on the beach and then afterwards we would lie side by side, touching each other?"

"But, Candy, it was different then. Can't you see that?"

"Yes, but it doesn't have to be," she said. "We're still human, aren't we?"

Please, Candy, don't do this. Not now.

"Stop it, Candy," I screamed, pushing her massaging hands on my chest away. "Please..."

I quickly turned, fumbled around with the door handle, and finally opened the car door. Then I leaped out and ran toward the lights of Boston. It was as if someone else was running and I was watching.

From behind, I could hear her voice blending in with the howls of the icy, wintry wind. "Vinnie, come back! You don't understand..."

Think of nothing, I thought as I hurdled over large pieces of driftwood. Think of nothing. Then suddenly I tripped, stumbled forward, and fell. Fatigued, I just lay there, thinking I don't care about anything.

After a couple of minutes I turned over on my side and stared at the sea. I wondered how and why the waves kept folding over one another, with perfect harmony and order, so unlike my world now.

Finally I stood up, brushed some wet grains of sand and long strings of slimy seaweed from the front of my coat. I then shivered, as the skin underneath my pants now felt wet and cold.

Across the street that ran in front of Wollaston Beach, I saw a bright red neon sign blinking "Pro Bowl." Slowly, I started to walk in its direction.

I looked at my watch. It was almost eleven. Uncle Louie, I thought, I need to see him—view him—before Longo closes.

When I reached the bowling alley, I called a cab. I guess I was a glutton for punishment.

5

I rang the doorbell, and on the second ring Longo opened the door. For a long time, he just stood there and stared at my face suspiciously. The strong fragrance of both fresh and dying flowers hit my nostrils, and blasting loudly from a built-in hi-fi system, was a girl's high-pitched voice singing a rock song with lyrics that caught my ear.

> *I talk babe, you listen,*
> *You talk babe, I listen,*
> *Hoping each time*
> *It will glisten,*
> *But like the unending*
> *Circle of time,*
> *It goes on and on*
> *And it's not*
> *Worth a dime.*
> *I talk babe...*

"Alice, turn that damn thing down," he yelled over his shoulder, and then turning back to me said, "Sorry, man, we're closed, all the family's left for the night." The phony smile of a department store's salesperson was spread across his face.

"Oh," I said.

The phony smile was now frozen on his face. I figured Longo was somewhere in his late forties. He was wearing a V-neck T-shirt over a slim, but hairy, tightly-muscled chest and a pair of brightly colored plaid slacks. I thought he looked like a man who had just gone through a complete transformation in looks and lifestyle. But his sad, dark-brown eyes seemed to contradict this new look.

I now felt a little sorry for him. I remembered his nickname was "Turk" because of these dark eyes that went along with a narrow, perpetual five-o'clock-shadow face, a hawkish nose, and thick, black hair that now seemed dyed and styled.

"Hey, who are you?" he asked, with a puzzled look on his face. The phony smile was gone. Serious now.

"I'm Vinnie Serr..." He didn't let me finish as he quickly steered me closer to a tiny lamp that hung over a stand-up writing desk where visitors signed in.

"Holy shit, Vinnie, I didn't recognize you," he said apologetically. "God, the last time I saw you, you were wearing short pants. Jesus, I must be really getting old." He then grabbed my hand and shook it vigorously.

I nodded and smiled.

"I heard you were coming," he said, "but I thought someone said you would be here earlier."

"I was, but I got held up," I said.

"Could I get you something, wine or food?" he asked.

"No," I said.

He kept staring at me and shaking his head. "Vinnie, Vinnie Serrano, where does the time go?"

"It goes," I said.

"You sure you don't want anything?" he asked again.

"No," I said. "But I would like to sneak in and see my uncle for a minute or so."

"Sure, man, you got the whole place to yourself," he said. "The show must go on," he added in a joking tone of voice.

I laughed.

"Hey, Alice," he shouted in the direction of a half-opened door on his left, "come on out. I want you to meet someone."

Right after, from the door he was staring at stepped a matronly-looking woman, wearing a sky blue, quilted robe over a nightgown of the same color, and slippers with fluffed blue cotton balls on top. I figured, like Longo, she was also in her forties.

"Hon, meet Vinnie Serrano; Louie Serrano was his uncle."

"Hi," she said, hesitating in the doorway.

"Hi," I said.

She smiled. Her blond, coiffured hair looked dead and fake like the wigs that mannequins wear in store windows. I thought the heavy mask of white makeup she was wearing made her look more whore-like than she already looked.

"Vinnie, Alice is my new love. I traded my old one in," he laughed and winked at me.

She attempted a girlish giggle. It failed.

"I hope you don't mind my appearance," she said in a sleep-filled voice and as she looked down at her robe.

"No, not at all, I understand," I said.

"I think she's tired from learning how to run a good Italian funeral," he laughed. "Germans don't do it this way. Do they, hon?"

"No, they don't," she said smiling. Her blue eyes looked weary.

"Are you hungry?" she asked halfheartedly as if this was expected of her but she disliked doing it.

"No, I'm fine," I said. "I just want to see my uncle and then leave you people alone, so you can get some rest."

"It won't be any trouble," she said woodenly.

"No, thanks again."

"See, she's learning," Longo beamed.

"Well, I guess I'd better go back in and finish cleaning up the dishes before I fall asleep on my feet," she said. "That's why, honey, I had the music so loud. It was keeping me awake. See you later..." She mumbled something. I figured she had forgotten my name.

She turned and left, closing the door behind her. I thought about the young, blond woman in the cab. In twenty years would she look the same?

"A smart woman," he said proudly, "an interior decorator for Jordan Marsh for twenty years."

"Is that right?"

"Yep," he said quickly, "nothing like the dummy I had before."

Longo grabbed my elbow and steered me to a room on the left. Out of the corner of my eye, I could see a glow of superiority come over his face as we approached the dimly lit room. His eyes were now shining like polished black marbles, and his mouth had taken on a cocky, sly smile. I felt sure he was relishing the thought of directing the melodramatics of people's lives in the next few days.

At the entrance of the mourning room, he turned toward me and said with frustration in his voice, "I'll tell you, man, he was really a mess when I picked him up from the hospital, especially the nose." I felt he was talking to me as he would to a colleague in the same line of work.

"They think it got that way because of the way he fell when he had his heart attack. I just don't know. Shit, every night it discolors on me because all the insides were screwed up. I wish to hell I could've used an artificial nose. They're tremendous. But Concetta wouldn't hear of it. So please don't get upset at my job, okay?"

"Hey, don't worry," I lied.

He was talking as if he didn't hear what I just said and was having a heavy conversation with himself.

"I guess to come to think of it I'm kinda proud of the work I've done on that nose. There you are..." Suddenly, he stopped in the middle of the sentence and said, "Oh, shit." He pounded on his squeezed forehead with the palm of his hand. "Jesus, I got another body I'm supposed to pick up tonight. I must go, or hell, man, I'll never get any sleep tonight."

"Don't let me hold you up," I said. "I won't have any problem being left here alone." That was another lie.

"You sure?" he asked.

"Yes," I said bravely, and now thought about Jimmy and his dissertation on noses.

"Well, if you need anything Alice will be in the other room," he said.

"Okay, thanks." Jimmy is crazy, I thought, but not a murderer. *No way God.*

He patted me on the back, turned, and headed toward the apartment door.

I walked in and stood for a long while in front of the red-cushioned kneeler, which was placed near the middle of the coffin. I couldn't look at Uncle Louie's body. I wasn't ready. Instead, my eyes scanned the room. The sound system was back on again.

I search in vain
Among my friends,
Lovers and strangers too,
They talk, babe, I listen,
I talk, babe, they listen,
So like me and you.

A reddish, soft-glowing light, which enveloped the coffin, was created by small floodlights glancing off a wild red and black wallpaper design. It was eerie. But warm.

The center of the room was mostly occupied with black metal folding chairs; "L O N G O" was stamped in large, white letters across their backs. They were neatly aligned in rows of four on each side of the room. On one side of the room were about ten to twelve chairs placed against the wall. I figured this was where Aunt Concetta would sit and receive the phony condolences of people.

Finally I knelt down on the kneeler, looking at Uncle Louie for the first time.

"God, Uncle Louie," I said, "I feel so sorry for you. Now I wish I'd talked to you more... but you said only 'hello' and 'good-bye' to me when you visited my father... why didn't we say anything more... there's too much lipstick on your lips... and Longo was right: your nose looks like shit. ...hey, Uncle Louie, that pinstripe suit with wide lapels and new white shirt you're wearing are too big for you, and those unseamed cordovan shoes... Jesus, you just don't look right in those things... you always wore an old tweed suit coat and underneath you usually wore one of your soiled green polo shirts... yes, and always that thick rope belt that held up your dark gray working pants... that rope belt... I always wanted to ask you about that... I hardly know you... I can't believe Jimmy would do this...."

I want to laugh... come on, Vinnie, why do you always have to at times like this... stop it... please, God, help him... Are you looking down at me, Uncle Louie... I know, I know, you're probably saying we're all damn nuts... but what is it like where you are... God, I wish

I could talk to you about that... you know, I'm writing a book about heaven... Is there a hell... I still can't figure out how I'm going to deal with that. God, how I envy you... Hail Mary full of grace... No... Uncle Louie, did Jimmy do this?... Oh, God! Help me!

Now I focused my eyes on a fresh, glowing red rose that was hanging out of a narrow milk glass vase. It had been placed behind Uncle Louie's head, so that it leaned against one of the coffin's satin-lined corners. I reached over and read a note that was attached.

> *To Uncle Louie, A gentle man, he gave me*
> *so much. I'll miss him more than anyone will.*
> *Love,*
> *Candy*

Candy's massaging hands, slowly moving down my body flashed across my mind, but quickly I forced it out. I concentrated on Uncle Louie again.

I remembered those late-night conversations he had with my father in the kitchen. I was always glad Grandmother Serrano had taught me formal Italian, because that's all they used on those nights. Smoothly and rapidly, the words flowed from their mouths as if they were singing in an opera. I thought it was nothing like the jerky sounds of the English language, where too many words need some kind of tongue action.

Sometimes when they drank too much of my father's homemade red wine, their voices would increase in volume and intensity. And if it was too loud, my mother would get up and remind them that I was asleep.

Which, of course, I wasn't. I was always too interested in what Uncle Louie was saying to my father about his troubled world.

A very real part of Uncle Louie was his strong belief in the Italians' code of ethics, especially those things dealing with man's honor and respect. And yet, the full-time working Italian American fathers in the North End who had the honor and respect of their families were increasingly absent in his life. Often he would say to my father that he was no longer a man, but only an Italian who had been castrated of human dignity. He never held a permanent job because of his refusal to learn the English language. As a result there were only the most menial jobs available to him. Sometimes he would work at the statehouse as a part-time doorman. At other times, sympathetic grocery store owners in the North End had him sweep out their stores in the early morning hours. Then, on many sun-filled mornings, instead of returning home after sweeping out ten to fifteen stores, he would sit on a cement bench in the bocci yard, gazing thoughtfully into space for hours.

The inability to support his family like other men in the North End caused a bitter sense of shame and guilt to crop up inside him. And, to relieve some of this guilt, he became a servant in his own household. Ever since I could remember, he had always cleaned Aunt Concetta's house for her, gone shopping for groceries, washed and ironed her clothes, and so on.

Another fact of Uncle Louie's troubled world was related to material possessions. Everything he and Aunt Concetta owned was bought either by her or some member of the Cassallano family. This indignity was greatly aggravated by the fact that her mother and father owned the apartment they rented and lived below them. Because of this, their apartment was never empty. There was always a Cassallano family member around, which created more, more, and more hateful resentment in him, each time someone came to visit. The only place, he would tell my father, where he found some privacy was taking a shit. And that, he said, was often taken away, when the Cassallanos consumed too much food and drink.

I thought about the tortured face Uncle Louie had while he was alive, and which was now hidden underneath Longo's makeup. His cross was the Italian American world he lived in. To outsiders, this world supposedly offered love, affection, emotion, and communal sharing. To him, it was all a lie.

"Remember, Uncle Louie," I said, "the story you told us about Italians in America always wanting to be shining red apples instead of olives? I think it was one Christmas Eve. They laughed and called you stupid. I didn't.

"I listened to every word you said as you went on to tell us that when shining red apples get ripe, they get soft and rot; but not so with olives—they become firmer and more beautiful. They still laughed, especially when you said that ripened olives give off a glow that warms like the sun... ah, yes... beautiful... I thought for the first time in my life I was hearing real poetry. And they kept laughing... I'm so, so sorry I never said anything to them...

"You know, I remember once reading a poem by Emily Dickinson, and she said she carried a huge anger in her heart. The words really hit me, Uncle Louie, because of what I was feeling at the time... And now I think you, too, carried a huge anger in your heart... God, how I wish I'd talked to you more... How could Jimmy, the son of a bitch, do this? God, please don't let it be true... I don't need any more conflict...."

6

I opened the door of the East House and walked in. The East House had begun to look old and run down, which I hadn't noticed earlier that day when I came in with Jimmy. The crimson rug was threadbare; the institutional green walls were chipped and cracked, revealing the white plaster underneath; and the few grayish, overstuffed chairs that lined the walls were stained black by greasy heads, bringing to mind the Vitalis age of the past.

I walked by the registration desk, where a lettuce-faced old man sat looking off into space. I felt for sure he was sleeping with his eyes open. Then I reached the elevator, got in, remembered Jimmy's room number, and pressed the button for the sixth floor. Slowly it moved up, shaking all the way. I had all sorts of images of getting stuck between floors.

After what seemed like an unbelievable amount of time, the elevator stopped at the sixth floor and, thank God, the doors opened. I wished afterwards that they never had.

When I stepped into the corridor, I noticed a small crowd gathered in front of Jimmy's room. They were all looking down. As I moved closer, I saw Jimmy kneeling on top of a frail-looking boy. He was slapping the boy with such violence, it scared me. The boy didn't resist.

Soon reddish-blue welts started to appear on the boy's already swollen face, while blood dripped from his forehead onto his snowy white hair. I thought quickly about running out of there and going back to West Virginia. Who needed this.

"Stop it, stop it, he'll kill him, oh, God...," cried the girl Jimmy had introduced me to earlier that day.

Many of the people in the crowd seemed like they did not want to disrupt what was happening in front of them. They were probably happy it was the boy and not them, who was getting the shit knocked out of him. But a few of the people did press around the girl in sympathy. Now there were tears in her eyes.

Suddenly, Jimmy stood up, face flushed with anger and, as if he was drunk with his own power, he started to kick the boy in the ribs, then in the stomach again, then in the face. One punishing kick followed another. After each kick, the boy grunted and yelped like a dog who'd been hit by a car.

Jesus Christ, there was a boy being murdered. Doesn't anyone care? Help the poor kid out, Vinnie, go ahead. I can't. I'm scared. Look at Jimmy's eyes. He might kill me. Coward, another voice rang out in me.

Someone yelled from the crowd, "Get the cops."

Jimmy was now tightly clutching the boy by the neck. The veins in his hand seemed ready to burst. He held the boy's body up, perfectly still and erect. The expression on Jimmy's face was similar to the pictures one sees scattered throughout a fishing magazine. Proudly and gleefully one could see fishermen standing next to their prize catches, showing off to the world not only their struggle but also their accomplishment. To be stronger and more powerful than something was their goal.

I decided, life or no life, this had to stop. But as I was getting ready to move toward Jimmy, Jimmy's girlfriend got there first. She jumped on his back and started to pound at him with tiny clenched fists.

It startled Jimmy at first; he staggered with the boy's neck still in his hand, then he laughed as he wheeled around and pushed her against the wall. Slowly she slid down the wall until she was in a sitting position. "You prick," she cried with hurt. I hated that word, especially coming from a girl's mouth.

Finally Jimmy let go of the boy's neck. A dull thud followed after the boy's body hit the floor. Jimmy then stared at the boy as if he was challenging him to get up. The boy only groaned with pain.

"If you want more, my dear friend, come back again. It was fun." He laughed and turned to the crowd. "Come on, the drinks are on me."

I stayed behind. Jimmy's girlfriend was now on her knees, sobbing while she tenderly placed the boy's head on her lap. I could see small cakes of dried blood scattered throughout the boy's white hair. His eyes were swollen shut. It reminded me of the pictures of what Joe Frazier looked like after one of his fights with Muhammad Ali.

Somewhat dazed and still sobbing, she asked me to help her carry him to the elevator. So we each took one of his arms and placed them around our necks and dragged him slowly to the elevator. Then I pushed the elevator button and waited for it to reach our floor.

"That's it for the asshole," she said, pale-faced and tight-lipped. For two years I've been all over the goddamn world with him. And every time a guy talks to me, he thinks the guy wants to fuck me. Well, no more. I'm finished."

I said nothing. Only nodded.

The elevator doors opened. Slowly we walked in, and leaned the boy against the rear of the elevator where he sank down into a Buddha-like position. I held the elevator doors open as she squatted down beside him and looked up at me. "You don't have to come down. I'll get someone downstairs to help."

"Okay."

"I would be ashamed to call him my cousin."

"I guess so."

"God, if you only knew how crazy he is," she said, as she gently stroked the boy's bloodied hair.

"I think I do," I said. "Are you sure that you'll be okay?"

"Yes," she said, holding back tears that were welling in her eyes. "I appreciate your help, just tell him for me that he'll never change. I was stupid to believe he would."

"I will," I said, "I hope everything works out."

She nodded sadly. "Thank you."

"Take care," I said, as I now released the elevator doors and watched them slam shut.

"Hey, Vinnie, never mind that slut, come on," Jimmy shouted from behind me.

I turned and saw him standing in front of his room. As I headed in his direction, he ducked back in.

I stood outside the opened door and looked in. I could see arms and legs bobbing and weaving in a thick layer of smoke. Also, loud piercing voices were trying to outdo a kind of bizarre, wild, often screeching rock music.

I figured why not. I was feeling depressed and the noise and people might help. So I walked in.

"Cuz, I'm glad you came," Jimmy said, as he pushed his way over to where I was standing. "This party needs a touch of intellectualism to get it going."

"I could see that as soon as I arrived."

He laughed and then introduced me to a guy and girl that were pressing close to him. The guy had an ape-like face and was built like a hulky guard on some professional football team. The girl was small, broad-shouldered with light brown hair, cut in the style of the Olympic skater Dorothy Hamill. She wore an open-necked, white blouse with a Kelly-green vest over it and a matching short skirt. She had a large oval face and a flirtatious gleam in her greenish eyes. Her name was Tatum Ryan, and muscleman's was Dave Conklin.

Jimmy leaned over and whispered in my ear, "Tatum, man, is a good screw. Try it, you'll like it."

I felt my face get immediately hot and tried hard not to change the expression on my face. I wondered if she suspected what he just said. Jesus, Jimmy, why do you say things like that? *I know now, you did kill your father.*

Putting his arm around Tatum's shoulders and nodding in my direction, he now said, "Tat, Vinnie went to Harvard. Didn't you go to Radcliffe?"

"No," she said coldly. Her body stiffened as she moved from underneath his arm.

He looked puzzled. "Well, I'm sorry, for some reason I thought you did. Anyway, Vinnie was too smart for Harvard. Right?" He winked at me but didn't wait for my reply. "He's now a big shot professor in West Virginia and has written several books in mathematics."

"Just two," I said humbly.

"Whatever," he said. "I just wish to hell someday you would write about Italian American people. I hate all of this Mafia shit they now write about. It's bad for us. Man, what we really need is a Fitzgerald or Hemingway. Someone like that, who can really get into our souls. A lot of money could be made, a whole lot of money, man."

"True, I..."

But he wasn't listening, as he quickly patted me on the back, turned around, and started talking to a fat-ass girl in back of him.

A lot of dancing was still going on and the rock music was playing louder than ever. I thought about asking Tatum to dance. She seemed more relaxed now since Jimmy turned his attention away from us.

However, she made the first move. She reached out and grabbed my hand, and, without saying a word, she led us to an empty space near a window.

She went and got me some wine. And after finishing about two glasses, I got the courage to dance with her. Because my dancing skills were still in the twisting age she taught me how to move and rotate my pelvis. She said it was called the funky something rock.

I loved it. Every time Tatum's body brushed against mine, I shook with excitement. Once she whispered, "I'm glad to meet someone who isn't into himself, like the rest of the people here."

After a few more dances, the loud rock music stopped. I was grateful, as I was starting to feel dizzy and sweaty. We sat down on the floor. She leaned over and asked, "Did you really go to Harvard? I know how Jimmy exaggerates everything."

"Yes, I really did," I said. "Lasted about half a year. There was a difference of opinion, you might say, concerning what I should be doing. Harvard thought I should be attending classes, while I thought I should be spending my time in johns. I figured, hell, they were the best places at Harvard for meeting some famous scholar and not worrying about status and all that stuff. Of course, you know who won."

"Are you serious?"

"Yes," I said. "I don't tell that story to many people."

"Come on, you're putting me on," she giggled with some hesitation.

"No, I'm not," I said. "In fact after a while my close friends started calling me the John Rat."

"Well, did you ever meet any of your so-called famous scholars?"

"No," I said. "All I met were guys looking for dates on Saturday night."

"Now I know you're putting me on," she said, followed by a laugh that sounded more like a scream than anything else.

I laughed.

"You're too much," she said, still half laughing. "Tell me, what happened after you left Harvard?"

"I went to a small Catholic college in New Hampshire where we studied during the week, got drunk on weekends, and then asked for forgiveness on Sunday. For four years, this routine changed very little."

"Seems boring."

"It was."

"What did you do about your sex life?"

"Nothing, it wasn't allowed. Priests reminded us daily about the benefits of being chaste. We were saving ourselves for the saints we would marry."

She laughed, "I bet."

"May God strike me dead if I'm lying," I said, wanting her to think I was kidding.

"Vinnie Serrano, I like you," she smiled widely, "would you like to get out of here and go to my place? And please don't consider me fast."

"I don't," I said, "I think it's an excellent idea."

"Good," she said as she stood up, "but first I got to go to the bathroom. I'll see if there are any scholarly Harvard types hanging around in there, in case you still want to realize your fantasy. Okay?"

"Okay," I laughed, as I stood up and watched her move through the crowd, full of self-assurance and sexiness. Another first, I thought, first being in a hotel with Angie and now the first being asked by a woman to come to her place. Too much.

I looked over to where Jimmy was standing, talking to a group of people. I moved closer, to hear what he was saying.

"You might say it was right in front of his nose." Jimmy laughed to himself. Some of his audience laughed too. I guessed it was because they thought they were supposed to.

"Come on, Jimmy, don't stop now," an anxious voice shouted from the audience.

"I'm sorry," he said shyly. "A good teacher has to get his students interested. Right, Vinnie?" He looked over at me and winked.

"Right," I mumbled... *God, what should I do...*

Soon I felt myself trembling and getting sick to my stomach. *Please. Oh, God. Help.*

"That's it, people," Jimmy said still smiling at me. "Today's lecture on Nosetivity is over. Study hard, like all good students do. Okay?"

Someone handed Jimmy a drink. He finished it in one gulp and headed in my direction.

When he reached me, he put his arm around my shoulders and said with a forced grin on his face, "Let's talk where it's quiet, okay?"

I nodded obediently.

Then everything happened so fast. He dropped his arm from my shoulders, strongly gripped my elbow and quickly guided me across the room toward the bathroom.

When we reached the line of people who were waiting to get into the bathroom, he pushed me past them and started knocking on the door. "Hurry up, I got a person who is having a heart attack."

"Okay, Okay," a husky female voice on the other side of the door yelled back. "I'm coming." The voice belonged to Tatum.

A few seconds later, she opened the door. "Are you serious, Jim? Oh, hi, Vinnie," she said, now turning her eyes on me. "Are you really having a heart attack? You look so pale."

"No," I mumbled weakly. I imagined myself pushing Jimmy aside and running out with her.

"For Christ's sake, it's not his heart," Jimmy said angrily, "I only said that to get you to open the fucking door. Can't you see that the poor son of a bitch is going to blow his lunch?"

But before she could answer, Jimmy had pushed me past her and was slamming the door close behind us. Then Jimmy shoved me ahead of him with such force that I bounced off the bathroom wall. "Wha-what, what's the problem?" I stammered, as I staggered around, realizing now that I was scared shitless.

The wild look in Jimmy's eyes was the same as it was when he was beating up that poor boy.

"You always thought you were hot shit," he finally said. The muscles in his neck were taut and tense. "Like, you were too good for us."

"I-I don't know what you mean."

"You know exactly what I mean."

"I really don't."

"Cut the shit, Vinnie. You always acted aloof when you were with us guys. And you know it. We all hated the way you used to stay in the background, as us guys talked about fucking or balling someone. Always acting like some self-righteous bitch."

"I never meant it to be taken that way."

"Sure that's why you corrected us guys when we didn't say the *th's* in *length* or fucked up the *n't* sound in *couldn't* or *shouldn't*. Don't give me that. You knew exactly what you were doing."

"I don't know what you're saying," I said quickly, "Look, Jimmy, if the real reason you're saying all of this is because you're worried about what I know, forget it. You're my cousin. My God, Jimmy...."

"Cousin! Shit! You would still screw me, cousin or no cousin. Everyone in this world is out to fuck over the other guy."

"Oh, wow, you really have been hurt to feel that way," I said, hoping now that I could change the subject from me to him. "God, if relatives can't trust each other then it's a sad state of affairs."

"Yeah, maybe so," he said, "I just wish I could believe you." The fight seemed to be going out of his words.

Thank you, God. Everyone always said that I was better with my mouth than my hands.

"You could, Jimmy," I said, "there's too much of the same blood in us for me to be lying. If you need help, I'm ready to help. And I mean it. No bullshitting."

"Help is really not what I want," he said, as he started to nervously pace back and forth in the small bathroom. "I just need someone to talk to about him. That's all. I'll never forget the simple-ass grin on his face while he was choking and gasping for his last breath. Sometimes I think the son of a bitch worked on getting me to hate him over the years so that I would be his executioner. Always making fun of me, with those screwball stories of his. Once, I remember this time when, after beating the shit out of me, he told me he should've killed me as soon as I was born, for I was no good. Do you believe that shit? Telling this to a kid about seven or eight." He shook his head in disgust. "Then, when I was about fourteen, he started to tell everybody that he didn't have a son named Jimmy, the devil took him in birth. The hurt from those things and others was unbearable. A father saying those kinds of things to a young kid. God, I had no other choice but to hate him."

I shook my head. "It's sad, but I also had some of the same kind of problems with my father."

He stopped pacing and laughed weirdly. "We Serranos just didn't make it in getting loving and accepting fathers, did we? It's the burden we were born with." His eyes suddenly got watery as his words now came out strained and choked. "I just wish I could describe to people how it is to live with someone who never uses your name. It was always you bitch, bastard, cocksucker, lazy-no-good-for-nothing. His best words in English you know."

Soon small streaks of water ran down his cheeks, as he continued to speak, almost too softly. "Vin, it's so, so hard to live with someone who tells you from the moment you wake up until you go to bed that he hates you. Just a smile, just a nice word, just something, but all I got was his hate, misery, and ignorant peasant ways." His voice was no longer audible, as his glassy eyes searched aimlessly, while he tightly clenched the skin of his bottom lip between his teeth. Then, almost simultaneously, he ran his fingers nervously through his thick hair and braced up, as if someone reminded him to do so. He seemed to be desperately trying to change the subject and mood within himself and with me.

"I think I understand," I said.

"Vinnie, you have to be strong," he said confidently. All traces of his tear-filled emotion of just a little while ago were gone. The same cocky, bold son of a bitch was back.

"It's all in here," he added as he pointed to his head. "That's why I'm so passionate about Ziegler's Theory of Nosetivity. It's getting me through. Very few people in this world have strong convictions about anything. And that's the problem. You see, I believe the great American ideals went down the drain when the WASPS got kicked in the balls in the Sixties. And now it's a battle for people's minds. Someone once said that the greatest calling for all men is to lead. Nosetivity is only a small part of it."

I really wanted to share my ideas about the book I was working on and its implications for the world, but I was scared that he might feel I was playing the condescending intellectual game. And I didn't want that.

"Damn, Vin," he said, "I just wish we had spent more time together when we were younger."

I nodded. "There was so much we should've done when we were younger. But the past is over. Somehow, we must forget and move ahead."

"I should've listened to my mother," he said. "She said you could've been a good influence on me. Maybe I would be some famous scientist now," he laughed. "Still there's one good thing, I've gotten free of him! And my mother doesn't have to take his shit anymore. Shit, enough depressing thoughts, I'm going out and get really fucking drunk. Want to join me?"

"In a little while," I said, "I got to take a leak."

"Okay," he said, as he turned and headed toward the bathroom door. But just before he opened the door, he turned around and said in a colder tone of voice, "Vinnie, I could very easily forget about us being cousins, if I hear you said anything." He chuckled to himself, turned, opened the door, and left.

I followed a few minutes later. Tatum was waiting. "Is everything okay?"

"Yes," I said, wanting her and all the sympathy that existed in her. "Let's go."

"Okay."

We left.

7

The stench of boiled cabbage hung heavy in the air, while Tatum led me up two flights of dimly lit stairs. We walked down a long hallway. A husky, gruff bark of a dog came from behind an apartment door as we passed by. From another apartment a strong baritone voice blurted out something about the busing problem; it blended in with the monotonous muffled sounds of boom then pause, boom then pause. I remembered the flashing red neon sign, "The Flys," which was beside the door where we came in.

We reached her apartment door, and she opened it with her key. I followed her in. From one corner of the room, a fairly large rectangular-shaped aquarium threw off a soft greenish light. She went over and turned on two Tiffany-style lamps that stood at the ends of a rust-colored sofa. The room looked expensively decorated.

"Wait here," she said, "I'll get some wine." She crossed the room toward a small kitchen. On the way over she told me she had majored in art education at Wellesley.

I took off my coat and examined one of the lamps more closely. I noticed that each glass panel on the lampshade had been meticulously painted by hand. Each one represented an event that eventually led up to a scene where a group of people dressed in stiff, Victorian clothes were having a picnic in a serene lush-green English-looking countryside. I wondered if she had painted the scenes. They were really good.

"I've been trying to get this wine bottle open, but it just doesn't want to work for me," Tatum called from the kitchen.

"Okay," I said and joined her in the kitchen. When I reached her, I gently took the corkscrew and wine bottle from her hands. Trying to act cool and experienced, I played with the corkscrew until I got the screw part started in the cork; but, as I was clamping down the lipped-cup of the corkscrew over the rim of the bottle, I clamped my left forefinger instead. Jesus Christ did it hurt. And soon blood was spurting out all over the place. I was terribly embarrassed.

"Nice play, Vinnie," I said with a sigh.

"Don't worry," she said seductively, "I'll take care of it." She kissed my finger and sucked the blood off. Then she took my finger out of her mouth, led me to the sink and ran cold water over it for a couple of minutes. Once the bleeding had stopped, she wrapped my finger in a white cloth napkin. I thought it looked like I had stuck my finger inside a cue ball.

Then to be cute, I tried sticking my cue ball finger in my ear. I laughed. She laughed. But suddenly our laughing stopped as I pulled her close to me. We kissed. She held me tight, almost too tight. Her body now shook violently. It scared me.

"I'm glad you made the first pass," she said, gasping for air and still shaking. What the hell, I thought, that comment is out of the Fifties.

With our arms locked around each other, we moved from the kitchen to the sofa. The cue ball on my finger fell off in the process. She still shook uncontrollably. I prayed she wasn't a damn kook who was having a neurotic convulsion.

We sat on the sofa, kissed again, and before I knew it, I was down and she was straddling me on my face. I couldn't breathe. This was too fast for me. Then I felt her moist tongue swishing around in my ear. I loved this. My body tingled.

Her body was no longer trembling. She was strangely calm and confident as she took charge. "Let's get naked, Vinnie."

"Okay," I said.

While we undressed I didn't look at her. I was scared.

Gently, she pushed me back down on the sofa. This time she came down on me by planting her hands besides my head and leaned forward ever so slightly so that her large breasts loomed over my face. I reached up and cupped one of her breasts in my hands and kissed it lightly. So great. I was free. Totally free then. I sucked hard on them until it hurt her, but she said it was okay.

Later that night, I woke up and felt her fingers slowly drawing imaginary circles on my chest. I found it hard to speak. Then I brought my wrist up to my face and looked at my watch. "Jesus, it's almost five in the morning," I said, sounding a bit panicky. "Wonderful, Vinnie, your parents were only expecting you twenty hours ago. I got to go."

"Do you have to?"

"Yes, I must, even though I would rather stay here."

"I wish you would too."

"I must," I repeated, as I sat up with her head still lying against my chest. She got the message, as she now leaned back against the sofa. Then I quickly stood up and dressed in front of her. *Get your ass moving, Vinnie, this woman is nothing, really nothing. She couldn't hold a candle to Chris. Get out.*

She asked me if I was close to Jimmy's father. I said, not really, but he was close to my father. She said she couldn't see how Jimmy was partying when his father had just died. I said it was a long story, and it was too complicated to get into now.

She got up and came over to me. "Could you do anything like that? You know, enjoy yourself when your father just died?"

"No," I said, feeling a bit weak and wondering why she asked that question. I hadn't realized how tired I was.

"Good," she said as she placed her arms around my neck and kissed me lightly on the forehead. "Please promise you'll call before you leave Boston. I want to see you again."

"Sure," I lied.

"I don't want this to turn into a one night affair," she said.

"Okay."

"Then you'll promise you'll call?"

"I promise."

I kissed her on the nose, turned, and headed toward the door. She followed. As I reached for the doorknob, she tapped me lightly on the shoulder. I turned, and she kissed me with the same trembling emotion of a few moments ago.

I also felt something trembling inside of me.

8

I walked the streets of the North End until I heard the bells of Sacred Heart announcing the seven o'clock Sunday mass. You can't avoid it any longer, I thought, go and get it over with. Show him he can't hurt you anymore.

Now, as a light snow started to fall, I headed toward my parents' apartment on Hanover Street.

My hand was on the doorknob, as the door opened from the other side. It was my mother. A tiny, pretty, bleach-blond woman. She was wearing a simple but expensive-looking black dress with a string of pearls hanging over her lemon-sized breasts.

"Hi."

"Hi."

Our voices were strained and stiff. I leaned over, kissed her lightly on the cheek, and closed the door behind.

"I was worried," she said. "I expected you much sooner."

"I'm sorry," I said, as we moved through the living room and headed toward the kitchen. "I went to see some friends in Quincy, and one thing led to another, and before I knew what was happening, I fell asleep on their sofa. The plane ride took a lot out of me."

"You should've called," she said, struggling not to show anger.

You've had much practice in keeping your feelings locked deep inside of you, haven't you, Mom?

"Well, I just couldn't because of the circumstances," I said helplessly, as I settled myself on one of the chrome-legged kitchen chairs. My elbows on the table, I rubbed my eyes with my fingertips. "God, I'm tired."

"Have some coffee," she said, as she moved over to the stove.

Is this it, Mom, after eight years? Have some coffee. Why, Mom, are you so scared of me?

"Okay."

She came over to the kitchen table and placed a cup of coffee in front of me.

"How about some nice homemade cookies?" she asked, as she walked over to the kitchen cupboard. I remembered how happy she would be when she was helping Aunt Concetta prepare a large feast for the Cassallanos. Serving was what the Italian woman was all about. And, of course, cleaning. I would be amazed at how many times a week my mother scrubbed the kitchen floor, vacuumed the furniture and rugs, and washed the outside steps, which were hopeless because of their age. Over the years, she trained my father and me to take our shoes off before we entered the apartment. I wondered, quickly, if she was worried now because my shoes were wet from the snow outside.

"Please sit, Mom, you look tired," I pleaded. "Never mind the cookies, the coffee is good enough." *God, can't you see, Mom, how difficult it is for us to speak to each other. Never mind the damn cookies, tell me what you're really thinking.*

Holding a cup of coffee in her hands, she came over and sat down across from me. I looked at her. I could see the toll of living with him had started to show, especially the deep lines fanning her eyes. She looked tired and beat.

"How's Aunt Concetta doing?"

"I'm worried about her," she said, nervously twisting the coffee cup in her hands. "I hope everything will go all right with the funeral and all."

"It will, don't worry, Mom, she has been planning it for years."

"Vinnie, please, don't you start. One's enough," she said, feeling sorry for herself. Her eyes jumped to the bathroom door, which was only a couple of feet from us. The other door in the kitchen led to my pint-sized bedroom. I could see a yellow light shining from underneath the bathroom door. He was in there.

"I'm just so happy I have the brothers I have," she continued, with great affection. "They've been a godsend for Aunt Concetta during this sad time. You know, they made all the arrangements for Uncle Louie's funeral without anyone ever asking them. They've been wonderful."

Sure that's because Aunt Concetta has bought them off with free meals and gifts.

"I wonder what they are expecting in return," I said with a bit of sarcasm in my voice.

"Come on, Vinnie, be nice," she said, weakly defending them; but, somehow, I felt she felt the same inside. "They're my brothers."

"I'm sorry, Mom." She looked so tired. Then I surprised myself at what I did next. I reached over and stroked her hand with a gentleness I've never had for her before. *Why can't I say what I'm feeling? God, she's my mother.*

Both embarrassed, our hands quickly slid apart. Then she shifted the subject. "Vinnie, I've been worried. I don't want you to start with him. I don't care what he says. Right now he's mad, because, he figures, a son who comes home to make up should at least be here on time. But let him be. Please."

"Make up," I said unbelievingly. "Don't tell me he's starting on that shit again."

"Ssshh, he might hear you," she said. "Whisper." She leaned over the table, stretching her head closer to mine, "And please, Vinnie, don't use that language. I don't like it. It sounds so dirty."

Yes, Mom. Have you forgotten the time you called me a cock-sucker, when I walked into your clean apartment with mud on my shoes. Have you?

"Okay," I said begrudgingly, feeling anger build up in me.

"Now, whatever he says, just listen. I don't want this to be another day to remember like that time. I still feel so bad that your wife had to see it all.

Don't worry she's a saint, you know. They breed on troubles and sufferings.

"I won't start. I promise."

She sighed with relief as her eyes filled with tears. "Thank you, thank you."

The phone rang. She stood up and went over to the phone hanging on the kitchen wall. Then with her hand on the receiver, she turned to me and said, "It's probably Aunt Concetta." Tears were still brimming in her eyes. "With all her troubles she still calls. That woman, I swear, is a saint."

"Hmm."

She picked up the receiver and started talking to Aunt Concetta. While she stood sideways, head tipped against the receiver, my thoughts turned to Aunt Concetta. I thought about how she used people in her attempts to become rich and successful.

I remembered it was the talk of the North End, how she saved herself twelve thousand dollars by using her brothers in renovating a run-down apartment building. She paid them nothing. In fact, it was said that they bought the materials.

I remembered one summer, when she gave me a job at twenty dollars a week for cleaning up a smoke-damaged apartment building. I heard she had bought it for almost nothing. Ten to twelve hours a day, Grandfather Cassallano and I worked our asses off, trying to get the coal-black soot off the walls and floors. I remembered going home each night and spitting up black phlegm for hours on end. When I used to complain to my mother, she would say I should be thankful that I had a job. Moreover, she would say I should even work harder because Aunt Concetta was family. Of course, Aunt Concetta knew this too. *Except only too well.*

Later that summer, in the middle of August, Grandfather Cassallano died of a heart attack. I knew that the carrying of refrigerators, sofas, mattresses, bedsprings, and so on was part of the cause. Soon after the funeral, my father, in one of his frequent attacks on Aunt Concetta, screamed the same thing at my mother. "The money-hungry whore killed her own father."

"Mario, stop." She was hurt. "How could you say that? She's been so good to us."

"What do you mean?" he exploded. "Damn you, Anna, she gives us a few meals a year. And that's only because you kill yourself for her. Big deal."

"You don't appreciate anything."

"And you don't want to hear the truth," he shouted back at her. "That woman will do the same thing to you as she did to your father. Mark my word."

"You talk crazy," she said, trembling with anger.

"Okay, you wait and see," he said. "Everything I say comes out true. I..."

They went on like this so many times when they argued. I would turn over in bed and fall asleep, pretending that it was all part of a bad dream.

After that summer, Aunt Concetta used to joke with me about being afraid to come back to work for her because she worked me too hard. She was right. So many times I wanted to tell her to go fuck herself, but instead I just nodded, smiled like a nice boy, and accepted defeat.

The holidays were the times when Aunt Concetta supposedly showed her gratitude to the family. Everyone was invited to spend them with her. She would buy the food, and her slaves, especially my mother, would cook it. On Christmas, her gifts always seemed to be the most pricey: brand new fifty-dollar bills for each of her brothers and expensive clothes for their children. Shit, I used to think, why not, what's a couple hundred dollars in comparison to the thousands of dollars her family had saved her as she became one of the biggest landlords in the North End. But her real job was being an editor. She was bright and educated.

My mother, Anna, worshiped Aunt Concetta and did anything she asked. I believed, for some reason or other, she had resigned herself to being subservient to Aunt Concetta for the rest of her life. Only once, I remember, did my mother express any frustration over Aunt Concetta's way of doing things. One night, lying in bed, I heard loud whispering going on in the kitchen. My mother was complaining to her brother Nick about every few months having to go along with Aunt Concetta to Cape Cod. She hated these trips, she said. They were boring, for Aunt Concetta used to leave her alone in the motel room, while she went off for two days and nights and helped a young author edit his manuscript. The business with the author was never questioned by her or her brother. The doing nothing was her problem. She whispered sadly, "But she is so good to me. What can I do? I just hate sitting around, doing nothing." Her brother Nick was very sympathetic. When I left eight years ago, not only was Aunt Concetta making trips to Cape Cod, but also to Maine, to Vermont, to upstate New York, and to other secluded places where young authors could hide from the world, and where they could screw their editors in their spare time.

"Vinnie, VINNIE, did you hear me?"

"No, what?" I said with my mind still somewhere between thoughts of Aunt Concetta and my mother's loud voice.

She was standing next to me, frowning. I looked up.

"For God's sake, Vinnie, sometimes I think your father is right, you live in a different world."

I wondered, when she said things like this, if she had something in common with him, hate. When I was younger, I felt that was the only way she could get close to him. Bitch about me. It helped them to forget the real feelings they had for each other.

"I'm sorry, Mom," I said. "I told you I didn't get much sleep last night."

"Always excuses," she replied disapprovingly.

I closed my eyes and turned my head away.

Silence.

I opened my eyes. She was sitting across from me, shaking her head. "What I said," she went on, in a softer tone of voice, "is that Aunt Concetta wants you to come over there for supper tonight. She's been telling everyone how wonderful you are to come all the way from West Virginia for Uncle Louie's funeral."

"I'll see," I said. "I don't know if I could put up with all of them. At least not now."

"Please Vinnie, you've got to go," she pleaded. "She's been so good to you and to me through the years. How would it look?"

Mom, I never wanted any of those gifts. She just sent them, hoping it would relieve the guilt she had for shitting on you. Hell, I would've sent them all back if it wasn't for Chris. The silverware for our wedding, the clothes for the kids, the fifty-dollar bills on their birthdays, the toasters, the electric ovens, the encyclopedias and so on, and so on. Every single one of those damn gifts I would've sent back, if Chris hadn't convinced me that you would've been terribly hurt if I rejected your sister like that.

"Hell, Mom," I shook my head. "I don't know if I could put up with all those loud-mouth brothers of yours, and then watch you wait on her like she was some kind of royalty."

"Vinnie, please," she said.

"Okay, but sometimes, Mom, you must admit that your brothers are too much to take all at one time."

"I know," she said apologetically. "But they have changed since you last saw them. They really have."

"Well, I just can't believe Uncle Phil has changed. Always trying to prove the Cassallanos are smarter than the Serranos. Mom, I'm above all of that now. Understand?"

"Yes, I know you are," she said, "But believe me, he's changed. He teaches in Braintree and loves it. You'll see he's not as loud as before."

"I hope so,"

"Listen, Vinnie," she said as she leaned forward, motioning for me to get closer. "If Phil starts anything, do what I said to do with your father, just listen, keep your mouth shut, and pretend that whatever he's saying, he's right."

Like all good Italian boys. Right, Mom?

"Let me just see how I'm feeling after I get a couple hours' rest. Okay? I'll probably be there, so don't worry."

"Good," she sounded relieved as she leaned back against her chair, her arms stretched out in front of her, crossed at the hands.

Just then, I heard the sounds of his gargling in the bathroom.

"Ssshh," she said, bringing her forefinger up to her pursed lips. She leaned forward again bringing her arms close to her chest.

I shook my head. "I just can't believe that he's still mad. You would've thought after eight years he would've mellowed a bit."

"Please, Vinnie, he might hear you," she whispered. "We've been talking too loud."

"Okay."

"He has mellowed some. But since Uncle Louie's death, he seems lost." Again, she motioned for me to bring my head closer. "He's drinking worse than ever."

"Why?"

"Sometimes I think it's because his business is not too good," she said. People, instead of getting old shoes fixed, buy new ones and throw the old ones out. So now he has a lot of free time during the day to think about himself and whatever he does on those nights he disappears."

"Does he still do that?" I asked, somewhat surprised. I wondered, with all his free time now, if he ever thought about that night.

"Yes," she nodded sadly.

"Where the hel—I mean heck, does he go?"

"I don't know, and I don't care anymore," she said bitterly. Her whole mood shifted. "He goes his way, and I go mine. I'm not going to spend the rest of my life worrying where he goes at night. No more."

She pushed the kitchen chair back, stood up, and went over to the stove and poured herself some more coffee. I could see her face blush and tears brimming in her eyes again.

I stood up and went over to her. She waved me away. She was embarrassed. Setting the coffee cup down on the stove, she turned, stared at me for a second, and then rushed past me into the living room and toward her bedroom door. I followed. She opened and slammed the door behind her.

I knocked. "Mom, you okay?"

"Yes," she answered weakly. "I'll be fine in a few minutes. I'm just tired."

"You sure?"

"Yes, I'll be okay," her voice trembled. "Please don't make a fuss. He might hear, and that's all I need."

"Okay." I obeyed.

I turned and looked around at the living room. It could've been a showcase for a Mr. Clean ad. Nothing ever looked out of place. On one side, a golden yellow contemporary sofa stood against the wall, with glass end tables at its sides. On the top of each table was a large, milk-glass lamp. I thought, they probably paid for everything in cash, for my father, except for what she just told me, had a good business—owning a shoe repair business and the building it was in. My mother also worked, since I could remember, as a secretary at the North End Community Center. It didn't pay much, but, along with what my father made, it gave her enough money to decorate the apartment the way she wanted it.

She was always reading *Better Homes and Gardens, Good Housekeeping* and other similar magazines, which now were all neatly arranged in a row on the glass-top coffee table in front of the sofa. I thought how many times she must've dreamt of having her own home with lots and lots of rooms to clean and decorate. Of course, he was against moving and buying a home. Everything they needed was there, he used to say.

Anyway, we were never hurting for money, like some of the people around us. In fact, they paid for my undergraduate and master's degree work. However, after that time, everything stopped, and my mother was forbidden to send me anything. Whatever she did, it was done on the sly.

On each side of the small archway that led into the kitchen, there was a chestnut, low-backed chair. Over each chair hung a painting. Several years ago, I bought one of them for their anniversary. It depicted a small clear lake, surrounded by long thin pine trees reaching into a cloudless sky. I thought at the time that the lake looked friendlier, more personal, than the omnipotent sea that surrounded us. The other painting was of a tiny village, nestled against a steep hillside. My mother told me that a close friend gave it to her. She said my father liked it because it reminded him of the village in Italy where he came from.

Underneath the two narrow windows that faced the street, was a bookcase my father had made for me when I was in high school. It was as new-looking as on the day he gave it to me. On the first two shelves there were pictures of me at my first communion, confirmation, and graduations, plus pictures of my children and a black-and-white wedding picture of Chris and me. On the third shelf, lying down on their side, were the two textbooks I had written. Books from my early years in college filled the rest of the bookcase. To one side of the bookcase, in the corner, was a large TV.

A few minutes later, the bedroom door opened. I turned around. Mom walked out.

"I'm okay now," she said in a firm voice while her bloodshot eyes said just the opposite. "Just promise me you won't start with your father, Vinnie."

"I won't," I said. *Tell me, Mom, was it true what they said about you. Were you too nervous to have me?*

"Over and over I hear the same thing," she said dejectedly. "How you took his hard-earned money for your schooling, and how you promised him you wouldn't get married for at least three years after you got your PhD. Then, how you had the nerve to get married before you finished. God, Vinnie, I've heard it so many times, that I know every word by heart."

"I'm sorry you have to put up with all of that. I'll tell you, if he starts with that stuff and that you're-no-good stuff again, I'm leaving."

"He won't," she said, as we moved into the kitchen.

"We'll see," I said, as I sat down again on one of the kitchen chairs. She moved closer to me and softly said, "Sometimes, I wish you gave in halfway. I know, what's done is done. But, Vinnie, you don't know what it's like, not being able to see your son, his wife, and your grandchildren. It's not right."

I looked at her. I thought she was going to start to cry again.

"I know it's been hard on you, Mom, but he wanted it that way. The kids only know you as the grandma in Boston who sends them gifts on their birthdays and at Christmastime. How do you think I feel watching my kids grow to love only my wife's parents. It's unfair. Paulie once asked me what an Italian was. Do you believe that? That is really sad."

She laughed under her breath. "Tell him about your father, then he'll really know. Right?"

"Yeah, that's right," I smiled superficially. I heard the bathroom door open. Quickly, my mother backed around the kitchen table and sat down again. I looked to my side. My father walked toward us. He looked so much smaller and older than eight years ago. His forehead now had creases, one above the other. Time had also given him two deep ruts that went in a crescent fashion from the sides of his Roman nose to the corners of his huge lips.

"Hi, Dad," I said, trying hard to sound friendly.

He nodded.

I watched him as he veered to the sink, his chunky hand combing his thick, graying black hair, his deep-seated brown eyes avoiding mine. The tension that now hung in the air was like the feeling one gets watching two fighters trying to stare each other down just before the beginning of a championship fight.

At the sink, he ran the water and then checked it with his forefinger every few seconds to see if it was cold enough. When it was, he stuck a glass underneath the spurting waterstream, and, with one huge gulp, he emptied the glass. For a long moment, he just stood there, his back facing me, staring out the small window over the sink. Some middle-age flabbiness was pressing hard against the hipline of his black pants. Still, he was well-built. When I was younger I remember everyone saying that he looked like and was built like the fighter Rocky Marciano.

"It's been a long time," I said, just to say something. I hated it. It sounded like a line from a soap opera.

He said nothing.

My mother said nothing. She just sat there with an expression of deep sadness on her face.

He drank another glass of water, made some funny sounds in his throat, and continued to stare out the window at the small piece of gray morning mist that was caught between our apartment building and the building in back of us.

I remembered how I used to eat lunch with him in his small shoe repair shop and how, after school, I would stop back and perch myself on one of his elevated shoe shining chairs and listen to him tell stories about Italy. He'd kid a customer about making good, or bitch about the Irish and the local government. I loved it. I especially loved it when he got into an argument with one of his friends. His face would flush beet red, and his eyes would pop open like an owl's. Then, gesturing with a shoemaker's cutting knife in one hand and his black apron flopping around his solid legs, he would destroy his opponent—one, two, three—with his tongue. Sometimes he would look over to me, to see if I was looking. God, how I loved him then.

I now heard the scraping of the kitchen chair against the floor; I looked over and saw my mother standing up. "I'm late for mass," she said, "I'd better go. I just put some clean sheets on your bed, Vinnie, so you go in and have a nice rest and I'll see you later at Aunt Concetta's. Okay?"

"Fine."

"Go, go help the big shot," he shouted, without turning around.

My mother pretended she didn't hear him. "You two have a nice long visit." She smiled quickly, as if she was delighted because she had an excuse to leave.

I nodded. *Thanks a lot.*

She turned and hurried out the kitchen. However, a moment later she returned. "Here's an extra key," she said, as she handed it to me.

When she left this time, she looked back and brought her forefinger to her pursed lips, reminding me about the promise I made earlier.

Soon after, I could hear her hurried footsteps going down the narrow, wooden steps, the ones she couldn't get clean and that now creaked with age as she stepped on each one. Finally, I heard the door at the bottom of the steps slam shut; the sound of its glass pane, shaking loosely in its frame, echoed faintly.

"How have you been feeling, Dad?" *Please, God, I prayed, let him speak. I can't stand it. I was scared. I wished she would've stayed.*

Finally, he turned halfway around and said rather stiffly, "Not good, all this funeral business for my brother has taken a lot out of me. They pretend they love him now, when every one of those sons of bitches has put more than one nail in his coffin."

He turned all the way around and his eyes met mine. "I was going to tell them all off last night, but I had too much respect for my brother's wake."

"Well, it will be all over after tomorrow," I said sympathetically. Then you won't have to deal with them anymore."

"It won't, it won't be over," he said loudly. "My brother only wanted to have a place of his own where he could raise his family, without the blood-sucking Cassallanos around. But Miss Big Shot didn't want to, because she wanted to be around people who would kiss her ass."

"Perhaps, he's better off dead," I said, hoping I could get him to see that I was supporting him.

"Maybe," he said. "But I just wish, I had told them off a long time ago."

"Why didn't you?" I asked, knowing as soon as I said it, that was the wrong question to ask.

"You know," he shouted.

"You're not going to start with that stuff again," I said. "I'll leave. Remember, we've gone through this before." I wanted to run out of the house, but I thought about my mother.

"Look at your own family, Miss Big Shot would say," he shouted louder, as if he was pleading his case to a jury. "A lazy bum who treated you like shit. He took all your money for school, and then he lied to you."

"Please, Dad."

It was too late. When he got mad he heard nothing but the savage beating of his heart. "Mister Hot Pants couldn't wait," he said sarcastically. "Sure, those goddamn Irish didn't want to lose a good catch. Any mother or father would want the same thing for their daughter. They're smart. Hell, they figured, with you they could be set for life."

"That's not true," I said defensively. "They've got enough to take care of both of us."

"You always have an answer," he shot back. "A good education means your son becomes a good bullshitter."

I said nothing. I felt my stomach turning while my throat tickled. I'll be damned, I thought, if I'll cry in front of him.

He leaned against the sink, his arms bent and lightly gripping the front edge. "You think your father knows nothing except shining and cutting leather."

"Come on, Dad," I said.

"No, you couldn't listen to me eight years ago," he said, lecturing more than anything else. "Without a family you would've been able to save and invest your money. A doctor. A lawyer. That's what you should've become, not a school teacher. There are millions of them."

"I'm a professor, not a school teacher," I said.

"No difference," he said. "You all have to work for someone."

"Well, I really don't care," I said. "Money is not that important to me."

"You're crazy," he shook his head in disgust. "Look at Paulucci's son, he's a doctor now. He makes three hundred and fifty thousand dollars a year. Last year, he built a new home for himself and his father in Newton. But no, you had to get married right away, buy a big house, a big car, and have kids."

"So?"

"What if I did that?" he asked in a taunting fashion. "Where would you have gotten the money for your education? I was lucky I worked for myself. I was able to screw the other guy before he screwed me."

"That's a terrible way to look at the world," I said. "You got married a lot younger than me."

"Sure, but like it or not, son, it's a dog-eat-dog world," he said, almost affectionately. "That's America and that's why you'll never have anything. You always trust people. I don't trust anyone."

Then he started to pace the kitchen floor like a caged wild animal, firing up his anger with each step. I had almost forgotten how quickly he changes from one mood to another.

"You don't know what you put me through," he said savagely. "You don't know!"

"Hell, what do you want from me," I exploded. "Because I got married. What the hell are you talking about?"

Then I stood up as he backed up a bit, "I never gave you any trouble. I never stole anything. I didn't murder anyone. I never did anything that would embarrass you. Jesus. I went on to school, got my PhD. You wanted me to get a good education. Okay, I disobey you once concerning something that you should've been very happy about."

He moved toward me, I thought he was going to hit me. "You didn't do all those things for me, you selfish son of a bitch."

"You're just like Uncle Louie," I said helplessly.

"So, what? I'm proud to be compared to my brother. He was not a liar and not a bum, like our sons."

"Hell, man, I never asked to be born to you," I said completely crushed. I could feel my face burning.

"That's right," he said. "Mister Sensitive, get mad now. I didn't mean that. I was just talking." He backed off, leaning against the sink, his head shaking in disgust.

"Talking, my ass," I shot back at him. Tears were in my eyes. I thought of Jimmy, and Uncle Louie saying he didn't have a son.

"You're like her, you take everything so personal," he said, feeling sorry for himself. "I can't talk to you. Go, go where you have to go." He turned, bent over, opened the cupboard underneath the sink and took out a bottle half-full with dark-red wine.

With my heart pounding like crazy and tears running down my cheeks, I turned, ran to my old room, and slammed the door behind me. The room was gray. I leaned against the door and heard him mumbling something about what a shame it was that father and son couldn't talk. He always did that, I thought. *Destroy someone and then afterwards pretend it's the other person's fault. God, I hated him.*

I moved limply across my small room to a frost-covered window and pressed my tear-streaked face against it. The cold frost felt good against my burning face.

I was twelve, I saw him in the distance walking north on Hanover Street. I thought I would try to catch up with him, thinking he was going to the Roman Social Club. I loved it when he let me watch him play cards. It was like peeking in on a secret society with all its rites and ceremonies. I saw him turn down Wall Street, away from the social club. I was disappointed; but, for some reason I continued to follow him. He went into an apartment building. I followed and watched him knock softly at a first-floor apartment. Before long, a woman opened the door. She was huge. Tall and big breasts. Affectionately, my father patted her back, as she closed the door behind them. I went to the door and looked through the keyhole. I saw my father kiss her and undress her. Their arms and legs were tangled all over... Enough and enough. I ran out. Full of repulsion and hate. I wanted to kill him. As I ran, I remembered Sister Louise, saying that we all have some sort of cross to bear in this life, and there was nothing we could do about it. It was God's will...

I would lie awake, night after night, concentrating hard on what my mother and father would be talking about in the kitchen. Nothing at all was ever said about me. The thing I did notice was that my father was especially nice to my mother those nights he yelled or screamed at me. Sometimes, when he was drunk enough, he beat me with a razor strop until I was black and blue. What made matters even worse, it made me feel like an orphan.

When my father did start to talk to me again, after these nights of beatings, he was mean and belligerent. Not helping my mother; forgetting to flush; spending too much time reading; leaving crumbs after a late night snack. These important things all became good excuses for my father to unleash his anger on me.

But it was my cross. And I knew that for sure about a year later, when he started to yell at me for not closing the downstairs door.

"Lazy bastard," he'd shout as I headed for my room. "If the nuns only knew that their Mr. Smarty Pants still can't clean his ass right without his mother cleaning up after him."

"Why do you hate me so much," I said coldly. And before the words were out of my mouth, he was grabbing me from behind and hurling me against the kitchen stove.

"Mario!" I heard my mother scream as I sank down to the floor and cried like a baby.

I remember my father left that night and never came home for three days. My mother said that he was sleeping in the shop because he couldn't face me.

Only one other time would he come after me, and that was the day I brought Chris home. Still, in the years following the not-closing-the-door incident, his anger could boil over at me. He always came close to hitting me, but always stopped short of it.

I'll never forget the months between flunking out of Harvard and finally deciding to go to Saint Boniface in New Hampshire. I expected the worst. But for some reason, he left me alone. Sometimes I even felt that he wanted to reach out and comfort me.

I wondered now if that's why I promised him that I would wait for at least three years after I finished my schooling to get married.

Such a stupid promise, I can't believe he's still upset about it.

I could see that it was getting brighter outside. People and cars were starting to jam the sidewalks and streets of the North End below. My head started to pound, slowly at first and then it started to pick up, as a fire seemed to be igniting in my stomach.

I took a deep breath and prayed to God for no more thoughts of that night, for not closing that fucking downstairs door. Then I went to my bed, took off my shoes, pulled back the covers, and slid in with all my clothes on. The sheet underneath felt cold but it smelled clean and fresh. I pulled the top sheet and blanket up until they covered my head. I closed my eyes, and sleep finally came.

I heard a telephone ringing. I shook my head. I didn't know where I was or where the telephone was. I opened my eyes. I looked for a bedside table that wasn't there. Then I remembered, I was in my old room.

The phone kept ringing. Finally, I got up and hurried toward the kitchen.

I picked the receiver up. "Hello," I replied, still groggy from sleeping.

"Vinnie." It was my mother. "It's seven o'clock, and they've already finished eating."

"God, is it that late?"

"Yes, Aunt Concetta's been asking about you all night," she said irritably. In the background, I could hear loud talking. I pictured Aunt Concetta sitting at the head of her enormous, oval mahogany table. On occasions like this, when the whole family was present, five extension boards would be inserted. It stretched from one end of the living room to the middle of the kitchen. Two sets of louver doors, attached to the walls and separating the kitchen from the living room, would be opened to make this possible. I wondered if her living room furniture was still covered with transparent plastic. I remembered how cold the plastic felt in the winter.

"How did it go?" my mother asked.

"What?" I asked dumbly. My thoughts were still with Aunt Concetta's table.

"Your father didn't say two words during dinner. Now he's asleep in one of the chairs. I think he had too much to drink. What happened?"

"Nothing, just that he started with that same old crap again. I'm sorry, I just couldn't take it anymore."

"You'll never learn, Vinnie, will you?" I could hear her breathing heavily into the receiver.

"Mom, don't start. I had enough with him," I said, feeling sorry for myself.

"Okay, but get over here now," she said with authority.

"I will," I said. "Let me take a quick shower, and I'll be right over."

"Okay, okay, just get over here, please," she pleaded, in an anxious tone of voice.

I hung up. I stood there for a moment, thinking some more about the arrangements at Aunt Concetta's. The table would be covered with a very expensive linen tablecloth, but like on the living room furniture, a piece of transparent plastic would be placed on top of it so that it would be protected from greasy human hands, tomato sauce, meatballs, and so on.

The chairs on each side of the oval-shaped table would be arranged in a hierarchy, going from the red-velveted dining room chairs, to multicolored straight-back kitchen chairs, to dull brown folding chairs. Sitting on Aunt Concetta's left would be her mother, her brothers, and their wives; seated on her right would be her sisters—my mother and Candy's mother when she was alive—and finally the rest of the family: Jimmy, Rose, Patsy, nieces like Candy, cousins, and when Uncle Louie was alive, he would be placed with my father almost directly opposite from Aunt Concetta. Then it was obvious who was at the head and end of the table.

I thought about the food on Aunt Concetta's table, and I got hungry. The house would be filled with the aroma from the many different dishes, which contained one, or a combination of, baccala, spareribs, sausage, meatballs, flank steak. Each dish would have been tenderly cooked for many hours in a sauce made up of tomatoes, parsley, garlic, and oregano. And somewhere near would be a large serving platter of spaghetti, covered with that same sauce. I remembered how, once Aunt Concetta started to eat, the powerful jaws of her four red-cheeked brothers would begin to savagely grind away. Then everyone started chewing, chewing, eating like animals, eating fast, talking fast, never listening to each other, arguing, never completing a sentence. Each time it was a terrible letdown for me. The props for the show were great, but the show always stunk.

I wasn't hungry anymore.

I took a hot shower. The sheets of hot water pounding my body felt good. After letting it rip at my body for a long while, a warm relaxed feeling took over. My father had exhausted me. The depression of last night was gone.

I got out of the shower and wiped the steam from the mirror on the medicine cabinet. I looked at myself. A tired-looking man with dark circles under his eyes stared back at me. You could have taken his picture as an advertisement for Alka-Seltzer. Look at that face. The plop, plop, fizz, fizz will work wonders.

Then I decided to shave, and as I started to lather my face more thoughts of Aunt Concetta came to mind.

Aunt Concetta was working full-time as an associate editor for Apollo Publishing Company on Beacon Street in Boston. I had learned from my mother's letters that Apollo was impressed with my aunt's ability to recognize what the public wanted to read. In fact, my mother said, she had been personally responsible in the last two years for getting two of Apollo's books on the *New York Times* bestseller list. Aunt Concetta had a knack for business, too: in the last twenty years she had built up a solid base of customers for her antiques store in the North End. Even though Rose, her daughter, ran it, she didn't have the head for business, according to Concetta. For sure, Concetta was the smartest of all the Cassallanos. She was the valedictorian of her high-school class, and later she took courses at night and got her degree in business administration from Boston University.

On holidays and weekends, and whenever she could get free, she worked in the antiques store. Aunt Concetta loved to barter with customers. Sharp, loud, abrupt and almost impulsive was the way she dealt with them. They loved it, especially the rich Jewish ladies from Wellesley. For a few moments she gave them a chance to revert to their poverty days, when they had to fight for every penny they spent. I remember once being in the store, and a large woman walked in, her fingers flashing with expensive-looking stones, and a mink stole covering her fullback shoulders. Before long, she was arguing with Aunt Concetta because a certain item—I can't remember exactly what it was, an ashtray, a lamp, a figurine, something little like that—anyway, she was disturbed because, she said, she could get it in New York for fifty cents. "I don't need your business, go to New York," my Aunt Concetta kept telling her. Finally, she had worn the large woman down, and, begrudgingly, she bought the item at the price Aunt Concetta wanted. Afterwards, Aunt Concetta turned to me and said, "Cheap Jews, they have more money than they know what to do with, and then they come in here and argue with me over fifty lousy cents."

Through the years I had picked up many rumors about Aunt Concetta. One was that she got the job years ago at Apollo because of her relationship with the president, who was Italian and originally from the North End. They said he gave her the job in order to get her into bed, something he couldn't do while he lived in the North End. Everyone knew that she had stopped sleeping with Uncle Louie after Jimmy was born. The plastic-covered sofa was Uncle Louie's bed for the last thirty years or so. Stories about her going to bed with famous Mafia leaders, singers, and actors were whispered throughout the North End. It was even said that she went to bed with John Kennedy when he was in the Senate. Of course, there were those trips to Cape Cod with my mother. All in all, whether or not these stories were true, one thing was for sure, she must have had a very active bed life.

Another time, I heard that one of her brothers' daughters got raped at school by a student who was her cousin. It was said that the very next day the student, the parents, the two brothers and sister were on their way to Arizona. Later, it was said the reason they left so quickly was because Aunt Concetta threatened to expose the family in the newspapers as a group of sexual deviants. Italians will do anything to protect their family's reputation. And Aunt Concetta knew that. The funny thing about all of this was that it was a well-known fact that her brother's daughter was one of the biggest whores in the school.

The success of her antiques store, the huge amount of rental property she had been able to accumulate, the position at Apollo, and even the rumors of her love life had all given her a great deal of status, power, and influence in the North End. Last year, my mother had written me that Aunt Concetta had run for city council and lost by only a small margin. But now, my mother wrote, she has the mayor's support, and with that she thought she could win next time around.

I thought about how generous she had been to me through the years; because of this, it was hard not to be nice to her, even though I hated the way my mother waited on her. Before I left, eight years ago, I started to feel uncomfortable around her. She, like her brother Phil, was persistent in trying to convince me that the Cassallanos were smarter than the Serranos. I remembered that a couple summers before I left, I was helping her clean up some old brass bedposts she had just bought. The day was hot.

The sweat poured off me as I tried hard to get the black-greenish tarnish off the posts. After a while, she came over to me and asked, "That's the kind of work you like, huh, Vinnie?"

"What?" I didn't understand. She said nothing as she lowered her eyes and smiled benevolently at me. That expression said it all. "Don't bother with the mind, Vinnie, you don't have it. Stick with hard physical labor, that's what Serranos are good at."

9

I opened the door that led up to Aunt Concetta's apartment, and slowly I began to climb the stairs. They creaked just like at my parents' house.

On the first landing, I could see and smell the wet rubber boots and shoes that were scattered along the wall outside Aunt Concetta's apartment. One boot was standing alone in the middle of the floor as if someone had kicked it there on purpose.

The sight of the wet rubber boots and shoes, lined up outside her door, brought to mind Aunt Concetta's fetish about keeping everything clean. Hers was even worse than my mother's. No one was allowed to enter the apartment with shoes on because of her shining hardwood floors and expensive oriental rugs. Only she was allowed to. Each day she carried a clean, black silk handkerchief so that when she came home she could wipe off dirt, grease, dog shit, or whatever from the bottom of her shoes. Aunt Concetta was the kind of woman who would have the black waters of the harbor cleaned, if they didn't move so damn fast.

I took off my shoes and placed them next to a pair of snake-skin cowboy boots. Then I opened the door. The room got deathly quiet, as I closed the door behind me. I looked around. The family seemed to have grown, with all the children of Aunt Concetta's brothers now old enough to sit around the oval table. In one corner of the room, I saw my father sleeping in a wingback chair. In front of him, sitting at the table was Candy, who smiled at me like a silly little girl. I felt tense.

I tried to relax as I walked over to the head of the table. I leaned over and kissed Grandmother Cassallano on the cheek, and then did the same to Aunt Concetta.

Grandmother Cassallano was a small, skinny woman who had a face unusually smooth for someone her age. She mumbled something in Italian, about how terrible it was to be old. Without waiting for her to finish, Aunt Concetta interrupted, "Thank you for coming, Vinnie."

"I'm glad I could," I lied.

Then Aunt Concetta waved in a regal manner to her brother Phil, and ordered him to bring his chair over to me so that I could sit next to her. While he fussed a bit about having to do this, I thought that Aunt Concetta hadn't really changed much in those eight years. She was still a good-looking woman for being in her late fifties. I guessed she knew it, too. She was wearing a fashionable, black dress with ruffles at the wrists and collar. Her hair was dyed deep black. It looked as silky as a sixteen-year-old girl's. She had firm breasts, very few wrinkles, and a fine, stately figure that could tempt any young adolescent.

Phil placed the chair between Aunt Concetta and Grandmother Cassallano. We said hello. He was all Italian. Black hair streaked with gray, and dark brown eyes. He was also a fat slob: fat and hair squeezed out over his belt, because the navy blue golf shirt he was wearing was too short for his stomach.

"How's your wife and kids," she asked. Her voice sounded more sophisticated than I remembered.

"Fine," I replied as I sat down. Out of the corner of my eye, I saw Phil's fat body heading for some folding chairs that were leaning against the wall. I knew he wouldn't bother me, as long as Aunt Concetta was controlling the conversation.

"I told your mother you were lucky to find such a nice Irish girl like Chris. We would like to get to know her. How long has it been since your wedding?"

"Eight years."

"That's too long."

"Yes."

"Maybe I'll come visit you with your mother."

"Okay."

"Something to drink, Vinnie?" she asked, her kindness superficial.

"No, thank you."

"Please have something," she insisted, still not meaning it. Italians were supposed to do this.

"Okay, a little white wine," I said, just like I was supposed to.

"Good. Anna, bring some white wine for Vinnie," she called to my mother in the kitchen. Somehow I had missed seeing her, standing there in front of the sink and smiling at us with a broad grin on her face. She was happy now. Her Prodigal Son was talking to her Moses.

"Your mother tells me that you've written two textbooks in math."

"Yes," I nodded.

"Who is publishing them?" Her voice was quite businesslike now.

"Smith and Brothers."

"Oh yes, a fine textbook company, I know a couple of their editors. We don't deal in textbooks, you know, because there are just too many publishing companies competing for the educational dollar. But anything else, if it will sell, we'll publish it." I noticed her hands as she gestured; they were mannish, long and muscular, like Jimmy's in a way. "The public market is the most challenging place to work in," she said. "Are you thinking of writing another textbook in math?"

The room was still very quiet. Everyone seemed to be listening intently to what we were saying.

"Not really," I answered. "I have an outline of a book in my head, but not a math book. Something I've been thinking about for a long time."

"Have you shared it with any publisher?" she asked.

Before I could answer, my mother was placing a glass of wine in front of me. I looked up. She smiled proudly and then moved to one side of me. "No, but lately I've been thinking about doing that."

"What is it about?"

"Well, it's kinda hard to describe at this point, but basically it is about Heaven."

"Heaven?" she looked puzzled. "It's not one of those evangelistic kind of books? There are hundreds of those on the market."

"No, no," I said, shaking my head. "What I want to do is to prove the existence of a higher-ordered world. A world of Truth—Truth, that's Heaven. Not the kind of Heaven we see advertised on bumper stickers. That's emotional therapy. I'm hoping to put together a book that explains Heaven together with consciousness and cosmic energy."

"A philosophical treatise, huh?"

"Sort of, I guess."

"When did you get the idea?"

"From a book by a Russian by the name of Ouspensky. He wrote it almost a hundred years ago. A fantastic book."

"You know, after listening to you," she said pensively, "it reminds me that my Jimmy is also interested in something that is very esoteric. Did you know that?"

Yes, and did you know also that he's trying to practice what he preaches?

"Yes, we talked a little about his ideas last night."

"He says he's on to something big. Something he says will change the world. Well, I don't know about that. You know, Vinnie, how Jimmy loves to exaggerate. A couple months ago, I gave him a manuscript to read. And now he thinks this Ziegler fellow who wrote it is the new Messiah. My poor Jimmy is so impressionable. It seems, every other day he's into something new. At least he is keeping busy. And, you know, he could be doing a lot of other things a lot worse."

Killing is a wonderful way to keep busy.

"Yes, it's a wonderful way to keep busy."

"Jimmy thought I should publish Ziegler's work, but I'll tell you what I told him. And that is, we publishers take an awful chance in trying to sell something like you're talking about, and what Jimmy is all hot and bothered about."

I was upset because she had the nerve to compare my thoughts with that sick stuff Jimmy was talking about last night.

"I know."

"It won't sell unless you really simplify it for the public."

"But I think that's the whole problem," I said in an argumentative tone of voice. "In the process of making it simple, we lose the difficult truths. Do you see what I mean?"

"Yes, but I know a lot of publishers would argue that people want to escape from the drudgery of their lives. They don't want to think about what you call difficult truths, because it makes them too depressed."

"I don't care," I said sharply. "What these publishers usually give the public are lies, and more lies. And, I think that's an injustice."

"I can see you're really serious about this book."

"Yes, I am," I said. "Quite serious."

"Well, then tell me more."

"It's not the right time, but 'forgetting the material world.' That's what it's about, and if the reader really works hard at understanding what I'm saying, he'll come to see that there's a chance for his soul to be in flight toward Heaven, while his body still lives on in this greedy world."

"Those are very noble ideas, Vinnie, very noble indeed."

"Oh, I don't know about that," I said.

"Perhaps you're right," she said, "and perhaps the public just might be getting tired of the perverted junk they are now reading."

"I hope so."

From here she shifted to lecturing me about the art of good writing. She told me that she reads manuscripts selfishly. She looks for new insights or some kind of confirmation of something she already knows. And, that writers today write psychoanalytical nonsense, no beginnings, no middles, no ends, et cetera, et cetera.

I sipped at my wine, half listening, and half thinking about her fat-cheeked brothers. They would go home tonight and brag for hours how Aunt Concetta held her own in a conversation with Vinnie who had a PhD in mathematics. Just another fine example of how smart she really was. I was sorry I didn't really show them what I really know.

Now she was on the subject of my book again.

"I like the idea behind your book," she said, "especially the fire in your eyes when you talk about it. Why don't you send me an outline of it, okay?"

"Sure," I said, not believing it. "I really appreciate it." I glanced over to my mother. The expression on her face was one of deep gratitude.

"Oh, don't worry about it, Vinnie," she waved me off. "Perhaps someday you could do me a favor."

"Okay." I felt elated and yet at the same time uncomfortable because of the benevolent look on her face.

"I'll show it to other editors," she said. "But listen, if I'm going to convince them about the marketability of your book, the outline has to be simple. Sorry. Vinnie, you just wouldn't believe how illiterate some of these editors are."

"I'll try," I said.

"Good! Get something to eat, Vinnie," she said, shifting her tone of voice to one that sounded like an overprotective mother. "You look washed out."

"I really..."

"Anna," she interrupted, calling to my mother, "please get your son something to eat, he looks terrible."

"Really, I..."

"Please eat something, Vinnie, or I'll get mad," she said strongly.

"Okay," I said sheepishly.

"Thank you again, Aunt Concetta." She didn't hear me, she was leaning over and saying something to Grandmother Cassallano. Only the bowing and kissing of her hand was missing. Somehow, I felt that would come later.

I followed my mother. As we stepped onto the kitchen floor, my sock-covered feet started to slide all over the damn place, as if I were trying to walk on ice. Quickly, I grabbed a kitchen chair and sat down at the table. Ahead of me, my mother moved with the artistry of a skilled skater. Hell, I thought, she's used to these slick-waxed floors. It takes years of practice. She asked if I wanted a meatball sandwich. I said yes.

I looked around as she moved to the refrigerator. The bright white walls, the marble-like tiled floor, the crunched-up aluminum foil wrapped around stove handles, cupboard handles, faucets, and inside of the stove burners made me think of a sanitized control room for a spacecraft. I thought about all the rich Jewish social workers who worked so hard through the years to clean up the greasy Italians. How proud they would be now.

My mother placed the meatball sandwich in front of me. "Eat," she said, "this will put color in your face."

"Thanks," I smiled at her.

The noise coming from the living room was getting louder. Everyone seemed to be interrupting just like I remembered.

After a while, some relatives attempted to come over and say hello but my mother snarled at each one of them. "Leave him alone, let him eat in peace." I loved her for this.

One time, I heard someone yell from the living room, "Anna, leave him be, and stop fussing over him, he's not a baby anymore."

I drank another glass of wine. I started to feel real good about what Aunt Concetta was planning to do. I thought I could even put up with her pretentious ways, if millions of lost souls found something in my words on Heaven.

Half dreaming about these millions, anxiously awaiting this next book from me, my mother placed another meatball sandwich in front of me. I hadn't even finished the first one yet. I told her one was enough. She argued.

"Anna, university professors can't get overweight because of all the hard work they do." I heard Phil's sarcastic voice booming from behind. I turned around. He was smiling like a bully. His fat lips had tomato sauce smeared all over them. A truck driver. Yes. A teacher? Never.

"Phil, leave him alone," my mother said. "I don't want another eight years to go by before I see my son again."

He sat down at the table, across from me. "Oh, stop worrying about your son, Anna," he said. "University professors need to be strong if they are going to save the world."

"It's okay, Mom," I said.

"'It's okay, Mom,' listen to that," he said, taunting me.

I said nothing, as I stared down at the table.

My brooding worked. In a repetitive tone of voice he instantly changed the subject, though I knew it wouldn't last for long. "Hey, I overheard you talking to my sister. It looks like you're into some deep stuff with that book you're planning to write."

"Yeah, it looks that way, doesn't it," I said, half-detached from what I was saying.

"You know, someday I hope to go on and finish my PhD in education."

"Good," I said, without any real enthusiasm. I thought he should fit in quite well with all the other dummies in education.

"I could've been working on it now if I didn't spend so much time commuting to Braintree. I wish I could've gotten a job teaching here in the North End. But the Catholic schools didn't have any openings. And there's a good possibility that all the Catholic schools in the North End will go public in a year or two. And if that happens, that means blacks. I looked up, his dark eyes were bulging, his face twisted with hate.

"So?" I said coldly.

"Well, I'll tell you, Mister Professor," he said, as his voice quivered with pent-up emotion. "If people thought it was bad in South Boston, wait and see what happens here. Just two months ago, a black tried to move in with a white girl, and in one night they were burned out. I'll tell you, the Italians won't stand for any blacks taking over their neighborhood. There'll be more killing here than they ever thought of having in South Boston."

"It's a reality you have to face, Phil," I said. "Like it or not." For some reason, I could never bring myself to call any of my mother's brothers "uncle." Perhaps some of my father's hate for the Cassallanos had rubbed off.

"Not me, buddy," he retorted, "not this guy anyway. I won't be forced to live with them, and I'll be damned if I'll teach them. It's liberal professors like you who have given the blacks the feeling that they're better than everyone else."

"So what," I said, "after three hundred years they deserve the right to feel better than everyone else. It's about time."

"That three-hundred-year stuff is pure bullshit," he shot back. "We've given them more time than anyone else to make it. Sure, I know they were slaves, but still they had a good head start on Italian immigrants like my parents, who worked their asses off for their children. The blacks' problem is that they are too damn lazy to make it on their own."

"I don't believe you said that," I said, shaking my head in disbelief. "You sound like a bigoted Southerner who was around in the Fifties and Sixties."

"I don't care who I sound like," he said, cocksure, "I won't give them any respect, until they work for things just as I had to. Believe it or not, I don't really hate them. Look, I teach with one in Braintree, and we get along fine. Even he agrees with me. I'm just saying I'm being discriminated against when a black gets ahead of me because of his color."

"I think you're scared, Phil," I said, "to accept the fact the scales have to be balanced in their favor, until they have the same equal opportunities as we do. And that may mean busing black children to all white neighborhoods or giving jobs to blacks even though there are qualified whites for them, or whatever. Their time has come to reap the benefits we've enjoyed so long."

"That is bullshit too!" he exploded as a red flame took over his fat face. "Hell, they're taking over in politics, in businesses, in education, in everything, even in the rackets. What else do they want, my home, my children, my religion? Tell me, what else do they expect to be handed to them?"

"You're being melodramatic," I said.

"No I'm not," he answered, as the flame intensified across his face. "I'm just asking for my rights as a citizen of this country. This country is founded on the rights of Americans: for example, the right to choose to send their kids to a school in their neighbor-hood, where they will be with their own kind. And that's really the issue."

I glanced over to my mother who was now standing near the sink; her worried eyes pleaded with me to stop.

"No, the real issue is that you can't accept blacks. Period."

"Would you have your daughter marry one?" he asked, smiling in a triumphant way.

"That's not the point," I said sharply.

"Oh, come on, Vinnie..."

Before he could finish the sentence his red-headed, roly-poly wife interrupted in a strained, nervous voice, "I could hear you yelling all the way in there, leave poor Vinnie alone. Can't you see he looks tired?"

"We're just talking, right, Vinnie?" he asked, laughing.

"Yeah, I guess so," I said dull and tired-like.

"Aunt Concetta asked me to come in and stop you from pick-ing on Vinnie," she said impatiently.

"All right, all right," he said, placating her. Then turning to me he said, "Someday, Vinnie, I would like to have about four hours with you. Then I think I could straighten you out about blacks."

"Come on Phil, please!" she pleaded with him.

"Of course," he mimicked a sophisticated voice, "you must tell me what professors think about while they sit on their asses all day." With that, his wife angrily shoved him in the direction of the living room. He laughed as he turned and winked at me as if he was kidding all along.

Immediately after he left, I caught my mother motioning to me that someone was standing behind me. I turned around and saw Candy's sad eyes peering into mine.

"Vinnie, I need to see you," she said. Her body shook.

"Okay," I said.

She looked over to my mother. "Aunt Anna, I'm going to take Vinnie away for a few minutes, okay?"

"Sure, honey," she smiled affectionately. "It might be good for him to get away before Phil starts up again."

As Candy went to tell someone to watch her kids, my mother hurried over to me and whispered close to my ear, "Vinnie, be nice to her, she thinks so much of you. She's had such a terrible time with the divorce and all."

Candy came back, then we excused ourselves to Aunt Concetta and left. Outside the door, we found our shoes, put them on, and avoided eye contact as much as possible. For a moment I thought about the mockery that was going on inside. There they were, supposedly in mourning, supposedly preparing for Uncle Louie's funeral, but no one, not one fucking person ever mentioned his name. Even in his death, I thought, they're pretending, as they did when he was alive, that he didn't exist. Strangely, they are involved in the activity, but like so many other things in life, the content is absent.

10

Outside, snowflakes floated down in a hushed silence. As we walked down Hanover Street, Candy kept a tight grip on my arm. She suggested that we go to her car, which was parked down the street a bit, so that we could sit and talk. She said she would put the heater on. I said fine. I really didn't care.

She got in on the driver's side and reached over, to unlock my door. The ignition choked at first, then sputtered, choked, and sputtered again, but finally, the monotonous rumble of the motor penetrated the embarrassing silence between us. Hot air rushed from underneath the dashboard, and the defroster slowly melted a small uneven circle on the windshield.

"First of all, Vinnie, let me apologize for the other night," she interrupted my thoughts in a sincere tone. She turned and looked me in the face.

"Hey, I loved it, but I've got so many things happening," I looked away.

"I wish, we were young again," she said.

"I know."

"When will all of this end, Vinnie. When?" Her voice now seemed full of loneliness and sadness. Her eyes seemed silver in the reflection of the streetlights.

"Candy, it takes a long time," I said, trying to muster a supportive tone of voice, "but in the end you'll be a better person for it. Remember what I told you last night? Just look at how far you've come already."

"Oh, thank you, Vinnie. You're so nice," she said, with tears now running down her cheeks. "I pray for the day when all this is over."

"It will be. And you'll be thankful someday, for having gotten through it," I said, reassuringly.

"Vinnie, I'm so selfish at times. Here I am, trying to talk to you about more important things, and I end up talking about my own personal problems. I'm so sorry," she said, as she lowered her head, crying a bit.

"That's okay, don't worry about it."

"Vinnie, you're so understanding."

"Tell me, what important things did you want to talk to me about?" I asked.

"I don't know if I could get into that now." She was gaining her composure, "Vinnie, let me ask you just one favor."

"Sure."

"Once I get started, please don't stop me," she said. "If you do, I'll probably start shaking my leg like anything and never finish."

"I understand."

"Also, Vinnie," she added, "it may be difficult at times for you to accept what I'm going to say. But, Vinnie, you know me. I wouldn't tell you anything unless I thought it was true."

"I know don't worry," I said.

"I might be a little crazy, but I would never lie to you," she said. "I love you more than a brother!"

"And I love you, too," I said, growing impatient. *Get on with it, get on with it.*

"Here it goes," she said. "You remember last night I told you that I got very close to Uncle Louie during this past year."

"Yes."

"Well, as I got closer to him certain things came out. He shared a great deal with me." Her voice trailed off for a second, as she gazed out at the snowflakes melting on the heated windshield. She turned and began again. *I wished she never did.* "Vin, Uncle Louie told me about that night you followed your father. He said that your father liked that whore, Maria, before he got married. And he always knew this. But he thought when your father got married, it would go away. But it didn't. It got worse.

She stopped for a moment. Then she began, again, "Vinnie, do you want me to go on? I'll stop if you want me to."

"No." Another voice inside of me resounded. *Help, God, help me.*

"Okay," she went on. "Well, anyway, Uncle Louie felt quite relieved when your father stopped seeing her. But then your father started to go to the wrong bars on State Street. And Uncle Louie worried about something happening to your father. So, whenever Uncle Louie could, he followed your father to those bars. He would wait outside until your father came out with someone. If the girl looked harmless, Uncle Louie went home. If your father and the girl had people following them—bad people, you know what I mean—Uncle Louie would follow them to a cheap hotel on Washington Street. That's where your father always took these girls. Uncle Louie knew the room your father always used. So when he thought they were in it, he would go and listen at the door. If everything seemed okay, he'd leave. Vin, you don't know how much Uncle Louie loved your father, and how it killed him to see your father pick up any cheap whore who walked by."

I felt myself trembling. Her words were like hot coals burning the bottom of my stomach.

"Anyway, I know it sounds so stupid, but over the years your father had convinced himself if he paid for your education, you would forget about what you saw that night you followed him. Vin, he knew you saw him that night. Jesus, I'm getting off the reason why I'm telling you all this," she said, mad at herself.

"I'm such a scatterbrain. Well, here it goes. I think, it all happened when you were in your second year at Saint Boniface. When I think about it, it was inevitable. Uncle Louie stopped over one night looking for your father, and he found your mother crying. She stopped when he came in and treated him very coldly, like she usually did, because of Aunt Concetta's brainwashing. But Uncle Louie said he saw something in your mother's eyes that made him come back on nights he knew your father was safe with his whore. Before long, one thing led to another, and they fell in love.

"Uncle Louie really understood a woman's feelings. I envied your mother. He was completely faithful to your mother except for one Saturday night, when I went crazy. It all began the day after I had an agonizing meeting with my lawyer, Michael's lawyer, Michael, and his fat-assed wife. I was shaking so bad afterward that my lawyer had to drive me home. All they talked about was whether or not I was capable of taking care of my own kids. I was so sick, I didn't sleep at all that night. And the next day, Saturday, everything seemed to go wrong. My leg was shaking like hell. I was yelling at the kids like a madwoman. And I was even seriously considering suicide, when Uncle Louie stopped over, like he usually did on Saturdays. He had started doing this, right after Michael left me. He would help me clean, shop, take care of the kids, or do whatever I asked him. He was a dear. You know, I was never close to him before the trouble started with Michael. But after, except for you and my therapist, he was really the only other person I could talk to. So many times I wanted to tell you on the phone how good he was to me. But I was scared that if I started talking about him, I would end up telling you what I just told you tonight. And I couldn't do that over the phone.

"Anyway, this Saturday, when he came over and saw the kind of shape I was in, he immediately took the kids over to the park to play. I tried resting while he was gone, but I couldn't. All I could see in my mind was Michael's wife looking at me, as if I was some kind of freak or something. I took all sorts of pills. Nothing seemed to help at first. Then, probably from the combination of not sleeping and the pills, I finally passed out on the sofa.

"When I woke up, it was late at night, and Uncle Louie was sitting in a chair watching over me like a worried father. I don't know what happened to me after this. I don't know if it's because I never really knew my father and had a father complex. I don't know. All I know is that I went after Uncle Louie like a wild animal. I think I scared him at first. I know I scared myself. But, he was so wonderful. I had never been loved like that before. So gentle. Afterwards, while he slept, I knelt beside the bed, staring at him. I thanked God for giving me a chance to experience such a warm love. A love, I know, I will never feel again. Also, I know, because I'm addicted to sex. My therapist also believes this. In fact, I get so lonely and depressed I have to find a guy to screw the shit out of me. It's a bad habit. I get restless and bored.

"Anyway, Uncle Louie never came over again, but I wasn't mad. He gave me something I never had before: true kindness and gentleness. There's also something else he gave me. Vin, I'm two months pregnant with Uncle Louie's baby. I know it is his, because with others during that time I used a diaphragm. But that night I forgot, because of my crazy spell. Some of my so-called friends, and even my therapist, think I should have an abortion. But I never will. I don't care if the child comes out retarded. I could never kill anything that belonged to him.

"Finally, Vinnie, here's the other real reason why I'm telling you all of this. A couple weeks ago, I was at a single's bar on Bolyston Street, and I ran into Jimmy. He was there with some skinny girl and some other weird-looking people. He invited me over to his table. After a while, he got feeling pretty good and he started talking about killing people by sticking tubes up their noses. I just thought it was a bunch of crap Jimmy was throwing around, in order to impress his weirdo friends. You know what a shithead he is. I didn't think anything of it until the other day, when I got up the courage to go to Uncle Louie's wake. And God! I couldn't believe what I saw. His nose, it was awful. Just awful, Vin..."

She stopped talking. Her body shook, and she cried. Then, just as quickly, her mood changed. No more tears, and her shaking stopped, as she straightened up her back against the door. She seemed to be mad at herself for letting me down.

"Vinnie, I think that idiot, that crazy idiot Jimmy killed his own father." Her voice was hard and cold. "Unbelievable. But it's true."

I gazed outside at the falling snowflakes, as my body now started to ache and sweat, as if I was coming down with a fever.

"Vinnie, are you all right?"

"Yes, I'm okay," I said.

"Vinnie, do you still like me?" she asked, tenderly stroking my arm.

"Sure, I still like you," I said. "I just need time to think about all these things. It hurts."

"I'm so sorry, Vinnie," she said. "But I couldn't go on without you knowing how nice Uncle Louie treated your father and me."

"I understand," I said. I was surprised at how calm I was acting.

She frowned. "Vinnie, I can't forget how kind and gentle he was to me. Please, help me, Vinnie, I don't know what to do..." She started to cry again.

"I will," I said. "But now I've got to go."

"Okay," she sniffled. "There must be something we could do."

"We'll see," I said, as I opened the car door and left.

Quickly, I headed away from the car, with no particular direction in mind. *I just wanted to forget her, and my father's whores, my mother and Uncle Louie, Jimmy... I wanted death.*

11

The next morning, I heard the voice of my mother break through the dark shadows of the previous night. "Vinnie, I'm leaving now. The funeral starts in fifteen minutes at Sacred Heart."

I forced my heavy eyelids open. She was standing between the foot of the bed and the open door. Then she motioned with her head in the direction of the empty wine bottle next to my bed. She asked coolly, "Did you drink all of that?"

"Yes, almost," I said, as the words rolled heavily off my tongue. I felt vulnerable, as she stood there, and my head crackled with pain from too much wine.

"Keep it up, and you'll end up just like him," she said sarcastically.

I said nothing.

"Some woman called this morning," she said, with a tone of suspicion. "I left her number over by the phone."

"Thanks."

"Will you be going back after the funeral?"

"Yes, I've decided to go straight from the cemetery to the airport."

"Can't you stay a little longer?"

"I can't, I have to get back, I'm teaching tomorrow." Somehow, I felt she knew that wasn't the real reason.

She moved around the bed, lowered her voice, and said, "I just want to tell you, while he's not around, that I'm planning sometime to come down to West Virginia with Aunt Concetta for a couple of weeks. Aunt Concetta feels it would be good for us to get away."

"Fine," I lied.

"I'm coming and I don't care what he says," she said, as if she was trying to convince herself that she really meant it. "If he wants to rot away here, bitching about everything, that's okay. But I'll be damned if I'll rot with him. I've got to get away from him."

"I'm glad," I lied.

"We'll stay at a hotel nearby so you won't have to worry about us taking over your house," she said. "I don't want to end up being a bossy mother-in-law."

"You're not going to do that," I lied. "You'll stay with us. We've got lots of room."

"I don't want to be any trouble for you."

"You won't be," I lied. "Now stop it, when you come, you'll stay with us." I couldn't stand this sudden wave of humility at my bedside.

"Let's not talk about it now," she said, waving her hand impatiently. "I've got to leave. Stop by at the cemetery to say good-bye."

"Okay."

"Bye," she said, as she turned and left.

I heard the downstairs door slam shut, got out of bed, and took off the turtleneck I was still wearing from the night before. I got my shaving kit and went to the bathroom. As I was shaving, I thought seriously about forgetting about the funeral and going straight to the airport.

Back in my bedroom, I put on some clean clothes from the suitcase: a new pair of dark-blue pants and another dark-blue turtleneck. Even though Chris hated the dark clothes I wore, she had packed them. Perfect wife, Chris, I thought, always trying to please. I got a good feeling, as I thought about how she fusses over me. At the same time a wave of guilt took over, as I remembered Angie.

I threw my old clothes in the suitcase, snapped it shut, and carried it to the living room. Then I decided to call and confirm my flight back to Pittsburgh, flight number 202, leaving Boston at 12:32 p.m. and arriving in Pittsburgh at 1:25 p.m. As I put down the receiver, I noticed a small piece of paper with a number on it, stuck between the phone and the wall. I wondered if Angie or Tatum had tried to reach me. The phone started to ring. After the second ring I picked up the receiver.

"Hello."

"Vinnie?" It was Tatum.

"Hi," I said, trying to sound surprised, "I was just thinking about you. Did you call earlier?"

"Yes," she said. "I was leaving to go out for a while. I thought you might be trying to get me." I couldn't believe she still wanted me, after blowing it like I did.

"I was going to," I said, "But there's been a lot happening around here."

"What are you doing now?" she asked, not really paying attention to what I just said.

"Right now I'm getting ready to go to a funeral," I said. I felt myself getting excited as I thought about her taking charge; the receiver started to slide in my hand.

"Have you thought about me since the other night?" she asked, and laughed in an irritating way.

"Yes, a great deal."

"I have too," she said. "Can I see you before you leave?"

I hesitated, "I don't know." I thought about how ugly she looked before I left. The excitement I'd felt for her a moment ago changed to disgust.

"I just want to talk," she said, sounding upset. Her persistence was also very irritating.

"Okay, how about meeting me at the airport?" I asked, "I just checked my flight, and it's leaving at twelve-thirty, Flight 202, Appalachian Airlines."

"Good," she answered happily.

"Okay, I'll meet you around eleven thirty, in front of the gate I'm leaving from."

Why did I do that, I asked myself as I hung up. Somehow, I had to tell her that I didn't want any part of her.

I went to the bathroom and took an aspirin for my headache, which was now spreading to the back of my neck. In the kitchen, I poured myself some hot coffee and chewed on a hard, Italian egg doughnut. The warm coffee and the doughnut going down soothed the dull burning in my stomach.

As I was getting ready to leave, I wondered where he, my father, was.

Outside, the icy chill felt good. The sky was flecked with pewter clouds; the snow on the ground was dirty from the morning traffic.

I walked in the direction of Sacred Heart. I thought of Chris, who had insisted eight years ago that we come back here in order to convince him to attend our wedding. I told her he would never come. But she felt if he had a chance to meet her, he might change his mind. It didn't matter. She still insisted that it wasn't right for a father to refuse to attend his own son's wedding. She wanted a perfect wedding. It would be bad luck, she'd said, if all the parents weren't there.

I knew something was wrong that day as soon as I'd opened the door at the bottom of the stairs. I could hear him yelling in Italian. He got louder as we climbed the stairs. I looked over to Chris. She looked scared. I asked if she wanted to turn around. She said no.

I opened the door and saw that he was sitting in the kitchen, as my mother stood in the middle of the living room. Her face was tense. When she saw us, her face turned white. We walked in and I closed the door behind us. I set the suitcases on the floor. He stopped his yelling, stared at us for a moment, and then turned away.

"Hi," my mother said, pretending everything was all right. "How was the trip?"

"Fine." I answered with uncertainty. Just as she was coming over to meet Chris, he started his yelling again.

"So he brought his whore home," he said bitterly.

"Stop!" my mother yelled at him.

"Goddammit, I don't believe this," I said, as I took a step backward. "Mom, I'm not going to stand and listen to this shit."

"Bastard, go, we don't care. And take your Irish whore with you," he said.

"Jesus," I said shaking my head. I turned and motioned for Chris to follow. She didn't. I was shocked. She walked straight to where he was sitting. "Chris, come back, you can't talk to him," I yelled at her. She didn't seem to hear me as she now stood in front of him.

His voice lowered a bit, but he was still shouting.

I turned to my mother who seemed dazed. "Mom, I'm going down to get a cab, please get Chris away from him." I picked up our suitcases and walked to the door.

"Wait," Chris pleaded.

"I'm going," I said, as I opened the door.

I could hear some of his bitter yelling as I hurried down the stairs. "He was never any good and never will be. Take him, I don't want him. You can have him..."

"Liar!" I screamed, as I looked for a cab. In a short while, I waved one down and told the driver to wait. I ran up the stairs again. Chris was still standing in front of him. I heard her trying to reason with him. He wouldn't let her. My mother seemed wilted as she leaned against the wall in the living room. I thought if she could, she would've melted into the wall.

"Perhaps you're right, Mr. Serrano," I heard Chris calmly interrupt his yelling. "But I know, Vinnie will try to be a better son. It would really help if you came to the wedding."

"I don't attend weddings of liars," he said, "and I don't listen to any Irish bitches, either."

I started for him, but my mother grabbed my arm. He took out some papers from an envelope he had in front of him.

"Look," he yelled, waving the papers in the air. "Look, almost sixty thousand dollars I spend on his education, and this is what he does to me. He brings home a whore."

Why did he have to destroy? Why, I said to myself, as I broke away from my mother and ran into the kitchen. I grabbed Chris's arm, and then, with all my strength, pushed the kitchen table against him. I heard him scream something about God, and then I heard a thud, as he fell on the floor.

"My God," my mother shouted, rushing over to him.

I stared at him, as he sat on the floor, looking bewildered. "Oh, God," my mother sobbed. "What are we to do? What are we to do?"

I turned quickly, took hold of Chris's arm more tightly and led her out. Everything in me was trembling. In the cab, neither Chris nor I said anything for a long while, as we headed back to the airport. I thought for sure she would call off the wedding because of what just happened. A few more moments later, however, I was surprised. She turned and smiled lovingly at me and then kissed me on the cheek.

I said somewhat weakly, "I'm sorry."

"Don't be," she said compassionately. "He's a sad person. A sad person. There's nothing one could do. Only pray."

"I don't know, I don't know," I said. "I couldn't believe how calm you were. Didn't what he said bother you?"

She took my hand and gently stroked it. "No, Vinnie," she said. "He's ignorant. I just feel sorry for him."

"Still, he shouldn't say those things," I said.

"Forget it," she said, as she kissed me again. "Vinnie, I love you," she whispered. "That's all that matters."

"I love you too," I said, realizing now that I didn't have to worry about losing her because of him. Virgins were going fast in the late Sixties. Thank God, I thought, as she pressed her soft breast against my side, I got one before they were all used up.

12

Black limousines were parked all around Sacred Heart like a huge black snake getting ready to slither through the streets of Boston. In front, huddled in tight circles, smoking cigarettes and drinking hot steaming coffee from white Styrofoam cups, were the drivers. All were dressed in black overcoats. Here and there, I could spy their starched white shirt-collars, uniformly adorned by thin, black ties. The men nodded, as I passed them and walked into Sacred Heart.

The walls were banked with vigil lights; pale candles in red glass holders sat in horizontal tiers on charcoal-gray pewter stands. A few were lit, but most of them were burned out. The ceiling was low like in a basement; the seating area was small in comparison with the average church, and there were too many fat columns stuck between the newly varnished pews. Still, I thought, as I took a seat near the back, I loved Sacred Heart. The quiet, the semi-darkness, and the feeling that someone was protecting me from his bitching, had made it a favorite spot of mine when I was growing up. Now, I felt that it gave me refuge from what Candy had told me last night.

Straight ahead, I could see the back of my mother's bleach-blond head, bowed in prayer. Next to her sat my father. He seemed to be staring blankly at the powdery-faced priest saying mass. On the other side of him were Candy and her mother. Candy slouched, as if her shoulders were giving way under her heavy burden of sorrow. Aunt Concetta, Patsy, and Rose sat in the front row.

The priest was now swinging a brass incense holder, as he slowly circled the coffin. The incense brought back memories of novenas, Ash Wednesdays, Holy Saturdays, and serving funeral masses for Father Charles. The aroma always seemed to make everything so holy and clean.

The priest now stood at the foot of the dark chestnut coffin and recited a prayer. "Oh, Lord, do not bring Your servant to trial, for no man becomes holy in Your sight unless You grant him forgiveness for all sins. We..."

But before he could finish the sentence, Aunt Concetta interrupted with a tear-filled shout: "Why, oh why, did you leave me, Louie? Oh why!" I could see Patsy and Rose trying to comfort her. Then she flung her arms into the air, sobbing, "Please take me with you, please, I love you."

The priest, seemingly undisturbed, kept on as if the interruption had been practiced many times before. "...therefore, do not let the verdict of Your judgment go against her...him," the priest nonchalantly corrected the pronoun, "whom the..."

Again, he was interrupted by Aunt Concetta's sobbing voice. "God, I want to die! Louie, please, oh God!" For a moment, she sounded so convincing that I believed her wailing.

The priest went on "...escape the sentence which he deserves, for during her earthly life... his earthly life, I mean, he was signed with the seal of the Holy Trinity. You, who have lived and reigned forever and ever. Amen." Then he bowed to the coffin, made the sign of the cross with the incense holder, and slowly walked back to the altar.

"Oh, Louie...," Aunt Concetta cried, her voice quickly trailing off, as she sank into Rose's arms. Soon Rose was rocking and gently patting her mother on the back like a hurt child. I thought about how Rose had changed. When I left, eight years ago, she was slim and sensuous like her mother, but now she looked fat and sloppy, like Phil. She seemed worn out as she leaned over her mother.

The priest came back down to the foot of the coffin, he bowed his head, and prayed, "Oh, God, who alone are ever merciful and sparing of punishment, humbly we pray to You on behalf of the soul of Your servant, whom You have commanded to go forth from this world. Do not hand him over to the power of the enemy and do not forget him forever, but command that he should be taken up by the Holy Angels and brought home to paradise so that, since he hoped and believed in You, he may not undergo the punishment of hell, but rather possess everlasting life. Through Christ Our Lord. Amen."

I rode up front with the driver. In the back, my mother and father sat, saying nothing to each other. I gazed out at the people, as we drove through the streets. They looked dull, gray, and neutral, like the day. Ahead, the black snake of the funeral procession crawled and twisted, over two narrow and heavy traffic congested streets, over one ramp, and finally onto the expressway. Other cars started to roar by us.

I kept staring out, but I saw nothing now. I was thinking about a get-together Chris had organized last month.

A long time ago, Chris had stopped asking me who to invite over, because anytime she did, I would argue with her for hours over their faults. So she just went ahead and selected those people she enjoyed being with. They were either her friends she had met in her Charismatic Prayer group or people in the neighborhood, like Frank and Wanda Stone.

Frank Stone owned a coal company. His looks reminded me of Mickey Rooney. Short, moon-faced, and portly. His wife, Wanda, was beautiful, with her tennis-player figure, tanned and lithe, big blue lollipop eyes, and curly black hair. She reminded me of Polly Bergen, the actress. Frank bothered me, but Wanda I liked. She was witty and intelligent. Something, of course, Chris wasn't. I remembered the times when Chris would tell me we were going over to the Stones' house for a party. I would bitch all the way over; but after I got there, had a couple of drinks, and talked to Wanda for a while, I started to enjoy myself. She constantly talked to me about being my "friend," but I knew better. She wanted me to make her happy, because Frank treated her so awful. I had many fantasies, where Wanda would finally come to me and say please take care of me. Then I would run off with her, and we would be happy for the rest of our lives.

At this one get-together Wanda seemed unusually quiet, so I felt there was no one whom I could talk to. None of the people there worked in the university, even though most of them were concerned about the effect the university had on them. But good ole Father Luke was there, as always. In the last year or so, he seemed to be always there for Chris's get-togethers. He was instrumental in getting Chris involved in the Charismatic movement. His talk was a mixture of "Praise the Lord, Hallelujahs," and quotations from the Bible. Father Luke had a cherub's face, framed by long black curly hair, giving him the look of a very holy man. Lately, he had been dropping over to the house for supper even when he had not been invited. Many times, he brought gifts for the children, for Chris, and even for me. I asked Chris once where he got the money. She said he had a good friend who was a successful movie producer, and he sent him money all the time.

I never found out what exactly went on at Father Luke's Charismatic meetings. All Chris would tell me was that it brought her closer to Jesus and God. From what I heard, it seemed to be similar to an evangelistic or revival meeting that some Protestant groups participate in. In my opinion, it was just a bunch of flakes playing touchy-feely with each other, like the sensitivity groups on the West Coast. Chris and Father Luke didn't take too kindly to my opinions about their group. One night, I called them the new "holy rollers of America," and for three days after neither Chris nor Father Luke spoke more than small talk to me.

The conversation during that evening was the same as at the others. Dull and boring. It included a discussion of the zoning laws in Wheeling; a rumor about an apartment-complex going up at the end of the street; a new fertilizer on the market that killed crabgrass with one spreading; the problem of dogs shitting on lawns; and the possibility of the university's football coach being fired. On and on it went.

No one ever talked to me about my work. One time during the get-together, the Pattersons from down the street said they saw one of my math books in the bookstore. The wife said the title looked impressive, and that she said to herself, "Holy cow, that's my neighbor." Another time, Father Luke asked about the new book he heard I was working on that dealt with Heaven. Before I even got out two sentences, he was interrupting me, "Wow, Praise the Lord, Vinnie, for giving you such a wonderful mind. He must really love you."

"Yes," I said, as he swayed away to get another drink. I wondered if he ever repented at his prayer meetings, for always having three drinks to everyone's one.

The only interesting part of this get-together was when someone brought up abortion. For once, I saw Chris take a stand that was intellectually sound and logical. I agreed with her. Her arguments were very convincing, especially when she talked about the rights of the unborn majority. In the background, after each time Chris made an important point, I could hear Father Luke mumbling quietly, "Oh, yes, oh, yes, Jesus." I wondered, how many of the guests here would actually go out and work for an anti-abortion and right-to-life group. Very few, I guessed, they were too busy with their own lives to do anything except give lip service.

Later that night, as we were in bed, watching Johnny Carson, Chris turned to me and said, "I thought, for once, you were enjoying yourself."

"Only for a moment or so, the rest of the time I was bored," I said, as I raised myself up and leaned against the bed's headboard.

"Well, I enjoyed myself," she said. "They're just good, common ordinary people, not trying to impress anyone with big words and philosophies. I don't care what you say," she added quickly, "I like them." She turned over, crept closer to the edge of the bed, and assumed the sleeping position she had been in for the last several months.

As I continued to watch Johnny Carson trying to act serious with a fat old man with bulging eyes, I thought about her feelings about the Rhythm Method. Discussions of pills, foam, diaphragms, condoms, were all out because, she said, they were unnatural, and went against her conscience and the Pope. She could not see how good Catholics could go to communion after using such things. Through the years, she had reached the point where she figured the only safe time was during her period. She feared any other time might bring a child. And she knew I didn't want any more. "A child must come in this world with love, not rejection," she said.

One night, she reached over for me and said, "It is safe, I have my period." The idea repulsed me, so I pretended that I had fallen asleep.

The next morning, lying there on her back as if she was waiting for me to wake up, she said, "I can't understand it, when we could do it you don't want to, and when we can't you want to! It must be the devil."

"Yes, it must be," I said, humoring her.

"You're not normal, not wanting it," she said bitterly. "We haven't done it for months. Don't you need it?"

I turned over, my back to her, and pretended I had fallen asleep again.

We were now passing over the Charles River, its emerald waters, occasionally being stirred by the wintry winds, looked beautiful. From the bridge, whose name I had forgotten, the pollution and shit that flowed into it was invisible. I remembered how I always envied the rich sons of bitches who owned sailboats and who flaunted the benefits of their position on hot summer days.

I stared at the reflections of our black-snake procession moving across the river's surface. For once, I thought, the reflections were not distorting reality. It was real. It was the inevitable reality of all of us who were following Uncle Louie's body to the grave.

Up ahead now, I could see the large, black, iron gates that stood open at the entrance of Saint John's Cemetery. The name was written on a small arch above the entrance. We drove through. On my right, near the front, facing the highway that ran past the cemetery, was a pile of freshly shoveled brown soil. It seemed out of place against the wintry background.

Most of the Italians from the North End were buried at Saint John's, and it seemed that all of them jockeyed for a plot near the highway. When I was young, I was told the reason for this was because Italians wanted a closer view of the outside world. But now I knew better. Guilt was the real reason. Italians figure it like this. The more visible, the more distinct, and the more elegant their gravestones were, the better the chance of their family members seeing it, and feeling guilty for being alive after they pass by. Thus, the mission of the front-row plot was accomplished.

Our limousine drivers rolled past Uncle Louie's gravesite and circled back, so that the procession would be facing the entrance when we left. The cars parked near a small stone chapel, which stood to one side of Uncle's freshly-dug, open grave.

In the chapel, the old priest who was wearing a frayed and dandruff-spotted black coat, led the people in prayer. No one listened. It was too cold and damp in the unheated chapel. The prayers were short, as if the old priest himself was trying to get it over with as quickly as possible. He shook with cold. On finishing, he lowered his head to the naked altar, genuflected slowly, then turned to Longo for further direction.

Outside, Longo asked us to assemble in a large circle around the grave. The coffin now stood on a silver-barred lift, which was directly over the cold, dark, empty hole. I wondered how long it took the gravediggers to dig the hole, especially in this kind of weather.

A light snow started to fall. The wind got colder. The skies got grayer. The old priest, pulling the frayed collar of his black coat up for protection, placed a purple stole around his neck, then, leaning over the coffin, he mumbled more prayers. The funeral guests looked at Longo for their cue and mumbled along, when he mumbled.

I looked around at some of the other gravestones. The names were different; their dates of birth and death were different; the gravestones were different in shape, size, and quality. But, we all knew, like the image of the funeral procession passing over the Charles River, that there are no differences when we face it. *Its warm and eternal arms make us all the same! No differences! No pains! No hurts! No hates! No memories! Only warmth and peace!*

On a knoll behind Uncle Louie's gravesite, I could see a gravestone where two vases with fresh-cut flowers had been placed next to a shining statue of Santa Claus. I immediately felt sad. I thought about Linda or Paulie lying there. I quickly turned away.

I could not believe what I saw next. There was Jimmy, standing with one arm tightly locked into his mother's arm, staring sadly at the coffin in front of him. I wondered how he'd gotten there, without me having seen him arrive.

While the old priest mumbled some more prayers, Longo handed out long-stemmed roses to the people in the circle. On his signal, we dropped the roses on top of Uncle Louie's coffin. The wind blew so hard now that the roses quickly blew off into the open hole. One of the drivers, who was standing behind me, pressed closer to me and said, "Tell Longo to get the damn thing over with. It's too fucking cold to play games with flowers today."

I nodded and smiled weakly.

Now the old priest was sprinkling some dirt on the coffin, but again, because of the stubborn wind, some of the dirt flew back into his face. Unruffled, he rubbed his eyes and said loudly, "From dust thou came, to dust thou shall return." Then he turned slowly, still rubbing the dirt out of his eyes. He walked in the direction of Aunt Concetta, but before he could reach her, she had moved out of the circle and was now standing at the edge of the hole. Looking up at the dull gray sky and with outstretched arms, she screamed, "Please my love, come back, please." No one moved. Suddenly she leaped onto Uncle Louie's coffin, as if she were jumping onto a horse.

Before I could stop myself, I was laughing. I couldn't help it. There was cool Aunt Concetta riding piggyback on Uncle Louie's coffin. Her arms and black panty-hosed legs were tightly wrapped around the coffin, and one side of her face lay flat against its shining surface. There was a look of what-the-fuck on most of the faces, as the mourners started to crowd around the hole so that they could see Aunt Concetta riding her pony. Then, before anyone could stop it, the lift started to slowly descend into the hole. "Louie, I want to go with you," she sobbed on the way down. "Don't leave me alone, don't."

I started to laugh even harder when I saw Patsy leaning over the hole, cupping the sides of his mouth with his hands and yelling in a high-pitched feminine voice, "Mother, please get out, you'll catch cold. Please." Tears were in my eyes from laughing so hard.

Someone yelled from behind me. "Shame, shame on you. Don't you have any respect?"

As I tried holding my breath someone else yelled, "Get her a stick, you stupid bastards." Again, I exploded with more laughter.

Now Patsy, Jimmy, Longo, and even the old priest were getting down on the ground, swinging their arms wildly about the hole as they tried to reach for some part of Aunt Concetta's body. The closer they got to her, the more she pushed her face against the coffin, yelling up, "Let me be, please let me be."

Then Longo stood up and started to push the crowd back, "If you fall in, your damn shoes will scratch the coffin. Get back, get back!"

I closed my eyes, took some deep breaths and prayed, "Oh God, please let this stop."

When I opened my eyes, I saw Candy moving closer to the edge of the hole. She seemed to be in a trance, as she peered down at Aunt Concetta; her eyes were hollow and frightfully hateful. Suddenly, jerking her head back and then quickly forward again, she let go of a huge gob of yellowish phlegm, right on Aunt Concetta's back. She repeated this, spurting like a broken water fountain until only a fine spray came out.

Everything happened so fast, nobody had time to react. Candy, letting go of a Tarzan-like scream, suddenly threw herself forward and leaped into the hole. And just like that, Candy drove her head underneath Aunt Concetta's black dress and savagely bit into her ass. Aunt Concetta screamed with pain.

Many of us spectators circling the hole seemed to be in a state of shock. Aunt Concetta pressed her face closer to the coffin and unsuccessfully tried to grab one of Candy's legs in back of her.

"I'll kill you, you whore, I'll kill you!" Jimmy shouted down at Candy.

Tears streamed down Candy's face, as she brought her head out from underneath Aunt Concetta's black dress. "Fuck you!" she cried, looking straight up into Jimmy's eyes and quickly shooting up her middle finger.

Jimmy started to snap his thumbs and forefingers together, now desperately trying to capture Candy's nose. "Come here, you whore," he shouted, "come here."

Small muffled giggles were coming out of me. Oh, no, not again, no more. Then I was almost completely wiped out by the next scene. Out of nowhere, a midget-like man appeared, carrying a stepladder. He was wearing gray coveralls with "L A R R Y" stitched in blue over one of his pockets. On his back, in white lettering, were the words "St. John's Cemetery." Longo, on seeing him, pointed with a shaking hand to the hole. The man understood. He walked over and put the ladder in the hole. Immediately, Jimmy bounded down the ladder.

I couldn't take any more, so I decided to leave. Just as I was turning around, I caught a glimpse of Aunt Concetta struggling with Jimmy, like a frightened drowning person. Before long, her arms and legs went limp, her face went white, and her head dropped backwards. I thought she'd had a heart attack. I got scared. My laughing stopped. Carefully, Jimmy placed her over his shoulders and then slowly moved up the ladder.

When he reached the top of the hole, Longo helped him gently lay Aunt Concetta on the ground. Longo then stuck a tiny, frosted bottle under her nose. After a few seconds, she shook her head dazedly and waved it away. I saw her face flush with life again.

I thought about going down and carrying out Candy. But before I could, Phil was doing it. Her arms and legs struggled in every which way to get free, as he carried her up the ladder. Then, as he put her down, she kneed him in the balls. He doubled over with pain and groaned. "You stupid shit. What the fuck's wrong?"

Now, out of the corner of my eye, I saw my father approaching. Just as he was parallel to me, he stopped, keeping his eyes focused on Candy, and spoke to me. "They're crazy, the whole bunch of them. And you, too. I cannot believe my own son would mock my brother's funeral. God, do you hate me that much?" He didn't wait for my response as he shook his head in disgust and walked over to Candy. He leaned over and whispered something in her ear, as he patted her hand comfortingly. I wondered how long it would take before Candy became his new whore.

13

On the way to the airport, bits and pieces of what took place at the cemetery kept running through my mind. I started to laugh out loud, as I thought about Aunt Concetta riding piggyback, then Candy jumping in, then Jimmy snapping his thumbs and forefingers together, then the midget in coveralls. Up front, I saw the bulldog-faced driver looking into the rearview mirror, wondering if I was crazy or something.

So it was.

Two for crazy.

None for sane.

At Logan Airport, I walked down the long corridor that led to the gates of Appalachian Airlines. On the way, I stopped for a moment to look at some live lobsters scrambling around in a tank of light-green water. Only to be born and to be put to death; nothing else, I thought, ever complicates their destinies.

At Gate 27 I saw Tatum, sitting impatiently. As I waited in line to check in, she looked over to me, smiled, and got up. She walked toward me in an exaggerated sensuous way. No doubt, I thought, she was a bundle of erotic electricity. Too bad I blew it.

"I have two cups of coffee waiting for you," she said, touching my arm.

"Good. Let me check in first, okay?"

She smiled, turned around, and walked back to her seat. Jesus, I wished I had done it to her. I've never seen breasts as hard and straight as hers. For a quick second I imagined my lips on them, and then immediately I pushed the thought out of my mind.

After I finished checking in, I went over and took a seat next to her. She handed me a hot cup of coffee. I couldn't believe it. Her whole mood seemed to have changed. Her eyes reminded me of the demonic-looking eyes of dogs when at night a light happens to shine into them. They gave me the creeps. Her body was stiff and full of tension. "You shithead, Vinnie, you promised to call," she said angrily.

Why do girls have to use that word, why?

"I told you," I said, still feeling scared because of the drastic change in her mood "that a lot of things have been going down."

"You're a fucker," she said bitterly. "I don't care." I looked around to see if anyone was listening.

"Come on Tatum," I said, with a great deal of exaggerated self-pity in my voice, "I've had enough misery this weekend to last me for a lifetime."

"I don't care, you promised," she demanded, putting her coffee down on the stand between us and edging toward me. "I'm not looking for sex, and I know you think I am. I just wanted to spend more time with you because of Saturday night." She stopped for a moment and then began with a gentler tone of voice. "God, Vinnie, it was one of the first times in my life I've ever felt so close to some-one. And that is a good sign."

Thanks for the compliment.

"That makes me feel good," I said. "It's flattering for a mid-dle-aged man like me to know he still has something that attracts young, beautiful girls like you."

"Then why don't you come over to my place," she said. "You can catch a later flight back to Pittsburgh. I'll help you to relax."

"I would love it, but I can't," I said, taking a sip of the coffee, which had gotten cold.

"Why?"

"Because if I did that, it would only be for sex, you know it and I know it."

"It doesn't have to be."

"I just know it would," I said, shaking my head. "I just couldn't be with you without sexually attacking you. Even now, while I'm sitting next to you, I'm getting all excited. That's not right."

"Why, what's wrong with a little pleasure?" she asked, smiling.

"Well, it's my wife, my kids," I said sadly, "the guilt would be too much, I've already had a touch of it, and I just can't handle it along with my other problems. The pain is too great."

"Maybe if you let me help you'll feel better," she said, leaning forward, her knee touching mine.

"I can't, I really can't," I said. "Please understand, Tatum."

"Jesus, Vinnie," she said, taking her knee away from mine and getting mad again. "I understand how you feel about your kids and wife. Please believe me. I also have a person I care a great deal about, but that doesn't mean we can't be friends. That's why you're feeling so bad. You won't talk about your problems. You're just being stubborn."

"Please, Tatum, I just don't want any more pain," I said, trying to act beaten.

"I won't give you any," she said, in a tone that was too cold to believe. "If you're worried about me telling your wife, forget it. I'm not that kind of person."

"I know, that's why you're so wonderful," I said, hoping she would become warm again. "I know I could trust you. Perhaps when I work out some of these problems I'll get with you again."

"I know you never will," she said, unconvinced. "If you're serious, I want you to set up a date right now."

"Okay, I will."

"When?" she asked smartly. "The date and time."

"God, you really don't believe me, do you?" I asked, slamming the Styrofoam coffee cup down on the stand and spilling some on my hand. "How about January eighteen, six o'clock at night, and I'll meet you in the lobby of the East House?"

"Sure," she said, still not believing me.

That's it, I'm not playing any more fucking games with you.

"Hey, Tatum," I said, trying hard to control my anger, "I'm going to be honest with you. Look, you're a beautiful, sexy person, and any normal guy would be crazy if he rejected you. But, I'm not normal, see. I really don't like the whole affair business. Meeting in hotels and motels, sneaking around, shits."

"Yes, but..."

I didn't give her a chance to go on, because I still had some more things to say. "Another thing is that we're too different for each other. You're external and socially oriented. And that's okay, but you see I'm just the opposite. I'm inward, complicated, and I hate conflict. So it would never work." "Never," I repeated.

"How do you know I'm not inward?" she asked.

"Look," I said, losing my patience, "there's more guys deserving of your attention than me. Hell, give them a chance. Why me?"

She leaned back in the chair and said in a dreamy tone of voice, "You got a fantastic body. But most of all, I'm attracted to just plain you, you're so human. I could see that you love humanity and care about people. And that's important to me."

I tried to think if, in the few hours we were together, I said anything that could've prompted her to discover any such bullshit. I couldn't. I decided she was no different than a guy, when he's trying to hustle a woman.

"Well, I don't know about that," I said, embarrassed.

"You are," she emphasized.

"Hey, let's stop this shit," I exploded. "What the hell do you want from me? Everyone wants some part of me. My wife, my kids, my family, you, my leg, my arm, take it, take it. I can't stand it anymore." My heart was beating like crazy. I noticed that some of the waiting passengers were now turning their heads in our direction.

She looked frightened. Then she said in a shaken voice, "I don't want anything, I just want to be your friend."

"But can't you see, Tatum," I said, feeling guilty because of my outburst, "that it will end up as something more?"

"Yes, I see, but I don't think that is the real reason," she said. "I think, you're kinda scared of me. Right?"

"Perhaps," I said quietly, "especially when I think about the book I'm working on. I don't know. Perhaps I am scared that you might get in my way of completing it, and I couldn't have that. I'm hoping it will say a lot to the world."

"Vinnie..."

"Please, Tat, let me finish," I urged in a strained voice. "I think a lot of what you're feeling for me now is infatuation; I bet in a few months you will have forgotten all about me. I really do."

"No," she said sharply. "I know it's more than infatuation. I know it is. I just do."

"Well, you wait and see, it will wear off," I insisted.

"It won't," she said, with a trembling voice, "I'll never forget you. Can't you understand? I'm not asking you to be committed to me, I'm just asking you to be my friend."

Oh, come on, stop with that friend shit.

"I just don't know, Tatum," I said. "There are so many things I'm confused about. In a way, I think we're like millions of others who are searching for happiness. And that kind of happiness like we had in bed for about thirty seconds is not real happiness. I think real happiness is struggling and suffering to achieve a higher purpose in life. Everything else is not happiness but contentment."

I thought about sharing my ideas about Heaven, but I decided it would be a waste of time. "You understand what I'm saying?" I asked, as if I were posing a question to one of my students.

"Yes," she responded weakly. "Everyone I talk to seems so depressed."

"That's right," I said, reinforcing her like a good teacher. "Very few understand what it takes to achieve a higher purpose in life. No one wants to give until it hurts. A friend once told me that Americans are obsessed with fulfilling needs and more needs. I think she was right." Angie's nude body flashed across my mind. I leaned closer to her and whispered quietly, "Tatum, there's something else I want to share with you. Not too many people know about it yet. Not even my wife. It's something I've given a great deal of thought to over the last few years. Tatum, I'm thinking of becoming a Benedictine monk. Even when I was small, I always dreamt of becoming a priest. And, now of late, because of the pain this damn world has given me, I've been thinking the only way I could achieve the higher purpose of life is by becoming a monk. I want to be away from it all, so I could concentrate on my work."

"You're serious, aren't you?" she asked in a reverent tone of voice.

"Yes."

"W-well, she stuttered, "that's real real nice... If... it doesn't turn out for you, I'll be available to be your friend or whatever you please."

"Thanks," I said, feeling drained, empty but elated at getting her to fall for my story.

"Wow," she shook her head, "I just don't believe what a trip this has been." Then with one full motion she slid out of the chair, and almost in a crouch-like position, she ran out of the gate area into the corridor.

Great! Great!

The noise of the plane's engine became muted, the buildings were quickly passing by, and zoom, we were in the gray skies. In a little while, the seat belt and no-smoking signs went off. Across the aisle, a little girl was banging her blond mother over the head with a rolled up magazine. Then she stopped banging, started banging again, then stopped; she sat down, stood up, then turned around and stared at the passengers in back of her. Then she started jumping up and down on the seat, as if it were a trampoline. The mother turned and said something to a passing stewardess. Shortly, the stewardess returned with a small glass of chocolate milk, which she placed in the seat-back tray in front of the mother. The bribe was accepted. The little girl stopped jumping, turned around, and for a few moments got quiet as she drank her chocolate milk through a straw. But then, before the mother could stop her, the little girl was squashing the small plastic glass of chocolate milk between the tray and the seat in front of her mother. The mother, acting as if nothing was wrong, slowly reached down and picked up a napkin off the floor, then, slyly, she dabbed at the crooked chocolate veins running down her legs. The child was back jumping up and down on the seat again. I could see that the mother was well on her way to becoming what psychologists call a "warm and accepting parent."

The noise of the plane's engine had changed into a steady hum. I closed my eyes, leaned back, and remembered another time I told a girl about becoming a Benedictine monk. But quickly, I shoved it out of my mind.

14

Taking a long cold shower, I was thinking it had been a month since Boston. When I got back the only question Chris asked was "Did everything go well?" Uncle Louie's death and that Jimmy's a murderer were always there, and being pushed deeper and deeper in my mind.

I said, "Yes." And that was it. Death was not her favorite subject. I remembered one time I had asked her why she cringed when I mentioned death, or when we passed a cemetery.

"I don't know."

"Think real hard."

"I guess, I never really thought about it that much. I've always felt that way since I could remember."

"But there must be a reason."

"I don't know. Maybe it's because my mother used to drag me along with her as she looked for old cemeteries. I think she was obsessed with death. She loved to read the epitaphs. Sometimes, if she really liked one, she would copy it down. I remember one she liked so much, she had it framed. I wish I could remember it, but I guess I've blocked it out of my mind."

"But there must be something more behind your unwillingness to talk about death, than just because you didn't like going to old cemeteries."

"I don't know. I think it's really because it's so final."

"Is that really it?"

"Yes."

"I just can't deal with anything so final as death. Please, Vinnie, let's not talk about it."

"Okay, I won't."

The first week back from Boston, my stomach seemed to be burning all the time. Then, when I started to double over with pain, I decided it was time to see a doctor and find out how much longer I had to live.

The doctor took X-rays and, after looking at them, he said that a tiny shadow near the top of the stomach indicated that I had a peptic ulcer. And even if he was wrong, he added, it should be treated as if I had one. It was always better to play it safe in medicine, he said. He prescribed two tablespoons of Maalox every four hours and a Valium, to be taken at mealtimes and just before bedtime.

The Maalox gave me diarrhea after about a week, so I substituted two Tums whenever my stomach started to burn. The Valiums made me too drowsy during the day, so I didn't take them until night. I would take two of them, along with two or three glasses of dry red wine. This combination elicited the black clouds of sleep faster than ever. Now and then, a few weird dreams broke through the deep blackness, but most of the time, I slept like a rock.

However, in the morning, like today, it was hard to wake up. It was different from a hangover: it was sort of being in a half-awake, half-asleep state. Sometimes, long cold showers helped my body move as fast as my mind. Other times, it didn't. And perhaps it would be late afternoon before I really felt fully awake, even though I had already taught one or two classes and had attended all sorts of committee meetings.

I turned the shower off, stepped out of the tub and started to dry myself off. My thoughts went back to the doctor's visit, for he sent me to a stomach specialist.

The specialist was a good-looking woman. She looked to be in her early thirties. Her clothes were sharply modern, new, and looked expensive.

She asked a series of questions about the burning in my stomach: when did it start, when did it hurt, did certain foods bring it on, did tension bring it on, were my stools black, did I have problems sleeping, on and on they went. Most of my responses were quite vague. I couldn't get into the Boston trip and Jimmy killing his father, which I now thought was taking its toll on me. I was dying. And nobody would ever know why.

I looked in the mirror and thought about what the doctor said when she came back into the examining room. She said I needed "an avocation." I worked too hard, worried too much, and had too much ambition. "That's the story for the majority of American males," she emphasized.

She suggested jogging as an avocation to consider. I liked this idea. Then the good-looking doctor suggested going on a diet. Even though I was considered slim, she said, I was getting near the age where a middle-age paunch would start to appear. I was a potential high blood-pressure case also. She wanted to prevent it. I thought, it's all part of the pathological syndrome the medical profession uses to scare people. Everyone is a potential sicko. Sane people are potential nuts. Law-abiding citizens are potential murderers. And so on, and so on.

There was always the possibility that she might be correct. So, on the way home, I decided I would go on a diet. I knew what I had was a lot worse than she was telling me. I figured the ulcer diagnosis was just a cover-up, so she would have more time to show the X-rays to other doctors. I saw myself getting a phone call from her in about a week, and with remorse in her voice, she would ask me to meet her at the hospital. When I'd get there, I would be led to a room, where a stern group of doctors in their clinical, white coats would sit around a long, formal table. Once the door was closed behind me, they would jump up, bang their fists on the table and laugh, chanting in unison, "You have Cancer, you have Cancer! Too bad for you. You. Have Cancer!"

I did my jogging at night, before I took the Valiums with wine. Chris thought it was great about my running. She said she would even run along with me if she had time. But she had very little time of late, because she had just been appointed by Father Luke to be the liturgy coordinator for the Charismatic Prayer group. And praying for the world to find Jesus Christ, she said, was more important than her selfish wish to jog with me.

Fine.

After a while, the running became an obsession with me. No matter what, I ran. I ran from my house to a high school track that was two blocks away. Once there, I ran eight times around the track, and then I ran home again. It was exactly four miles.

The diet I finally decided on, I found described in a West Coast health magazine. It consisted of having a small glass of carrot juice for breakfast; then for lunch, a small lettuce and tomato salad, heavily covered with vinegar; and for dinner, a large glass or more of dry red wine, and another lettuce and tomato salad, again heavily covered with vinegar. The diet was based on what some South American Indian tribe ate. The majority of its members, the article stated, lived to be one hundred or more. It said that the daily use of the vinegar decreased the body's need for large amounts of starches and sugars, which the article claimed were a major cause of death in this country. Like many health food enthusiasts had been saying, it pointed out that before Americans became obsessed with Cokes and Milky Ways, rarely did they die from cancer or heart disease. I was convinced.

I now looked more closely at myself in the mirror. In just two weeks, I had lost close to fifteen pounds. I felt youthful, as I slowly passed my hands over my chest. When I got to my stomach I tried grabbing some fat from around my waist. I only had enough to hold between my thumb and forefinger. I thought I looked like I did when I was an adolescent. I really liked my body.

But Chris didn't like my new look. I watched her face in the mirror quickly change to a troubled expression. She thought I looked too skinny and sickly. With my long, black hair now hanging over my shirt collars and a gaunt look that was all eyes, she said I reminded her of Rizzo, the drug addict in the movie *Midnight Cowboy*. Which, of course, she hated, because it was too depressing and dirty. She also said in a half-cynical and half-kidding tone of voice that pretty soon she wouldn't have anything to hang on to, you-know-when.

After I left the bathroom, I walked downstairs to the kitchen and saw something written on the memo pad near the phone.

Went to the Friary
to help Father Luke
to organize a prayer meeting
for tonight.
love, C
P.S. Please pick up Paulie at school around four.
He had to stay to make up some work. Thanks.

As I drove toward Paulie's school, I thought about his condition. Four years ago, while running high fevers, he started peeing a lot; drinking a lot of water, a lot of Kool-Aid, and he started bumping into things, as if he were drunk.

I had read somewhere that peeing a lot meant diabetes. I was right. It was confirmed after we took Paulie to a doctor who was in Chris's prayer group. We also discovered that Paulie was going blind in the right eye. The left eye was fine. It was quite common, the doctor said, for young children who get diabetes to have their sight affected. He said Paulie would be able to live a normal life, as long as we watched what he ate and made sure he got his insulin shot each day.

I remembered one day, when we forgot to give Paulie his insulin shot, the school nurse called from school to tell Chris that Paulie was disoriented. That was the word she used, Chris said. I could hear the nurse sneer, as she went on to ask Chris if we had given Paulie his injection.

That was the last time we forgot, except for that one time later on. Chris made a large, red flag with "INSULIN" written on it and stuck it on the refrigerator, next to a picture of the Christ-child who had a golden halo circling his curly, blond hair. "Jesus will help," she said, "he has a special place in his heart for children who must suffer in this world."

And Jesus did, except, like I said, for that one time.

Because of his health problems Paulie looked scrawny and sickly. His face always had a pasty color to it. His weight and height were far below normal for an eight-year-old boy. He had my beaked nose and mousy hair. However, with his large brown eyes and tiny mouth, he was all Chris. He also had this deep, reflective look in his eyes, as if he were fifteen miles ahead of the person he was talking to. He was bright, even though he had missed a lot of school because of his condition.

As I pulled up to the school lot, I saw Paulie, tilting his head to one side as he studied each car that passed, searching with his one good eye for me. He wore glasses with a dark-tinted lens covering his poor eye, and a regular clear lens over his good eye.

I now stopped the car in front of Paulie. As usual, his clothes were wrinkled. One end of his soiled white shirt hung carelessly out of his chalk-covered pants, his hooded winter jacket was unzipped, and his navy-blue sweater had three buttons at the bottom without their matching button holes.

"Hi, Dad," he said, getting in the car and placing his books between us. Then he sat like he always did, on the edge of the front seat nervously drumming his fingertips on the dashboard.

"How you doing?" I asked. His teacher's remarks now flooded my mind. "Mr. Serrano, your son is very bright. You should thank God for that. God gave him a good mind to compensate for his handicap. In all my years of teaching, I've never seen anyone with such a zest and love of life. It was like every minute was his last. You should see how he plays in the playground. My Lord! He plays baseball every day, even though he gets hit by the ball a lot, because he can't see it when he's batting or catching. But because of this drive that he wants to be like everyone else, he pretends it doesn't hurt, when I know, inside, it's killing him... Sir, this would be the only criticism I have of Paul, he tries too hard to be normal. It's almost an unnatural drive he has for wanting to be like everyone else. He'll even take off his glasses sometimes and try to read. But he can't. I think he feels his diabetic condition will get better... but it won't, will it?"

"No," I said quickly and with finality.

"I hate staying after school," Paulie said with frustration in his voice, as he drummed a fast beat on the dashboard. "I could be playing outside, but no, I have to stay after school and do all that stupid work. Gee, Dad, I already know all of it anyways. It isn't fair."

"I know," I said reassuringly, "but it's only because you missed so much this year, it will be better next year."

"I hope so," he shook his head as he picked up the beat with his fingertips. I reached over and pulled his hands back. He stopped.

"Will I be able to go to the Steelers games next year?" he asked with a trace of doubt in his voice.

"Sure."

"When will you get the tickets, or are you just saying that, like you do all the time? You always promise me something, but when the time comes to doing it, you always say, you've got too much work to do."

"Come on, that's not true. Didn't I bring you to some university football games last year?"

"Only two. I wanted to go to all of them."

"I just couldn't, I had to finish..."

"See," he said quickly.

"Okay, but this time I've already looked into getting tickets for next year's Steelers games," I lied. "And we'll go to each one, I promise." Hell, I thought, how could he ever sit through one of those rough wintry days at Three Rivers Stadium? He couldn't.

"Thanks, Dad," he said happily. He believed me. He leaned over and kissed me on the cheek. "That will be a lot of fun."

"It sure will," I said, trying to sound enthusiastic.

"Dad, did you know that your birthday is on the same day as Franco Harris?"

"Is that right?"

Paulie picked up a book from the stack that lay between us, "I read it in here."

"What's it called?"

"*Franco, the Black Stallion.*"

"Sounds interesting." I pretended to care about the Pittsburgh fullback.

"I just can't wait until I'm old enough to try out for the Steelers, and I'll have friends like Franco. He seems like a nice Christian man."

As I stopped and waited for a traffic light to change, Paulie demanded, "Dad, please tell me again how you go about making it into a professional football team."

Hell, Paulie, you've asked me that question a million times before. Can't fathers and sons in America today talk about something other than damn professional football? Jesus.

"Well, Paulie, you go to a college or university on something called a football scholarship. Then, in your senior year, if you're outstanding, a professional team picks you up in something called the draft."

"What if I don't get picked? Could I still try out for the Steelers?"

The traffic light changed, and I steered the car onto the ramp that led onto the interstate.

"Yes, there are a lot of guys who try exactly that; but, Paulie, very few make it that way."

"Well, I guess, if I don't make it," he said, "then I'll become a coach or an announcer for the Steelers. I really like making up plays and seeing how they work."

"Well, that's a possibility."

"You know what I would do for the next Super Bowl game?"

"No, what?"

"I would have Terry Bradshaw practice passing all week in front of the press," he said, with a grown-up, professional tone of voice. "Then, after everyone goes home, I would have him and Franco develop some fancy running plays. I've already written out some and sent them to Chuck Noll. I hope he likes them. Dad, do you think he might use them?"

"He might," I said.

"You've been really thinking about this, haven't you?" I asked, as we got off the highway and headed toward Baywood.

"Yes, I think about them all the time in school or when I'm sick," he said proudly. "I've come up with swing and loop plays, and buttonhook passes; I've been working on 7-3-1, 8-2-1, and 5-4-2 defense formations on my electric football game. You should see it, Dad, I've even worked them with stunting guards or tackles. Sometimes I work them with linebackers blitzing, or with safeties blitzing and the linebackers staying back. You should see them, Dad, they're really great. Yesterday, I wrote up a beautiful shotgun play for Terry Bradshaw. I'm going to send it to him. I watched Roger Staubach use it during the season. I would have the guards trapping, the receivers treading the zone in the flat, then go down and out, bumping the defenders on the way. In the backfield, Franco would screen, Terry throws it to him on a lob, then Franco throws it back, then Terry can run downfield or throw it to his looping receivers. Great, huh?"

"Unbelievable," I said, "just unbelievable."

"Another thing, Dad," he was on a roll now, "if I live right in Pittsburgh and go to the university there, I can see the Steelers practice and play all their games. I could learn all their plays then, so when they draft me, I'll be ready to play."

I steered the car to the right and headed toward the entrance of Baywood. Small, white Colonial-style brick walls flanked the entrance, and "Baywood" was painted on them in large black letters. We passed through and headed to Mission Drive, the street we lived on. Each street in Baywood was named after something or someone in the space program.

"Paulie, you're only eight, and you have to realize like everyone else that you have limitations. You know, because of your condition, there's certain things you can, and cannot do."

"Yeah, I know," he replied. "Gee, Dad, you talk as if I was an invalid."

"I don't mean that." I was defensive. "I just mean that you have to realize that we can't all be what we like. If we did... well, never mind. I was just thinking of you, Paulie, because I love you."

"I understand, Dad, but I know I could do it." He said this with so much confidence that I almost believed him.

"Fine, as long as you realize that." I parked the car in our driveway in front of our white Colonial brick split-level home.

Paulie leaned over, touched my shoulder, and said, "Dad, you will try to get those tickets for me, won't you? You're not just saying that?"

"No, I will," I said earnestly, "in fact, I'll write for them tonight. Okay?"

"Thanks, Dad, I love you," he reached up and gave me a light kiss on my cheek. Then he picked up his books, opened the car door, and leaped out, slamming the door behind him.

I thought to myself, even though our genes screwed him up a bit, I felt proud that some of who he was came from me. And since the Boston trip, I found myself holding and hugging him more than I ever did before. He didn't seem to mind. There was something about the feel of that small frail body in my arms, something about his baby-soft skin against my lips. There was something in him that I loved more than anything else. Of course, the sad part was I never felt this way for Linda or Chris. It was like the secret part of me that was closed to them; it was open to him and only him.

As I approached the front door to our home, I heard loud, angry voices coming from inside. They stopped briefly when I opened the door and walked in. I went down the hall and into the kitchen. In one corner, I saw Linda standing with her hands clutching the back of a kitchen chair. Chris was facing her but turned around when she heard me come in. Her huge brown eyes were on fire. She seemed to be disturbed by my presence.

"Vinnie," Chris said, "now don't you interfere." Then she turned back to Linda and resumed her shouting. But somehow I felt she was really talking to me, wanting me to know what was happening. I wondered what her prayer group would say if they could see their saint now.

"A spoiled brat," she shouted. "That's what you are, a nasty spoiled brat."

I moved closer.

"Just doing as she pleases," Chris hissed, "just like all the rest of the spoiled brats on the street."

"But Mom, I forgot," Linda pleaded. "I really did." She was crying.

"What the hell is going on," I shouted. I felt myself trembling and getting ready to explode.

"Vinnie, stay out of this," Chris shot back. "I'm handling this." She started yelling at Linda again. I'll be damn if I'll be made a fool of by a seven-year-old brat. No way."

"Jesus, I want to know what happened," I screamed as loud as I could.

I think I scared both of them, as Chris turned to me and said with a calmer voice, "She lied to me, and I hate lying worse than any other sin. It cheapens everything."

"About what?" I asked, trying hard to control my rage.

"I've told her over and over again to stay out of people's houses, to play outside, Linda. But no, she had to go in. I saw her going in one of her friend's home. And I could even live with that. But she had to go and lie to me. She told me she didn't go in, when I saw her with my own eyes. That's what is driving me up the wall. My daughter is a liar.... What do they teach her in that Catholic school?"

I couldn't control my rage any longer. "So she lied," I shouted, lurching forward and grabbing a clump of Linda's silky hair between my fingers. Everything was blurred.

"God, Vinnie, please!" I heard Chris's voice, as if from a distance, alarmed and high-pitched. "Please don't interfere." She grabbed my arms in order to pull me away from Linda.

"I don't care," I yelled, as I whirled around and pushed Chris against the refrigerator. She let out a gasp. Then, still tugging Linda by her hair, I pulled her through the hall, up the stairs, and into her room. I locked the door behind me, and then, almost picking her up in midair, I threw her on the bed.

"Daddy, I'm sorry, I won't ever do it again." She curled up into a ball and buried her head between her knees. She knew, the worst was yet to come.

Now everything was completely white before my eyes, as I jumped onto the bed and screamed, "I'll teach you to lie, you bastard! Who the hell do you think you are?" Then I started to slap her all over with my open palms; then I switched to closed fists.

When I could think again, I could feel my hands stinging with pain. Her body had gone limp. I thought I had killed her. Quickly, I turned her over. Thank God, she was alive. She was gasping for breath, her face reddish-purple, she was sobbing and clutching her mouth. I wanted to tell her I was sorry. *It wasn't me.* Then I felt her body become rigid, as she looked up at me, with terror in her eyes.

I sensed someone in back of me. I turned. There was Chris, shaking her head in disgust. I wondered how she got in. The door was locked, I thought.

"For God's sake," she said bitterly. "Couldn't you see I was disciplining her? You would never treat Paulie that way. It's always her. Just something about women. It's in your blood. You bitch about your father, but you're just like him."

At least, she knew I wasn't to blame.

She went on. "Little girls need to be loved by their fathers. They don't need a yelling, raving maniac for a father. That's why I told you I wanted to do the disciplining with her. I want her to love you. But you won't let her..."

I blocked her out, as I turned back and looked down at Linda's small, crunched-up body. I could now see the tiny streaks of pale yellow flowing down her shaking legs. I felt sick and dizzy. My stomach started to burn. *So this is what university professors do in their spare time. What if my students could see me now? What would they say? This was only to happen in uneducated homes. Not in professors'.*

I leaped off the bed, ran past Chris to my study, and locked the door behind me. Then I went over to my desk and took out a small rust-colored vial of Valium from one drawer and a bottle of red wine from another. I had everything here that was needed to block out times like these. Immediately, I took three Valiums from the bottle and washed them down with a large gulp of wine. Before I waited for the darkness to come, I ran to Paulie's room to see If he was okay. Slowly, I opened his door, walked over to the bed, and noticed he was crying softly. I leaned over and said, "Did you hear all that?"

"Yes," he sobbed a little.

"I'm sorry, Daddy will never do that again. I love you." I hugged him tightly and cried on his shoulders and waited for him to go to sleep, then left.

Now in my study, I lay down on the burgundy sofa and waited for sleep to come. When I finally dozed off, I had a weird dream. I dreamt that I was sitting as a student in my own class. My seat was at the bottom tier of the auditorium, which was shaped like an amphitheater. At the podium, there was someone giving a lecture. Behind the instructor was a tall, black stage-curtain. Suddenly, the instructor vanished, and another person took over. Then that one vanished, too. Time after time, this was repeated, until I was able to prove to one of the instructors that I knew everything. So, finally, I took over. When I began to teach, I didn't feel too comfortable, because I sensed that something or someone was peering at me from behind the black curtain. The whole class saw it. But every time I turned around, it vanished, like the instructors. Soon, the students started to laugh at my antics. They laughed with much the same mocking laughter, I supposed, as when the Romans laughed at the Christians in the Colosseum. They drove me wild with rage. And, like a madman, I started to run up and down the aisles, striking and tearing the eyes out of everyone I could reach. It was a glorious feeling. Somewhere around here, I started to feel the tender touch of a woman. Soon, I discovered, there were two. One was full of lustful animal desire; the other only talked to me about the beauty of mathematical thought. As the first woman kissed me all over, the second one talked to me about how our lives should be centered on mathematics. She said the personal ordering and geometric representation of our lives and of our epistemology may lead to a better understanding of the infinite order of our cosmos. On and on she went. It was like she knew exactly what I wanted to say in my book on Heaven. It was all making sense, until a skinny, long-bearded man appeared. He started to pour a liquid on me and the two women. The women and I tried getting it off, but the more we did, the more the liquid spread all over our bodies.

15

The next morning, Chris's loud knocking on the door of my study woke me up.

"Vinnie, Vinnie, Vinnie," she called. I tried to concentrate on her tone of voice, to see if she was mad. I couldn't tell. Finally, I answered that I was up. I remembered I would be doing binomials with my classes that day. Also, I couldn't wait to apologize to Linda. To hell with my cold shower; I went to the bathroom, shaved quickly, and went down to the kitchen.

Chris was sitting in a kitchen chair, holding a cup of coffee. How her looks had changed over the years, I thought. Before, Chris's face was strong-looking with high cheekbones, wide chestnut eyes, and a high forehead. Her features gave her Irish ancestry away. Now her face looked sunken in and pale. Her once silky, shoulder-length black hair was thinning and graying. And there was some evidence now that middle-age was creeping into her hips and waist.

"I'm sorry," I said, as I sat opposite her.

"I am, too," she said. "We're not perfect. There's a noon mass at the Friary. Will your class be over by then?"

"Yes, but I'm meeting with a student at that time," I lied. "Sorry."

"That's okay." She sighed, with disappointment in her voice.

Silence.

I didn't like attending mass with her. In fact, I always liked it when I went alone to church, and nobody was there. It brought back memories of those times in Sacred Heart. Finally, our silence was broken a few minutes later when Linda came into the kitchen.

I was shocked. I expected a puffy face, swollen eyes, and all of that. Instead, she was smiling. I motioned for her to come over to me. She did.

"I'm sorry," I said, pulling her close to me and kissing her on the cheek. I thought I felt her body stiffen. "Honey, Daddy was only trying to help you grow up to be a nice girl, because I love you."

"I know, Daddy," she said, looking lovingly at me. She was in training to become a saint, too. I wondered how many people have lived in a house with two saints.

I also wondered what they would do, if they knew I had a crazy cousin who killed people by shooting shit up their noses.

An hour after class I sat in my office, listening to feet scuffling by and voices talking on the other side of my door, when Jarvis opened the door halfway and asked if I wanted to go to lunch. Thank God for Jarvis. I was feeling terribly depressed and jumpy.

Jarvis was in charge of teaching the statistics courses in the math department. Students gave him a very high rating on their annual student evaluations of professors. Also, it was said that he tried to screw every girl in his class. When I asked him about this, he said, quite seriously, "Not every girl." Then his face broke out in a wide smile, and he laughed like hell. I guess that was another reason why I liked him. I was able to realize some of my sexual fantasies through his stories or the rumors of his sexual exploits.

One thing I could never figure out was why Jarvis seemed to like me. Perhaps it was because he thought I was a genius or something like that, or because I had written two textbooks in mathematics. I could see him trying to impress some naïve, farm-fresh West Virginia girl by saying, "Yeah, Vinnie Serrano couldn't be where he is today, if I didn't help him develop his ideas for the textbooks, with the many late-night discussions I had had with him. I told him most of the things that are in there now."

Jarvis Kerns was tall, slim, blue-eyed, and blond. He was born in Kentucky and had a street-corner Americanized, British accent. He said his father was born in England and came to this country to set up a clothing store with his brother. Jarvis looked so innocent and childlike. I wondered how many girls got the shock of their life, when he was banging away at them like a half-crazed sex fiend.

We were sitting down to lunch now, when he started bitching about Art Fraiser, the chairman of the Math Department.

"He talks out of both sides of his mouth, just like the fucking dean," he said, matter of fact. "He tells me one thing, and then, as soon as I leave his office, he tells someone else just the opposite."

"I know," I said supportively.

"He hates conflict situations, and he'll mealymouth around, until he gets himself out of them." Then Jarvis shook his golden head and narrowed his blue eyes into slits and said, "Last week, the jerk called me in and said he'd heard I was screwing around with a girl in one of my classes. I guess, the boyfriend of this girl went in and told him about me. Well, I said, it was true. So what? Well, he said, I must remember the moral code of West Virginians. They won't accept that kind of behavior from their teachers. Maybe in Boston or New York, but not here. And then he said, which really pissed me off, that if I had a need to do things like that, I should be more discreet about it. That's unbelievable. I could fuck all I want, as long as I do it in some hotel in Ohio. That just doesn't make sense to me. It's hypocritical and he's suppressing my freedom. I won't have that. So I wrote the asshole a long letter, explaining how I felt. Well, he wrote back in his typical, content-free style and said exactly nothing. He said it was all a misunderstanding, but if that's the way I was going to construe his remarks, he said, so be it. The asshole."

"He's a Southern administrator," I said sarcastically. "What can you expect? They smile at you while, at the same time, they knife you in the back."

"You're right, Vinnie," he said, "damn right. And it pisses me off. I would like to say fuck it and get into something else, where I'm free of assholes like Art and the dean."

"Well, I've often thought about working only part time at the university." I was serious. "Then I would have to contend with the university crap for only half the time. I figure the other half of the time I would concentrate on my writing. In fact, if this new book I'm getting ready to write does well, I'm pretty sure I'll be doing exactly that. However, I doubt I'll ever make enough money to do it full time. However, I love teaching and would like to stay in it. It gives me a good high."

"Sounds great, Vinnie," he said, with wide-open eyes. "I'll be your business manager. We'll get a secluded little place on the ocean, where you could get away and do your writing, and where I could go and discreetly do my fucking around."

"Okay," I said calmly, realizing deep down that we never would.

"I'll check into property around North Carolina," he said. "I've always loved the Outer Banks, especially around Nags Head."

"Fine."

"Look, for six months a year we'll work for the damn university, and then for the other six you work on your thing, and I'll go out and sell your creative talents. I've always wanted to be a big-time book agent. I imagine they get more ass than they can handle. Hollywood, here we come, as they say in the movies. Hell, Vinnie, maybe then I'll finally get a shot at screwing Jane Fonda. I've loved her ever since I saw her playing a prostitute in, ah... what was that movie..."

"Why Jane Fonda?"

"Her eyes are so wild, just like a lion or lioness or whatever you call a female lion."

"Lioness, I think."

"Well, whatever, Vinnie," he said. "Let's talk more about this when we have more time, okay?"

"Okay."

A few minutes later, I told him I had to get back to the office. He said okay, but he wasn't ready to leave just yet. His eyes were staring at a table next to us, where a big-chested girl was flashing him a sweet, cheerleader-smile. That's a funny feeling, I thought, being a third party to two people who were getting ready to make love.

It was nearly one o'clock when I got back to the office. Fay had just called to remind me that I had a two o'clock appointment with a student. Her name didn't sound familiar. In the meantime, I decided to file some paperwork from my in-basket. There were three memos from Art, outlining new promotion and tenure procedures; then there were four memos from the dean's office superseding all of Art's memos; then there were three memos from the president's office, questioning the rationale used in the three memos from Art and the four from the dean; then there was Policy Bulletin No. 340 from the State's Board of Regents, which gave them sole power in outlining procedures for promotion and tenure, and this, of course, superseded all other memos written on tenure and promotion procedures. Then there were a few series of memos dealing with this Policy Bulletin No. 340, but I didn't bother to read them. I filed all of them under "Bullshit."

I leaned back in my chair, clasped my hands behind my head and looked around my tiny office. My desk and file cabinets were against one wall; against the opposite wall were a kitchen table that I used for my writing and a tall, metal-frame bookcase that was stacked with complimentary copies of mathematical textbooks. Across from the door were two medium-sized, aluminum-framed windows. They looked out on a parking lot, four tennis courts, two tall red-brick buildings, and some white clapboard homes, which were surrounded by leafless trees. In the distance, the West Virginia hills were streaked with snow.

The office walls had been painted off-white some time ago, but now there were many black scuffmarks covering the bottom half, from where I had placed my feet or moved furniture around. On some parts of the wall, dark-brown cardboard revealed itself from underneath the paint. I must stop Scotch-taping things to the walls. To a visitor, I thought, the office might seem cold and austere because of the marred walls and the dark-grey metal office furniture. But for me, it wasn't so. It was a place where I could feel secure and safe. In fact, it was really cozy. I had spent hours leaning against the counter-sized windowsill, looking out at the students get into their cars or at the stark-naked hills in the distance.

I stood up, walked over to the window, and looked out. I wondered about my comment to Jarvis that I loved teaching. I wondered if I really did. There was very little opportunity to see any sort of concrete results of what I did in the classroom. I used to feel some element of pride, when a doctoral advisee of mine came through his oral defense with flying colors. But this only happens once or twice a year. I wished I was like the professors in drama and music. At least they had a chance to show off their own talents in plays and concerts. Where do I?

I thought about him. Him. Always him. I remembered how his eyes would light up as he proudly held out a shoe in front of him. Pretending that he was talking to himself but really wanting me to hear, he would say: "That's a perfect job." *True, he was a perfectionist. I loved to watch him, as he concentrated on his work. Wrinkling his forehead in deep concentration, he would bend his broad shoulders over the overturned shoe, which lay on a black steel form that was worn to a shine. Then, taking a tiny nail from his tightly closed-up lips, he would place it swiftly in position on the new leather heel. With his free hand, he'd grip a small brow-handled hammer and drive the nail in with one quick tap. He repeated this process until the heel was fastened securely to the shoe. The quick sounds of his hammer coming down on the nails reminded me of a tap dancer I'd once seen in a movie. He sat in a white, spoked chair, and he rhythmically moved the sole of one foot from side to side, skillfully increasing the tapping sound as he went along.*

Here, at the university, I've never felt the same pride he had felt in doing his job as near perfect as he could. Here, we play silly little games, like using a little of this idea and that idea in committee meetings, so that we'll be noticed and then eventually get promoted. Here, we try to get personal and friendly with students; we try to find ways to get them to laugh in our classes, so then they'll say we're interesting and have a sense of humor. Of course, learning anything doesn't matter. Here, we learn to bluff, like Jarvis says, with such words as *humanistic, feedback loops, ad hoc, interfaces, ex post facto, operationalized, performance objectives, a priori, participatory democracy...* We pretend that these phrases are liberating us, when in reality, after much use, these words pass around us and become meaningless. Here, we learn to say "yes," because we know it's really difficult for the university to say "no" to someone who is constantly reaffirming its existence. So, we learn to balance the "safe" and "unsafe" areas; and, those who are unlucky enough to find themselves on either end are usually dismissed or forgotten.

I moved from the window, sat back down, and stared at the poster some students had given me a few years ago. Their signatures were to one side. The poster was a print of a painting that represented a black-outlined isosceles triangle with a red full circle at its apex. I was impressed by it. Even the artist's name sounded impressive. Santini Santanos. The poster was titled "The Soul of Man." I knew, in my mind I had the right words to describe the subtle ideas behind the painting, but, for some reason, they never came out. The only words that came out were words like *beautiful, magnificent, majestic, wonderful, touching, stimulating, exhilarating, meaningful.* All of them seemed to cheapen what the artist was trying to express, and what I was feeling. I wished sometimes I was like some of the art critics who wrote for the *New York Times*; they have so many more adjectives at their disposal than I do.

I thought again about my book on Heaven. I know that once I get started, I'll be able then to find the ideas to express what I'm feeling about this painting. In time, the art critics of the world will look to me for the interpretation of the abstractness of the abstract of all art. In my book, I promised myself, each and every sentence will be important. *Oh, God, I must get started writing. I must.*

16

I was feeling really good, as I walked back home on Mission Drive. I had just run ten times around the high school track, and I still felt I could've run ten more times without getting tired. Running gave me a break from my thoughts. When I wasn't thinking about Jimmy's disgusting act of killing his father, I was thinking of Angie or Tatum. Something was happening to me, and I was scared.

Stop it, Vinnie, please.

I saw that the Bodds, who lived across the street from us, had just turned off their lights. The only light they left on was the one in their second-story bedroom. Their drapes were always open; and, on some nights I could see either Jim's or his wife's head bobbing up and down in front of their powder-blue bedroom walls. The window was too high to see anything else.

Like clockwork, I knew their bedroom light would go off at eleven. Jim Bodd was a chemical engineer at Dupont in Wheeling, and his wife was a manager of a small boutique in the Baywood shopping mall. I often wondered what they did when the light was on in their bedroom. I tried to visualize them making love, but I couldn't. He was fat and short, and she was tall and nicely-built. I loved to listen to her speak. She had a slight English tinge mixed in with her heavy Southern accent. Jim talked like a gruff punk from Brooklyn. He was supposed to be one of Dupont's top engineers, but you could never tell by just talking to him. They had a fifteen-year-old daughter who was tall, dark, and beautiful. I couldn't believe that there were genes in him that could produce such a beauty. I decided she must've been adopted or that the wife had her from a previous marriage.

I reached my house and decided to sit on the porch steps. To my right, I spotted another neighbor, Ed Helchi, who was walking his German shepherd in my direction. I watched Ed, as he stopped in front of my house and waited for his damn dog to let go of one of his monstrous turds on my lawn. I remembered Chris's get-togethers where these monstrous turds were always a topic of discussion. He looked over, stared for a moment, and then waved.

"Hi, Vince, I didn't see you there. How you doing?" Ed reminded me of one of those male, potato-nosed cartoon characters one sees every once in a while in the *New Yorker*. He was tall and always slouched over. He had a PhD in something called "educational research."

"Okay, I guess. How about you?"

"Good," he said, pulling at his dog's leash so that he would follow him and stop sniffing at his turd. Finally, the dog obeyed, and both came over.

"Sit, sit," he now commanded the dog in a thundering voice. The dog refused until Ed quickly snapped the leash at him. The dog yelped with pain and finally sat for his master.

"Hey," he said, "I heard the Board of Regents has suggested no salary increases for the faculty next year."

"Is that right?"

"Yeah, but that's not going to hurt me," he said proudly, "I have some federal monies coming in for a new system of teaching educational psychology. I was working on it with a friend of mine who's in computers, Jack Faulks. You know him?"

"No, but I think I've heard his name," I lied.

"Well, he and I have worked out a system where a student plugs himself into a console and learns the basic concepts in educational psychology. Each concept is then tested. And if he misses a certain question on a test, he has a light-gun at his disposal, to call up any information he needs in order to correct his response. The system was originally developed by a group of professors at MIT."

"Sounds interesting," I said, with very little enthusiasm. I remembered reading a Board of Regents bulletin last year that explained how they were using a competency-based curriculum to train teachers. They were dividing up learning into such things as 1.1—The student will learn this, 1.2—The student will learn that, 1.3—The student will learn this and that, and so on. The whole process seemed asinine. I wondered how could any educated person accept that understanding could be divided up into neat little packages. Then I thought about the shallowness of people, like Ed, in education. And that was enough. I had my answer.

"We figure a pilot study needs about five hundred thousand dollars to make it go. But right now we're only asking for a hundred thousand, to do a feasibility study. We want to make sure we have a good idea, so that the five hundred thousand will be enough for the grant. The president likes the idea and so does my dean. They're talking about using it in a social-science class that all freshmen have to take."

"Is that right?" I yawned a little. Then I stood up and pretended I had to go in, but he didn't get the clue.

"Hey, Vince," he called to me. I turned around. "What do you know about item analysis and item discrimination, which is the feedback dimension of systems analysis?"

"I don't think I could help you," I said, "but I would be interested in the results." I put my hand on the doorknob and opened the door slightly. Finally Ed got the clue.

"Fine, fine," he said nervously. "Still, if you're interested, the consulting fee is pretty good."

"Okay, I'll think about it," I said. "Bye." I stepped into the doorway.

"Bye."

I stood there for a moment, then turned and watched Ed as he desperately tried to keep up with his dog, who was now barking and swiftly running ahead of him. "Franklin, heel, heel..." was the last thing I heard, as they both disappeared around Ed's house.

I softly closed the door again, sat back down on the front steps, and watched Bodd's house become completely dark, as their bedroom light went off. Their white clapboard-like aluminum siding looked gray under the streetlight.

Baywood was considered one of the better suburbs of Wheeling. It had a shopping mall nearby, neat dark-paneled restaurants, a private country club with an eighteen-hole golf course, a tennis club with indoor and outdoor tennis courts, and a dome-shaped school building with "classrooms without walls." I remembered a couple once telling me at one of Chris's get-togethers that they had lived in Baywood for eight years, and, except for passing though Wheeling to get on and off the interstate, they had been in Wheeling only once. That was to see the Osmonds sing at the Civic Center. They said Baywood had everything it needed. *And so it did, except for real people.*

The houses in Baywood ranged from seventy thousand to two hundred thousand. I thought about the people who lived in these houses. And, their things: their color-TV sets; their station wagons, or their second or third economy cars; their furniture; their dogs; their clothes; their children; and their crabgrass. It all looked so different in the day, but now, in the dark of night, they were the same.

I thought about Charlie Oates, the electrician who lived near the end of our street. It was said that he made more money than anyone else on the street. After last summer, when he put in an Olympic-size swimming pool, there was talk that he was connected with the Mafia. People just wouldn't accept that an electrician could be the richest man on the street. I could, especially after he charged me ninety dollars to fix my dryer.

Next to him lived the Carsons and their six wild kids. Directly across from the Carsons lived Peter Copeland, who was constantly reminding people that he was nothing when he started; but, by breaking his ass twenty hours a day, he now owned a chain of doughnut shops throughout West Virginia, plus two Laundromats, and a machine-shop in Wheeling. No one ever saw him, except on holidays, when he made it a point to go over to whomever was outside and tell them how hard he was breaking his ass.

Further down the street lived a gray-haired widow who supposedly wrote children's books. The only time anyone saw her was in the early morning hours, when she was walking her barking poodle.

Next to the widow lived Stanley Flankers. Stanley was a lawyer for Wheeling Steel. His Yale Law School background was stamped all over him. He had sandy hair, blue eyes, and he used just enough pomposity in his speech and manners to make sure you knew he was a pure Ivy Leaguer. His major interest, he once told me, was bear-hunting in Wyoming.

Next door to us lived the Bradshaws with their son, John, who was a bit weird. Bradshaw was a professor of history at the university. He spent, I heard, most of his time writing bibliographies on insignificant subjects. Now I felt my mouth breaking out into a grin, as I thought about Bradshaw, dressed in a suit, stiffly riding up and down the street on his ten-speed bike.

I missed Boston sometimes, even though it cast a huge shadow over me.

I had become terribly restless and edgy over the weeks since my trip. At the university, I tried to begin my book on Heaven. I wrote, "The meaning..." Nothing followed. I wrote the same words again. Again, nothing. Finally, I gave up.

I tried to read the simplest of memos, math journals, even novels, but I couldn't understand any of them. I would read sentences five or six times and not absorb any of it. After a while, I would just stare at the print on the page and think about nothing. I even found the local newspaper difficult to read. Only the column titled "People" was I able to take in. It told about famous people getting married, dying, divorcing, being sued, fined for drunken driving, placed in jail on a morals charge, and so on.

I started to buy the *Star*, which was simple to read and full of these neat tidbits. I read it between my classes. I didn't feel like doing anything else.

One day, I tried to write a three-line memo to one of my advisees concerning a question he had about a class being offered next term. It took me seven drafts before I could get the words in the sentence in the right order. After that, I decided, Fay could answer my correspondence.

I also found it increasingly difficult to take any interest in teaching my classes. I forced myself to go through the motions. I heard words coming out of my mouth, but I didn't know if they made any sense to the students.

The fourth week wasn't any better. I was as jumpy and restless as ever. On Wednesday, I got an appointment with the good-looking doctor.

She asked, "Are you having any problems with your sex life?"

"No, I'm just restless and nervous during the day, I can't concentrate. And I just can't sleep," I said, "and I need to, because I'm working on a very important project." *Jesus, why did she ask about my sex life? Is she hitting on me?*

"Okay, I'll give you something else," she said.

"But if you're still having problems in two or three weeks, call me. We might have to think about some alternatives."

"What do you mean?"

"Well, we might have to see if a psychiatrist can help you."

"Why?"

"There might be something in your subconscious that's going on, and he may help us get to the bottom of all of this. I don't want your ulcer to get worse. And if you keep up the way you're going, it will."

"Oh." I felt sick to my stomach.

"I know a very good psychiatrist," she said, as she wrote something on her prescription pad. "He's a good friend of mine." She tore off the slip and handed it to me.

I looked at the writing. The name of the pill was flurazepam.

That day I took one, and it helped me concentrate a little.

At breakfast when the kids were gone, Chris asked, "You seem so edgy and depressed all the time. What's wrong, Vinnie?"

"Nothing," I said, as I got up, turned away, and walked out of the kitchen. She followed.

"I know there is," she demanded, "please tell me, Hon. Since you came back home from Boston, you seem to be in a different world."

"Really, there's nothing wrong," I said, as I opened the front door, turned, and faced her. "On second thought, I don't know, maybe it's the book I've been working on. I just can't seem to get it off my mind. It's with me every second of every day."

She moved closer to me and leaned her head on my chest, "That's why you have an ulcer, Hon," she said affectionately. "You've got to learn how to relax. I think sometimes you think more of your stupid book than of me or the kids. I hate that book, Vinnie." I thought she was going to cry.

"Oh, come on, Chris," I said, pushing her back a little so I could see her face. "It's something I must do. Please try to understand that."

"I'll try," she said, "but I'll still hate it. Promise me, Vinnie, you won't start another book for at least three years."

"I promise," I said.

"I hope so," she took hold of my hand and brought it up to her breasts. "I feel, Hon, that this past year we've been really growing apart." For a brief moment I wanted to take her in my arms, close the door, and make love to her in the hallway. But then, I quickly thought that saints don't screw on floors. Oh, and she would probably interrupt our lovemaking with questions about whether or not it was the right time, and shit like that.

I reached up and brought her head back down to my chest. Then I stroked her hair and said, "Look, Chris, when the book is finished, I promise I'll take the whole family to Europe for a year. I'll get a job teaching in some university over there. The federal government has a great program for exchanging professors."

She took her head off my chest and looked up at me with worried eyes. "Vinnie, we can't do that for at least another couple of years."

"Why not?"

"Well, Hon," she said, lowering her eyes, "you know, my parents are not getting any younger. And I don't know if I could ever live with myself if something happened to one of them while I was away."

"I give up," I said, taking my hands off her hair, turning, and stepping onto the porch. I turned back and said, "Chris, that's the problem with you, you're always serving other people. Father Luke, your stupid-ass prayer group, your parents, but never us, your own family."

"You really mean, serving you," she said, half-smiling.

"No, damn it," I said, "I mean Paulie, Linda, all of us."

"I still think you want me to revolve my whole life around you."

"No, hell no," I said angrily. "Jesus, Chris, I got to get going, I'll be late for class. I don't know why we always have these types of discussions when I'm just leaving for work. Hell, we got all night."

"Do we?" she said sarcastically, as she stepped onto the porch with me.

Neighbors, look at your saint now. She can't stand the truth. She's losing her cool.

But she wasn't.

"Who spends all his time in the study or running?" she asked in a calm voice.

"Okay, okay," I said, knowing she had me. "Let's promise ourselves an hour a night."

"I hope we do it," she said blushing, "and I mean that more than one way. I'm horny, Vinnie. How long has it been? I was doing it in my sleep the other night." I couldn't believe she said that. The saint was masturbating. No. That's unreal.

"Whose fault is that?" I asked, as I still thought about her masturbating.

"Yours," she answered quickly. "You're the one who's so fussy."

This was getting us nowhere.

"Please, Chris, let's discuss this tonight," I backed off while I turned and walked down the steps onto the sidewalk and looked back. "I'll fuck you tonight. I promise."

"Vinnie," she said in a scolding tone of voice while she smiled, embarrassed, "I'll be waiting."

"Bye."

"Bye."

That night, as Chris took a shower, I fell into a deep sleep. God, I felt terrible the next morning, because I knew she was cleaning herself especiallyfor me. She knew I loved to make love to her when she smelled nice, and her skin felt soft and warm in my hands. By the time I came down to breakfast, she was gone. I found a note on the memo pad.

Vinnie,

Gone to Friary for Mass,

love you, C.

I wondered if she saw last night as a big test that would bring her closer to Jesus. He loved virgins, you know.

17

I saw Jarvis approaching, as he motioned for me to follow him. He was waiting for me at Dom's, a local college hangout. We sat down. It was late afternoon, after our classes.

"I was here two weeks ago and, hell, there must've been five hundred people jammed into this fucking place. It was wild, man. But I loved every minute of it. I made out like a trooper. I also met someone that night who has a lot going for her. Vinnie, I think I could even fall in love with her."

"Love, you *love* someone?" I was doubtful. "Come on, cut the shit."

"Why not?" Jarvis demanded, on the defensive.

"I just can't see you loving someone and giving up your freedom."

"I won't have to," he said, "I think she's the type who would understand that it's healthy to find sexual pleasure with other girls. She's a psych prof and really has her head together. She's not provincial and conservative like most of the women here. She is liberal, Jewish, and from New York. It's great. I can't believe how much we have in common. Vinnie, she's got me into reading and discussing Carl Jung, Freud, Adler, Skinner, and a lot of other psychologists I never heard of. And you know, Vinnie," he emphasized, "it must be serious if I'm reading." He laughed.

"I guess so," I said.

"Karen has..."

"Karen?" I interrupted.

"I'm sorry. Karen is the name of the girl I'm talking about. She's wonderful."

"Oh."

"Vinnie, she has really helped me to become totally involved with my experiences," he said. "Before, I would do a little grass, a little of this, and a little of that, and then screw. But now Karen has shown me how to go beyond the superficial level of things, and how to get deep inside of them. She says most of what we do is only rounding out our external self and that we must round out both the external and internal self. Isn't that great?"

"Yeah," I said, taken right from Jungian philosophy.

"Then afterwards," he continued, "I did it with her friend. Karen thought it was great."

I shook my head. "I don't believe it. You really did it with her friend while she watched? No. Unbelievable!"

"I sure did," he said proudly. "And we would've done it again if we hadn't run out of chocolate bars."

"God, I can't believe it, didn't you feel guilty? Doing it to her friend, in front of her. I just can't understand how you could do that. With chocolate bars?"

"That's because, Vinnie, you got all that Catholic shit in your background. Licking chocolate off a woman's body is great."

"Unreal," I said. "I would have had all sorts of guilt going through me." I remembered Angie and Tatum. Candy doesn't count.

"I think if you learn how to have an open relationship with someone, like Karen has taught me to have with her, it would be different. We have been able to share our innermost feelings. Vinnie, I don't think many marriages are like that."

I agreed, for it was something I never really thought of, but Chris and I had never been able to share our innermost feelings. And I doubted we ever would. That was not in her nature. Saints only shared their Innermost with God.

"Perhaps you're right," I said. "I know it's really hard for Chris and me to share our deep feelings."

"Karen says that people use love to control each other, like behavioral psychologists use M&M's to shape children's behavior. I think it makes sense."

"Would you marry her?" I asked.

"I don't know. We have been talking about her moving in with me."

"Unbelievable," I laughed. "I hope you work it out, Jarv."

He laughed, too. "Thanks."

Then he asked me if I wanted another beer. I said no. I hadn't started the first one yet. He crumpled the empty beer can in his hands to show me he had finished his. Funny, I couldn't even remember him drinking any of his. He got up and went over to the bar. I wondered what his Karen would do when she found out underneath his desire to fuck her was another desire to fuck her, and another, and another, and another. And that was it. Nothing more, nothing less. I wondered if any relationship could last under those conditions.

When Jarvis came back he started bitching about Art and the dean. He never got tired of bitching about his superiors. He said he had been working very hard on the statistical courses in the department, but still, Art and the dean were not satisfied. They wanted him to write the courses up using performance specifications, because next year the university was up for accreditation.

"I refuse to do that," he said, after taking a huge gulp of beer from his can, "It's a bunch of shit."

"I agree," I said. "So let's not talk about it. Okay. It gets us nowhere. I'm really down, and talking about the shit that goes down in that place makes me even more depressed."

"Okay," he said quickly. "No problem."

I felt bad because I was being selfish. He always had time to listen to my bitching about the shit in my in-basket. I was not a very good friend, I thought, I should try to be a better friend. He was always making the arrangements to get together. Rarely did I ever initiate these get-togethers.

Just as I was getting ready to tell Jarvis how much I appreciated his friendship, I saw him waving to two girls who were just coming in the door.

He leaned over and whispered, "That's Karen and one of her friends. I told her that I would meet her here. Do you mind if I ask them to join us?"

"No."

I wanted to meet the girl who likes chocolate. It might help me get rid of my depression.

He got up and brought them over. He introduced us. Karen was short, slim, and had a huge head of frizzy red hair. Her long nose gave away her Jewish background. The other girl's name was Julie. She took a seat between Jarvis and me; Karen sat on the other side of Jarvis. Julie looked like an Indian. She was tall with very high cheekbones and had long black hair in a braid down her back. She wore a peasant-dress underneath an oversized army-fatigue jacket. Karen wore a white blouse and a black skirt, which seemed to have come from Goodwill. Her black coat looked thin and threadbare.

Jarvis immediately started to talk to Karen, as if we were not there. I had the feeling Jarvis didn't want me to get to know Karen for fear I would take her away. He didn't have to worry. I didn't want her now. I was sure that she didn't appeal to me. For sure, the Indian-looking girl did, and she opened up the conversation.

"I used one of your textbooks in my undergraduate math class at Illinois State."

I wondered if she was the one who Jarvis fucked in front of Karen. I searched for a hint in her face that she was hot for me.

"Is that right? What's your field?"

"Psych," she said. "I'm Karen's graduate assistant."

"I see," I said. I wondered if maybe she and Karen had something going between them. There's some real weirdos, I heard, in the Psychology Department. I looked over at Karen who talked loudly to Jarvis. Her voice was hard and aggressive, like a New York Jew. They always scared me.

"Do you come here much?" I asked.

"When I have a chance," she said.

"I'm surprised I haven't seen you around campus before this," I said. "Have you known Jarvis long?"

"Only a month or so," she said. "Karen and I met him here one night."

"This doesn't seem like a bad place to relax and meet some people," I said.

"I guess so," she said, "if you have the time. Lately, I have very little time to myself. I've been working with children who have special learning problems. I love it, but it's exhausting. I come home each night and die."

"But I bet it's gratifying," I said.

"At times. But other times I wonder why we want to change them and make them unhappy like us?" Her face got immediately sad.

"I don't know."

"That's what I keep asking myself, as I work with them. So we help them become so-called productive members of our society. Then what? Who accepts the responsibility for destroying their innocence? Who?" She shook her head.

"I don't know," I said again, thinking, I'm not in a mood for a heavy philosophical discussion about dumb kids. I quickly changed the subject. "Hey, before we go on, tell me, is your home in Illinois? I'm curious."

"Yes."

"How did you end up here?"

"Well, it's kinda complicated," she said.

"I'd like to hear about it," I said, pulling my chair up close to her, because Karen's voice was getting harsher and louder.

"I got into a lot of different things at Illinois State," she said. "I really got into Sufi and Sufi dancing. I love Indian music. My friends and I used to dance every night, and we sometimes even performed for audiences. Those were lovely times. I really started to learn how to center my energy with the total universe. That's at the core of Sufi philosophy. I also learned how to read Tarot cards. Sonja, a good friend of mine, taught me. God, do I miss her. After a while I got so good at doing readings I started doing it for money."

"Do you still do readings?" I asked, interrupting her train of thought.

"Yes, only if the person really wants it done."

"I couldn't ever do that," I said. "I think it would scare the shit out of me, to know what's going to happen to me six months from now."

She laughed and acted surprised, "I don't believe it."

"Really. Maybe someday I'll have the courage to have it done, but not right now. I'm scared it will foul up the book I'm working on. And, you see, I don't want anything to get in the way of completing it. I know it's screwy, but that's the way I am."

"No, it isn't," she said, with more understanding in her voice. "You now have all your energy centered on something important in your life, and you don't want to lose some of that energy by worrying about the future and so on."

"I never thought of it that way, but I guess you're right. How come you're so good at reading cards?"

"Sonja says that some of us only see with our eyes, while others see and hear with their hearts."

"I like that," I said.

"I do too," she said.

"Did you do much drugs?" I asked

"Yes," she said, "for a while. But one time after a bad LSD trip when I went crazy, Sonja helped me to understand that I didn't need drugs. She said all I needed to do was discipline myself, to catch a glimpse of the beauty and grace of the world, like Moses did on Mount Sinai. She said God is subtle, but not malicious."

"So true," I said. "Beautiful." Except, my dear, I thought to myself, your friend Sonja stole it from Einstein.

"I finally understood, after Sonja told me this, that I could purely experience the world, if I practiced my seeing and kept my innocence. It's the purity, the innocence, that I hate to see those children I work with lose."

Jarvis and Karen now shifted their conversation to our side of the table. Jarvis looked over at us, and smiled at me, in a cocky sort of way like he knew all along that I liked to fuck just like him. I worried now that he had something on me. I wondered if he would tell people. No. I doubted it. I knew too much about him. I smiled at Karen, as she said something to me. I couldn't hear what it was.

I sipped at my beer, as Julie now talked and talked about another book she'd read that dealt with entering one's life.

Silence. *Time to make my move with Julie.*

"Let's go someplace where we could talk," I said. "The noise in here is too much."

"Okay."

"You live around here?"

"About a block away."

"Good," I said, as I stood up and she followed. I told Jarvis that we were going out to get some air. He glanced at me and then at her, with a sure-Vinnie-sure look on his face. He smiled.

18

Julie's room was small and dimly lit by a tiny lamp on the wall. In the middle of the floor was a sleeping bag with a patched quilt spread over it, and to one side were two large red pillows with arms. A small stereo system sat on top of a dark, wooden coffee table that was pushed against the wall. Next to this stood a home-made bookcase with shelves of raw two-by-four lumber strips, held up by red bricks on either end. It was lined with paperbacks, newspapers, and records. Also scattered around the room were many potted plants, either sitting on the floor or on small stands.

She asked me if I wanted some wine. I said yes. She went through a curtained doorway that was on the other side of the room. I figured that must be where the kitchen is, and where she kept the chocolate.

I took off my winter jacket, laid it over the homemade book-case, and sat down on the sleeping bag, cross-legged. It felt funny. A few minutes later, Julie came back with the wine. She handed me a glass and went over to place a record on the stereo. I thought I had heard the voice before. I couldn't remember where. She said it was Bobby Dylan. She loved him. She came back and sat beside me. We were both shy for a moment. I sipped at the bitter-tasting red wine. I hoped it would relax me.

I asked her if she had seen some of the beautiful rural areas of West Virginia. She said she had, and, in fact, she was thinking of going in on a farm near Morgantown with a friend. That would be great, I said, as I took another sip of the bitter wine.

Now she reached over, stuck her hand under the top of the sleeping bag, and took out a plastic-baggie full of dried-up brown leaves. It looked like tobacco. It wasn't. It was grass. Jarvis said everyone was doing it. Then she reached into the sleeping bag again and took out a package of old-fashioned cigarette paper. She placed some of the grass on one of the cigarette papers and licked one end of the paper, just like I had seen done in the movies. Then she rolled the joint on the floor.

This was the first time I had ever seen a real-life joint. I had heard a lot about them from students and Jarvis. I thought, I couldn't tell her that I had never smoked grass. Many times I had talked to Jarvis about trying it and seeing what it's like. But I never did. I guess I was just too scared it would affect my brain, which in turn would affect my writing. Jarvis said he had a friend in Salem, West Virginia, who placed small amounts of grass in chocolate chip cookies, and he thought when I got ready to try it, that's the way I should start.

She lit the joint and took a drag from the crumpled-looking cigarette. I was nervous. *Cool it, Vinnie, cool it.* She handed the joint to me. I took a puff and choked a little. She laughed. She then got up on her knees, leaned over and took another, as I held the joint. I tried again, and inhaled more deeply and slowly. I started to feel relaxed. I inhaled again. I was beginning to feel wonderfully loose. This is kinda nice, I thought, nothing like I expected.

"Everything okay?" she asked.

"Yeees," I smiled. I heard my voice a million miles away.

I took another puff.

"You look pale," she said.

"I feel fine, just fiiiiine..." I laid back on the sleeping bag and laughed at the way I dragged out the words. She laughed too, as she now stretched herself out beside me. She took the joint from my hand and took another long, deep drag. After a while, she placed the joint up to my lips again. I was feeling very, very warm as I started to dream of chocolate candy kisses, chocolate Hershey bars, solid chocolate Easter eggs, and solid chocolate Easter bunnies. Everything was becoming chocolate. Julie was turning into a chocolate princess. She was dancing on a chocolate stage.

I started to chase her, for I wanted to eat one of her arms. Then both of us started to melt into one large vat of chocolate.

"You feel better?" she asked.

"Yes."

She stroked my hair.

"God," I said, "I like that."

She smiled.

Then she French-kissed me with the suction of a thousand vacuum cleaners. I thought for a moment my tongue was being ripped from my mouth.

"Wow," I said, as she now took her lips away from mine and placed her warm cheeks against mine. "You're wonderful."

"Thank you," she said, gasping for air.

But then, abruptly, I moved from underneath her and with a great deal of effort I stood up. "I've got to get going, I really must," I said, sounding as if my tongue were glued to the roof of my mouth.

She lay there, looking at me in disbelief, with her bare breasts tilted to one side. Her face was flushed.

"I've got to go," I repeated again, as she sat up and stood up. She seemed to be in a state of shock.

I went over, picked up my jacket from the bookcase and slipped it on. I headed for the door. I was full of mixed feelings. On one hand, I felt bad because I knew I was going to lose her; but on the other, I felt pretty good about not having gone all the way with her. I thought, deep down, every guy wants every girl he meets to chase him; by not acting like an animal with Julie and by not doing it, it will make her want me even more. See, in the back of her mind, she's dreaming when I do do it, she'll get the best lovemaking of her life. I thought of Chris for a second, and of losing her if she found out.

I opened the door, turned to her, and said, "I'm sorry, I got so many things on my mind that's got to get done."

She said nothing for a moment as she walked over to me.

"That's your style, isn't it, Vinnie, hurry through life?" I detected a slight trace of sarcasm in her voice.

"I guess so," I said. "But that's me."

I reached out, pulled her close to me, and gave her a big strong hug.

"I'll see you," I said, as I turned and left her standing in the doorway. *Good going, Vinnie, you got out of that, great. I love you Chris.*

19

The next day Julie stopped by the office, as I sat wondering if I would ever be able to write again. I had wasted my morning, reading the *Star*. I found an article about John Kennedy's mistress kinda funny when she said she was writing a book about the affair in order to prove she wasn't a whore. Hell, I got another chuckle out of an article that described Richard Burton's drinking problem. He said he was so drunk last year that he couldn't remember the three movies he acted in. Also, he said he couldn't blame Elizabeth for leaving him, but in his heart he would always love her.

Back to Julie. After she sat down, the first thing I did was to tell her that there was no need for her to worry about coming to me as a professor or a friend because of what happened last night. I was too straight to do anything else. "You see," I said, "I would probably never touch you again. Julie, it would make it a lot easier for us to be friends, not lovers. Also, finally, the energy thing is very important. I just can't afford to waste my energy with the zillions of conflicts that go along with a married man having a mistress. My work is too important. You see what I mean?"

Then I went on to describe how I had only really given myself to my wife and to a beautiful Swedish-looking girl I met five years ago. I paused and bowed my head for a moment. I wanted to be really dramatic when I fed her the next lie about the beautiful Swedish-looking girl. "She died of cancer five months after I met her," I said sadly. "I really had a deep love for her."

Her eyes were close to tears. I thought the cancer thing really got to her. She said she understood everything I was telling her.

Also, she said she was glad I told her these things because she didn't think she could come to talk to me as a professor or friend with a crush on me. I felt like a teenager again.

In a happier tone of voice and with tears gone from her eyes, she said she had told Karen that morning about the crush she had on me, and how she was scared she would fall real hard if she took a class from me. Now I was sorry I blew it last night. She's really got it bad for me.

I decided it was time for her to go, so I stood up and impatiently looked at my watch. I told her I was late for a meeting. I picked up a file folder from my desk, hoping she would think that it contained the papers for my meeting.

She got the hint. She got up, turned, opened the door, turned back again, and asked with the awe-struck look of a teenager, "Did you know you have haunting eyes?"

"No," I said, embarrassed.

"You do. They are so penetrating."

"Better to see your soul, my dear," I said kiddingly.

She laughed. "Next time perhaps I could even read your cards and show you a new book I got called *Mind Games*. It's really interesting."

"Well, we'll see," I said. "The cards are definitely out, but anything that has the word *mind* in it I'm more than willing to explore."

"Okay," she said. "Bye."

"Bye."

The drawer was messy looking. Next week I'll start arranging the cards into categories, then after this is done, I'll stack them into nice neat piles and put a rubber band around each. I closed the drawer and sat down. *I wondered how that crazy, murdering fuck Jimmy was doing. Forget that world, Vinnie.*

I decided for sure I would start my book on Monday. Perhaps Julie's energy is already influencing me. *I hoped.* Hell, you can't tell, she might be some kind of mystic who has special powers to help writers like me get through their mental blocks. She could be my teacher. My Guru. I just hope she's not one of those white witches or Satan worshipers that I read about in the *Star*. The article said that they are popping up all over America, especially on university campuses.

20

In the bathroom at home, I looked at my face in the mirror and thought I looked like a sick, skinny Arab. Chris was right. The vinegar diet was making me look unhealthy.

"You're ugly, Vinnie," I said out loud to the mirror.

I shook my head, turned, and went back to the bedroom. I put on an old pair of faded jeans and a paint-spotted work shirt. It was Saturday, and I decided to do some work around the house. I was hoping it would help me relax.

On the way down the stairs I heard the muffled sounds of cartoon characters coming from the TV in the living room. When I reached the bottom of the stairs, I stopped and looked in through the wide doorway that separated the living room from the front hallway. Paulie was sitting on the floor, almost on top of the TV, and Linda was sitting behind him on the sofa.

"Get back, Paulie," I yelled. "The rays are dangerous." He didn't seem to hear me, as he was transfixed by the color figures jumping across the TV screen.

"Paulie, please get back," I yelled again, with more irritation in my voice. "Did you hear me?"

Finally, he moved back. He looked hurt. I wish they never invented the damn thing. Paulie and Linda sitting in front of that thing reminded me of the pictures of people from Third World Countries who sometimes stare into the camera expressionless and stonelike. They seemed already dead.

I turned and headed for the kitchen.

Chris was at the stove, making scrambled eggs. She looked over to me and asked, "Have a good sleep?"

"Yes." *What would I do without the pills.*

"Good."

"Want some eggs?"

"No, thank you."

"Still on that diet, huh?"

"Yeah."

"I'll tell you, if you got an ulcer like the doctor said, all that acid from the vinegar you have on your salads will make it worse."

"I don't know," I said absent-mindedly, as my mind searched for something else to say. "I just don't know. Perhaps you're right, my stomach has been killing me of late."

"Well, when are you going to stop that diet?" she demanded.

"Pretty soon," I said.

She came over, placed a large plate of scrambled eggs on the table, and asked, "Have just a little?"

I picked up a teaspoon and an empty saucer from the middle of the table, and placed a couple spoonfuls of scrambled eggs on the saucer. I hoped this would keep her quiet about my diet.

She sat down, opposite me. "Vinnie," she said warmly, "will you promise me that you'll be nice to the kids today?"

"What do you mean?"

"Well," she said, looking at me with worried eyes, "lately you seem to have no patience with them. I keep telling them it's because of the diet you're on. But something has to be done. It's causing all of us to be unhappy."

"Unhappy?"

"Yes, unhappy," she said, almost mad. "Every time you talk to them now, it's always to criticize them. 'Sit up straight, chew your food slowly, be quiet I'm working on my book...' My God, Vinnie, the kids are scared to move around in their own house."

She stopped for a second and then began again, in a gentler tone of voice. "And that, Hon, doesn't make for a happy home." *Has it ever been a happy home?*

"I'm sorry," I said, "I didn't realize I was causing so much unhappiness."

"Come on, Vinnie," she said, "don't start playing the poor soul game. I just want you to try to be nice to the kids."

It was always me. I was the problem. Never her. It must be nice to be perfect and saintly.

"Okay, I'll try." I got suddenly concerned that she would get mad and start slamming cupboards and screaming like she did that one time. "It's the book again. It's becoming a pain in the ass, Chris."

"I wish you would talk to me about it," she sighed. "Maybe I could help."

"I wish you could," I said sadly, "but it would take so much time to work through with you some of the background things you need to understand where I am in my thinking. I guess, also, the major reason, Chris, is that when I'm not working on it, I want to forget it for a while, because most of the time I'm thinking about it. I need a rest from it, really."

I am sure, I thought, that Chris thought that I had already started to write the book. She didn't know that most of my time, since I finished the last textbook, was spent writing one-liners. I wondered what she would say if she knew I couldn't even write a sentence now. But come Monday everything will be different. I hoped.

"Oh heck," Chris said, shaking her head, "I hate that book."

I decided it was time to get off this subject. "Hey, Chris, let's get off this thing about the book. I want to try to relax today and try to forget everything."

"Okay, but see how touchy you are?"

The saint still had to be on top.

"I'm not touchy," I said. "I'm just saying let's not talk about it anymore."

"I wonder why we can't talk anymore, Vinnie, without you getting mad."

"I'm not mad," I said, getting pissed off at her accusations.

"I have no one to talk to," she said, feeling sorry for herself. "No one."

"What am I doing now?"

"You always end up getting mad. I need someone to listen and be a friend to me."

"Oh, please, Chris," I pleaded, "let's not argue. I need a break. I can't take much more."

Just then the phone rang. Thank God. My head was throbbing.

Finally, Chris got up and answered the phone. It was for Linda. Chris called, but, of course, because the girl was getting stoned on TV, she had to go get her.

While Linda talked on the phone, I ate some scrambled eggs. Chris went over to the sink and started to rinse the dishes off before she placed them in the dishwasher.

When Linda got off the phone she went up to Chris and whispered something in her ear. Chris nodded yes, and Linda ran out happily without ever turning back to acknowledge that I was sitting there.

"I can't believe it," I said, feeling my anger rising inside. "Is she that scared of me that she has to whisper to you? I can't believe she hates me that much."

"She doesn't hate you," Chris said. "God, Vinnie don't be so dramatic."

"My God," I said, swiftly changing to a tone of self-pity, "it's terrible when your own kids won't talk to you."

"Oh, Vinnie," she said, "stop being such a baby. She only did that because of the terrible mood you've been in lately. Sometimes she sees me as a girlfriend."

Vinnie, we saints know how to treat children. Fallen people have to learn from us. Jesus loves us.

"How could you be a friend and still be respected as a parent?" I asked. "Someone has to help her, showing her right from wrong."

"I agree," she said, "but I believe you could find a middle-ground in being a parent and friend to your children."

"I don't know, I really don't know if you could do that."

"I do," she said. "It will make for a happier home."

I shook my head. "I think if you start doing that, it causes too many conflicts for the child."

"Maybe so," she said, "but at least try it, Vinnie. I would like to get through today without any yelling. Okay?"

"Okay," I said meekly. I was beaten. She won. *Saints always do.*

Before I left, she told me that she invited Frank and Wanda Stone over for a drink Sunday night. She tried to get them to come over tonight, but they couldn't because Frank was going to the Pittsburgh Penguins hockey game. I told her I wasn't really in the mood to listen to Frank's bullshit. She said she felt the same way. But, she said, Wanda needs friends now. Frank and Wanda haven't talked in weeks, she added. Their marriage is in bad shape.

"Wanda thinks," Chris said, "that he's having an affair. I don't know what Wanda is going to do. I don't think she'll leave him, because of the kids. It's a sad situation."

I took everything I could move out of the garage and placed it in the driveway. Then I swept off all the loose dirt from the cement floor and dumped it in a trash can. After that, I turned on the garden hose full blast, running the water almost parallel to the floor so it would force whatever dirt I missed into the large drain in the middle of the garage floor. After about an hour, the cement floor was almost dry, and I started to carry the things from the driveway back inside. I made sure that everything was put back into some sort of order. I liked doing this. It gave me a feeling of accomplishment. Also, like filing, such a menial task helped me to think about nothing. I needed that. Little by little, I felt myself starting to unwind, as I went about finding places for the following things: two bikes, one standard, one ten-speed; three hammers; two crazy-wheels, one good, one missing a wheel; one rusting wagon missing a wheel and handle; four tires, two worn pretty good, two fairly new; two shovels, two rakes, one lawn-mower; three transistors, all broken; one hairdryer, still good; planters; games: Scrabble, Racko, Monopoly, Planet of Apes, Battleship, Robin Hood, Hollywood Squares, and others; one gouged dining-room table and four matching chairs; one green army-truck; and one record-player and radio console, radio broken. Most of this shit, I thought, would be sold at our annual, street garage sale. That gigantic sale was when the new junkyards of America could be seen. Chris loved these sales because, she said, it gave her a great community feeling. I hated them, because it reminded me how greedy I was. I was first to open my garage door and also first to start selling hot dogs and cold drinks. "Fresh hot dogs, cold drinks, come and get them," I would shout every so often during the day. This, plus other neighbors selling coffee, sandwiches, and pizza, and the kids in the neighborhood running up to prospective buyers and begging them to see what their parents were selling gave the sale a carnival atmosphere. The first to arrive at these sales, early in the morning, even before we opened our garage doors, were the old ladies dressed in light, summer cotton dresses and always carrying huge black pocketbooks. They anxiously waited to get something cheap and useful like a chair, lamp, rug, table, toaster, and other things like that.

Later on in the morning came the couples from other suburbs, dressed quite informally from faded blue jeans cut-offs to long chiffon dresses. They bought like crazy, anything and everything they could load into their Chevy or Ford station wagons. Their kids, along with the kids in our neighborhood, were the best buyers for Linda's and Paulie's old toys and games. Like their parents, they too were learning how to worship material possessions.

Late in the afternoon came the affluent couples from Wheeling; the men were usually dressed in bright-colored expensive golf slacks and shirts, the women in sporty jersey-dresses or slacks, with blouses with large bows at the necks or seductively V shaped. They were the kind of people, I guessed, who did most of their shopping at boutiques. They looked and handled things in our garage disdainfully, as if they thought it was below them to buy the things we were selling. Only the Carsons, who sold antiques and Mexican jewelry, made out well with these people. These people reminded me of something I read that Socrates once said, after watching a procession of gold and silver: "How much there is I do not need."

As I was picking up a large, yellow Mattel crane from the driveway, Paulie came by to get his bright-red ten-speed bike, which was really too big for him. I turned around, smiled, and asked him like a friend, remembering Chris's comments, to help me place some of his toys back in the garage.

"But why, Dad?" he asked. He was too busy playing to be disturbed. "I'm playing with David now. I'll do it later, okay?"

"I am asking you now," I said, trying to control myself.

"But Dad, I don't like to do that," he said. "It's too boring."

"I don't like to do a lot of stuff either," I said bitterly, moving closer to where he was standing.

"Please, Dad, come on," he pleaded, "I'll do it later."

"Now," I shouted angrily, as I threw the crane down in front of him.

The crash scared him. But it didn't scare him enough.

"Come on, Dad, how about Linda?" he asked, sulking. "How come she can't help?"

"Because I'm asking you," I said, speaking with clenched teeth now.

"But, really, Dad, I just don't feel like doing that today."

"Oh God, I'm so glad I have children who are willing to help their father." My voice was full of sarcasm. "They're so wonderful. Go, I don't care what you do anymore. You asshole."

I walked into the garage and started picking up things and slamming them back down.

He followed. "Oh come on, Dad," he said, stammering.

"Go, go," I shouted, as I slammed a wrench down on a shelf. For a brief second, I wanted to pick it up and throw it at him.

"What do you want me to do, Dad?" he asked, crying. I could see his frail body trembling with fear.

"Never mind," I said, in a calmer tone of voice. Suddenly I wanted to run up to him, take him in my arms, and say I was sorry. I couldn't stand to see him hurt. I loved him too much. "Really, go and play, I'm not mad. I'll take care of this, it's almost done anyway."

"You sure?" His watery eyes were lighting up.

"Yes, go now."

"You sure you're not mad?" he asked, wiping the tears from his eyes with the back of his hand.

"Yes, now go play," I said, as I lined up some old paint cans on a shelf.

He came over to me and gave me a big hug and then got his bike and left.

You're still there... like father, like son... I hate this... Crazy like him... Please help me God... Nobody is doing anything about Jimmy murdering his father... What's wrong with me? Don't think about Boston, Vinnie, don't or you'll go insane... I loved playing with Jimmy when we were small... He was Durango Kid and I was Roy Rogers... Just forget it all... I didn't want it to be 1971.

21

"Hey," Wanda said, as she sat down on our powder-blue, crushed-velvet love seat, "I missed you guys. It's been too long." Wanda looked beautiful this evening. I just wished she wouldn't wear so much eye shadow.

"I agree," Chris said, taking a seat next to her.

I nodded, "Yes it has been."

I sat across from them on the sofa that matched the love seat, separated by our large, walnut coffee table. Chris had put out a spread of assorted cheeses, dips, potato chips, pretzels, and crackers.

Frank wasn't there yet. Standard operating procedure for him, I thought. He always liked to get to places late. I thought he did this in order to give people the impression that he was a very busy man. In so many ways, he was like Jimmy, insecure and needing tons of attention.

What the hell am I going to do about his murder? Forget it, enjoy yourself.

"My God, Chris your house always looks so immaculate," Wanda said. "My house always looks like a shit-house. You're so neat and creative."

"Oh no, I'm not," Chris protested weakly. "I only picked up a little. You should've seen this place a couple hours ago."

Wanda was really right. Chris had put a great deal of thought and planning into decorating our home. It wasn't too conservative or too avant-garde. *It was just right.* Her love for Colonial furniture and antiques was obvious. At first, one got the impression it was over-decorated, but after being in one of our rooms for a while, everything seemed to become a part of you. I guess, deep inside, I was really proud of her homemaking skills.

We drank some wine and talked about Wanda going back to school and studying music, and about a professor she had gotten very close to. She said she invited this professor over to dinner, but Frank ruined it afterwards by calling him "a fag."

But she didn't care anymore what Frank thought, she said. She meets this professor friend of hers for lunch every day and they have some wonderful discussions. "He's a good friend," she said, "and I don't care if he's gay or not, I like his company."

"Good for you," I said.

"I think you and he would get along great, Vinnie," she said. "He explains a lot of things in his music class by using mathematical analogies."

"I would love to meet him," I said.

"Okay," she said, "we'll all go to lunch. And you too, Chris."

"No, thanks," she laughed nervously, "gays make me very anxious."

Wanda and I laughed.

We drank some more, ate some more, and talked some more. I was really enjoying myself. It was so easy to talk to Wanda. If I were married to her, I would treat her like a queen. She was wonderful. I wished Chris would keep up on things like Wanda.

When Frank finally arrived, the mood suddenly changed.

"Okay if I fix myself a drink?" he asked, as he walked over to where the drinks were set up. Chris called this area in the living room the greeting corner. We were sitting in the conversation corner. There was also a study corner, and TV corner.

"Sure, help yourself," I said.

Out of the corner of my eye, I saw Wanda slowly sliding down onto the floor. Her eyes looked mean and hard. I could tell there was a great deal of bad feeling between them.

"What have you been doing today?" Chris asked.

"Working, working," he repeated proudly, as he turned with a drink in his hand and walked toward us. "Last night a coal operator's machine broke down, and I've spent half of today trying to get someone to fix it. I finally said, to hell with it. I couldn't find anyone, so I fixed it myself, and I probably saved myself a couple hundred bucks. No one wants to work anymore. Now they tell you that it's Sunday and they got to stay home with the family. Baloney! They're just plain lazy, I say."

"I know, it's really getting bad," Chris said. "It took me three weeks to get someone to fix our garbage disposal."

I wished he would go away. I was feeling so great before he came. Guys like Frank feed off people like Chris.

Frank shook his head as he took a seat next to me on the sofa. "I was supposed to get down to Morgantown this afternoon for a meeting on the new football stadium they're building. It's really going to be something."

Sneaky bastard. Here we go again. Now we will hear damn football stories all night.

I was right. On and on he went about how he almost won a game for West Virginia University against Penn State, and the great camaraderie football developed among men.

Twice during his unending bullshit, Chris asked for a gin and tonic, and once Wanda asked for a vodka and 7UP. For myself, I changed over and started drinking Scotch. I wanted to get drunker than hell so I wouldn't have to listen to him. At first, the three or four Scotches I had, mixed with the wine I had before, did do just that. However, after a while it seemed, the more I drank the more alert I became.

I looked at my watch. It was nearly three in the morning, and Frank was still going strong about his football-playing days at WVU. Wanda had fallen asleep on the floor. She was curled up like a baby. Chris was still sitting on the seat, looking half out of it, with a stupid grin on her face.

Now Frank stood up. Thank God, I thought, he was getting ready to go. But instead, he teetered past me toward the greeting corner for another drink. After he fixed himself another, he looked at Wanda sleeping on the floor, shook his head, and said, "She's always the life of the party." His tone was sarcastic.

Frank stood there for another second, and then he started to walk toward the sofa. But just as he was getting ready to take his seat next to me, he turned abruptly, and plopped himself down next to Chris in the love seat.

Frank turned to Chris and started talking. I felt like the other day with Jarvis, when he started talking to that girl. I was the third person again.

Frank said he hadn't realized how stupid people were, until he met this halfback he played with. He said he was so stupid that bright colors were painted on the linemen's asses, so that it would be easier for him to remember the hole he had to run through.

Chris giggled harder and harder, as Frank exaggerated how mad this halfback would get, when the linemen's asses got covered up with mud and grass stains. "Keep your asses clean," this halfback would shout over and over in the huddle.

Then it happened.

As Frank laughed along with Chris, he placed his hand on Chris's left thigh and rubbed it gently. I sat there, unbelieving. This was not happening, I thought. He'd never touched her on her leg before when he was flirting with her; maybe a light pat on the back, the shoulder, the arm but never, never on the leg. And God, she didn't seem to mind, either. *Holy shit! She wants him, too.*

Keeping his hand on her leg, he turned to me and laughed.

"You know, Vinnie, there's one group of people we poor dumb hillbillies are smarter than. You know what the halfback's name was?"

"No," I said coldly, wanting him to get the clue I was really mad about where his hand was.

"Angelo Cipriani," he said, with a shitty smirk on his face.

Chris giggled.

I forced a smile, hating him. I couldn't believe Frank was going to play the we-WASPS-better-than-you-ignorant-Italians game. He must be really hot for Chris's body to start that shit, I thought. For a moment I got scared, thinking perhaps his lust was so great that nothing would stop him until he got Chris.

He rubbed her leg again. Shit. She really did seem to be liking it.

"You know, Vinnie," he said, slurring his words now, "that I was near the top of my class academically. Not all jocks are stupid. And there wasn't a Guinea near me." He turned to Chris and laughed.

I could see that she was self-conscious, as she forced a polite smile. But why does she let his hand remain on her leg, I asked myself. Why? Is there a black, raunchy, sex fiend waiting for release underneath her white, pure, and saintly exterior?

I tightened my hand around my glass and took a deep, patient breath. Frank stared at me for a moment, as if he was expecting me to say something. But I didn't.

Now pressing heavily on Chris's leg, he pushed himself up and went over to the table with the drinks. I knew I had too much to drink, but Frank had had even more. I hoped that explained part of his behavior tonight. I remembered once Frank telling me he was going on the wagon, because of doing some awful things while he was drunk. That word *awful* elicited all sorts of thoughts when he told me, never thinking at the time, the "awful" would also happen in my house. After fixing himself another glass, he came back and sat even closer to Chris than before. "What I need is a good woman," he said, looking straight at Chris. "That's the only thing I don't have. Mine hates me."

"Oh, come on now, Frank." I remembered the look in Wanda's eyes earlier in the evening.

"Hey," he said, turning to me, "I'm not kidding. I'll tell you exactly why she hates me, I failed her by only giving her one silver bullet. The others have been duds. I..."

"Please, Frank." I thought about Wanda telling me a few years ago that two of their three children were adopted.

He now stood up, staggered over to me, and sat down. "Just listen to this, Vinnie," he said, grabbing my arm hard to make sure I gave him my full attention. "I can give her anything she wants, the best clothes, the best car, the best furniture, the best private schools for our kids, everything the best. That's the funny part. Everything the best. Two houses that are paid for, and televisions in all the bathrooms. People think I got it made. But I don't. None of that counts if you can't give your wife more than one kid..."

"Chris, how about some coffee?" I felt embarrassed that he was talking about his impotence in front of Chris.

"Sure," she said, more than willing to please. "It'll only take a minute."

Chris stood up and walked rigidly out of the living room, as if she didn't want us to notice that she had drunk too much. I hoped Frank would stay in the living room with me. I watched him, as his wandering eyes settled on Chris's ass. Soon, he was up and following her to the kitchen. Shit. So, I followed too.

Chris was placing the coffeepot on the stove as we walked in together. Frank went directly over and placed his hand on Chris's back and left it there as he turned to me and said, "I bet you didn't know, Vinnie, that I was offered a football scholarship to Yale."

"No," I said, as I moved to the other side of Chris.

"Well, I refused it," he said, turning and facing me, "because even with the scholarship money it would've been too expensive for me. But I know one thing. If I had gone, I would've made it through, not like some people I know who go and flunk out of Ivy League schools. Right, Vinnie?"

I said nothing. I finally figured out what the hell he was doing. He was baiting me like a high-school bully, trying to make me look bad in front of Chris, so he could win her over. And it was working. Look at how we were standing on either side of her, I thought. I was trying to show him that she belonged to me because she was my wife, and he was trying to show me that he was going to get her, because he was better than me in everything. It was so ridiculous playing these silly adolescent games.

"Well, some have it, and some don't," I said, trying to control my temper while not showing it. Also, I wanted to put him down verbally, but this sentence was the only thing that came out. I was mad at myself for being so stupid.

"Hey, why are we standing, let's sit down," Chris suggested, as she moved to the kitchen table. She sat down and Frank took a seat next to her, pushing his chair close to hers. I took a seat opposite them. I could see Frank's hand slowly moving under the table. I pushed my chair back a bit, and I could see his hand on her leg again. *I don't know how much more I could take. This asshole is trying to lay my wife right in front of my eyes.*

Frank continued his game. "You know that today I could sell my coal company for five million dollars and probably even more, if I hold out long enough." He was looking at Chris. "That's not bad for a poor hillbilly like me, you know." He brought his hand up from underneath the table, and now laid it on Chris's shoulders. His eyes were on her breasts.

"Will you sell it?" I asked, hoping his eyes would turn to me. They did.

"No," he said quickly. "I want to put enough money away, so my kids will have a good trust fund, and I'll be able to retire and go to Europe. Right now, I figure I could retire when I'm about fifty. Not bad, huh? Hell, what do you college professors make, fifteen thousand? I bet no more than twenty or thirty a year. Right? That's nothing. I only got a bachelor's degree and I'm making twenty times that."

"Well," I said, "like I said before, some have it and some don't." *Oh, shit, Vinnie, you should be destroying him verbally. What's wrong, Vinnie? You asshole.*

The coffee started to bubble over now. Chris got up quickly and turned the burner off. Then she came over and poured each of us a cup of coffee. After placing the coffeepot back on the stove, she turned and announced she had to go upstairs to the little girl's room.

I wondered why she didn't want to use the bathroom that was underneath the stairs. Perhaps, she was scared we could hear her peeing.

Frank, with a lust-crazed look in his eyes, hastily stood up and followed, as I did the same. I was scared there would be a scene. Thank God, Chris was already halfway up the stairs when I got there. Frank, from below, was yelling up, "Could I help?"

She looked back with an embarrassed smile, turned, and continued up the stairs.

Once I heard Chris close the bathroom door behind her, I turned and said to Frank. "Look, Frank, it's really getting late now, I got to get some rest. I got an eight o'clock."

"Sure, Vinnie," he said in a smiling, understanding tone of voice. "Go ahead, Chris and I will stay up for a while and talk."

He was serious.

That was it. "Hey, man, listen, did you hear me?" I asked loudly. "I think you'd better go."

We were both uncomfortable, as we stood there looking at each other.

"I guess you're right," he said, turning and walking toward the door, now he looked bent and very, very old. Then he stopped and turned. His eyes were red. I felt sorry for him.

"I want to thank you for putting up with such a shithead as me." His voice was full of self-pity. "I know you think I'm just a big braggart who's living in the past, just like other jocks whose glory days are over."

"No I don't," I said. "I'm just tired."

"I wish you would come out for breakfast with me," he said, sounding very sober. "There's a lot I could tell you about me, Vinnie."

"I would love to," I said, "I really would. But I don't like missing classes, Frank. It's something with me. You could understand that." I still had Chris letting him keep his hand on her leg on my mind. I couldn't let her get away with it.

"Oh, the hell with your classes," he growled. "Man, you've got to learn how to relax. Or you'll die before you're forty. Listen, I'll have this girl I know, she'll fix the best ham and eggs you ever had. Her place sits on top a hill overlooking a lake. It's a beautiful place. You remember that girl I introduced you to when we went for a drink at the Holiday Inn?"

"Yes."

"Nice, huh?"

"Yes."

"Well, she's great in bed. You want me to fix you up?"

"No, thank you," I said, trying to remember what she looked like.

"You sure you won't go?"

"No, I really can't."

"Okay, if you change your mind call me," he said. "I'm going to shower before I go."

"Okay I will," I said.

He opened the door, and the cold outside made me shiver a little.

"Beautiful cold, wash the shit off me. So long, Vinnie," he said, as he left.

I closed the door behind him and locked it, wondering how the hell could he expect me to go and watch the sun come up with him, after trying what he did with Chris.

I went to the living room to turn off the lights and check on the fireplace. When I got to the sofa, I saw Wanda still lying there on the floor. I had completely forgotten about her.

"Wanda, time to get up," I said, as I knelt down beside her and shook her shoulders lightly.

"Huh?"

"I'm going to bed. If you want to stay, I'll get a blanket for you and you can stay right here."

"Oh no," she said, forcing her eyes open. "What time is it?"

"Late."

I helped her get on her feet. "I'm sorry I fell asleep."

"That's okay. You didn't miss much."

"I know. I've heard those stories a million times before. Where is he now?"

"Home, I think."

"I'd better go."

Wanda, although looking a bit tired and pale, still looked beautiful. Something about the situation, about her just waking up in her slightly wrinkled mohair sweater, about her vulnerability, something about all of it, made me think about making love to her.

"Thanks, dear," she said, "for a nice beginning of the evening." Then she moved toward me and gave me a quick kiss on the lips. Her lips were cold and closed.

It didn't matter. Immediately, I felt warm and close to her; but, thank God, I no longer wanted her. Now my feelings for her were like one would have for a brother or sister. Finally, I thought, I could be a friend with a girl without wanting to go to bed on my mind. I felt tremendously good about that. I wanted to tell her.

"Look, Wanda," I said, "I just want you to know if you need a friend in your troubles, I'm here for you."

"Thanks, that's nice of you," she said. She looked affectionately at me. "I really appreciate that. I hope I can get you and David together. I just know you'll like him."

"Fine," I said. "Anytime."

"I'll see you later," she said. As she walked out of the living room toward the front door, I unlocked and opened it for her. She walked out, then stopped, turned, and said, "I love you, dear."

"The same here," I said.

She turned and left.

As I locked the door again, I thought about the words "I love you." Were they the I-love-you of a good friend or was there an itsy-bitsy part of Wanda that still wanted my body? I decided I couldn't think about that now. I had to get upstairs before Chris fell asleep.

After turning off the lights, I went upstairs and met Chris coming out of the bathroom.

"They left," I said coldly.

"They did," she said, acting surprised. "How come?"

"Because I kicked Frank out."

"No," she said unbelieving, "you didn't!"

"Yes, I couldn't take it anymore."

"I don't understand," she said, "we were getting on so fine together."

"You and he were," I snapped, "but not me."

"Oh, I think you're just over-tired, Hon," she said, smiling and not taking me seriously. "Let's go to bed, I'm tired, too." She walked past me into the bedroom, as I followed and closed the door behind us. Then she went over to the closet and took out a long, blue-flowered flannel nightgown, and, shielded behind the half-opened closet door, she started to get undressed.

"Jesus Christ," I shouted at her, "I don't believe you let him do that. I just don't."

Silence.

Then, with one hand holding her nightgown close to her bare breasts and another hand holding it close to her black hidden valley, Chris slowly slid out from behind her makeshift dressing room. Her face red, she asked uneasily, "What do you mean?"

"You know what I mean," I said. "Stop playing naïve with me."

She stared at me with a puzzled look on her face. "Really, Vinnie," she said, "I don't know what you're talking about. I can't remember anything happening."

She stepped backwards into the closet again and quickly finished dressing. Then she walked over to the edge of the bed, sat down, and looked up at me. The puzzled look was still there but now it was mixed with fear. "Honest to God, Vinnie, I don't know what you're talking about."

"Don't tell me you didn't feel his rubbing," I yelled, as I moved closer to her, so that I was almost standing directly over her. "I just don't believe you did that. In our home, I just can't."

"Vinnie, I swear," she insisted, with fear more than anything else now showing in her face, "I didn't know what he was doing. Maybe it was the drinks. You know I can't drink. I don't know. But honest to God, Vinnie, I never felt a thing. Gee, Vinnie, you know I wouldn't ever do such a thing."

"I don't care, I'm getting the hell out of here." I startled myself by what I was saying.

"Please, Vinnie, don't do this to me, please," she pleaded with a cry.

Angrily, I walked over to the closet, looked around for a second, and took out a suitcase that was buried in the back. I brought it back and threw it wildly on the bed, next to where Chris was sitting. Frightened, she threw up her hands, palms up like a shield, thinking I was aiming at her.

"That stupid hillbilly trying to lay my wife in front of my own eyes... in front of my own eyes. Jesus, I still can't believe it." Still full of anger, I went back to the closet again, pulled some shirts off their hangers, and threw them in the suitcase. I remembered a movie where William Holden did the same thing.

"Vinnie, the kids," she said, shaken, her eyes quickly jumping from me to the bedroom door. It was half-open now. The small heads of Linda and Paulie were peering in, with scared looks on their faces.

"What's wrong, Daddy?" Paulie asked.

"Nothing, nothing," I said, trying to act calm, "now go back to bed, Mommy and Daddy are just talking."

"But it's almost time to get ready for school."

I couldn't believe it. I looked at my watch. It was after five in the morning. I remembered that the school bus came around seven. The Catholic school children were the first to be picked up.

"It's still early," I said quickly, "you got another hour before you have to get up. Now go back to bed." I walked over and shut the door in their faces.

I heard Chris sniffling behind me. I turned and screamed, "Oh, shit, stop playing that Holy Mother of God role. Admit it, inside you're nothing but a damn whore who wants to lay every guy you see."

"Oh, God, no," she sobbed. Her head started to shake violently, and with her fists in a hammer-like position, she started to pound savagely on the upper part of her legs. "Please, Vinnie, I was only trying to be nice. I didn't know what was happening. Oh, God, help him to understand." Her pounding increased along with her sobbing.

"Sure, I understand," I said, mocking her. "You would probably let him screw you and then afterwards tell me that you were only trying to be nice. Love thy neighbor, right? Just like all good Christians, right?"

"Honest, Vinnie," she sobbed, "I didn't feel anything. Believe me! I promise I'll never invite them over again if you say that he did things to me. I promise..." She stopped her pounding but continued her sobbing, however, not as intensely as before.

I believed her. My mood shifted to contrition. Now I felt ashamed at my behavior. I knew, she was just too saintly to let anything like that happen. I decided it must've been the drinks.

I walked over and sat down on the bed beside her. Looking straight ahead and scared to touch her, I began to talk. "I'm sorry, Chris. I think, it's not so much what happened with Frank tonight that caused me to blow up, but other things that have been eating at my insides for a hell of a long time. You know,

Chris, sometimes, I think we have grown in different directions over the years, like you said the other morning. But then at other times, I think I'm the only one that has changed because of all the reading I do and the complicated questions I ask of myself, while you, Chris, my dear, seem to always remain the same. You're still the beautiful, simple, honest, Catholic girl I married eight years ago. And I don't mean that in a demeaning sense, hon."

"I know," she said, sounding calm, "but it's true, except for the beautiful part, I doubt that, especially after having had two kids."

"Oh yes, you are," I said, turning and looking at her. "Very beautiful, in fact. And that's why I think something is wrong with me. Maybe I'm flipping out. I've got a dedicated, beautiful wife and two beautiful children. What else could one ask for? I don't know. Chris, maybe I should've never gotten married. It would've been a better life for you."

"That's not true, Vinnie," she said strongly. "My whole life is devoted to pleasing you. I don't have anything else to live for."

She tried to place her arm around my shoulders. But I shrugged it away as I stood up. I wasn't ready for her comforting. At least not yet. There was still more to talk about.

I started to nervously pace in front of her. "Chris, there are things in my background you wouldn't believe, I'm so damn complicated. I don't even understand a tenth of what I'm about. Right now I just feel like saying the hell with it."

"Vinnie, maybe if I try to be a better wife..."

"But that's part of the problem," I interrupted quickly. "You always think that you're to blame. It's not you. It's me. I see things so differently. Look at how we see God and religion. It's not that I don't believe in God, I do. I think that's at least something going for us, but your beliefs are so absolute, while mine are so full of doubts and abstractions. You see what I mean?"

I stopped pacing, as she answered.

"I do, Vinnie, but it might help us to get closer to God and to each other, if we share our beliefs. I would really work on trying to understand how you see God, if you also tried. I mean it. Just be patient with me, because I'm so stupid at times."

"No, you're not," I protested. "Having kids, doing the house-work, washing clothes, preparing meals, and all those things, have made your mind lazy. Hell, how can you expect your mind to be sharp if that's all you do, day in and day out? Those things really dull the brain."

"That's so true, Vinnie," she said. "Every time I open a book at night, I fall right asleep after the first sentence."

"I don't know," I said, "on second thought, maybe it's best you don't do much reading. I really don't know if I could live with you if, after working all day with abstract mathematical problems and ideas for my book, you start bombarding me with deep intellec-tual questions. I guess, when I get home at night I really want a break from all of that. And I guess, when you really come down to it, the only thing I want you to do is to understand; when we do happen to talk about some intellectual things, and you don't understand me, I'm not being fake like you say sometimes. I really believe the things I'm saying. Okay?"

"Okay."

"And I think you're right," I continued, "we could learn and complement each other. The simplicity and the honesty you use in looking at the world could really help me in keeping in contact with the real world. Only Chris, accept me as I am. That's all I ask. And, of course, I will accept you as you are."

"Good," she smiled, "I doubt I could ever change anyway, because it's really almost too late for me to do that now. Really, Vinnie, I feel in my heart Jesus wants me to be this way. I just can't go along with all these modern ideas, especially in the Catholic Church."

I wished for once when we discussed things, she would leave Jesus out of it.

"Chris, that's another thing," I said, "we really must get this sex and rhythm thing worked out. It's not right the way we're doing it now—God, once every six months. We need to do it more than that, so that we can get closer together physically. Talking just can't do that for us, Chris."

"I know, Hon," she said, lowering her eyes. "But I won't take those pills or anything like that."

"Okay, but let's work out something better," I said. "Six months is really unhealthy. And to be completely honest with you, Chris, I don't like doing it when you're having your period. It's too messy. I'm sorry. There must be some other times we can do it."

I still can't believe, after eight years of marriage we still don't understand how the rhythm method works. That's really bad. It seems as long as I could remember, it always has been difficult for me to understand how a woman's period works. I don't know how many times I've read about this, and thought I understood it, but, an hour or so later, for some reason, I would remember very little of it.

"I'll get a thermometer and start taking my temperature every day," she said seriously. "They say that's the best way to be accurate. But remember Hon, for the last few years my period has not been regular, so we will be taking a chance. And, I know, Vinnie, how much you don't want another baby."

"You're right, but if we do everything that we're supposed to do in rhythm and still have a baby, I won't blame you. It's just something we'll have to accept."

"Good, I'll really try hard to keep track of my period. I know for certain, Vinnie, that when this white stuff comes out, like now, when I'm ovulating, it's not a good time. Sometimes I wish I could be like other Catholics who are able to use other methods of birth control without hesitation. I asked Father Luke to give me some things to read that would help me. He said there's very little available except for books that explore the philosophical roots of each approach. And I don't want that; I want something I could understand. My own mind still says you can't do it unless you use rhythm or want to have babies. The Bible says this over and over again when it talks about procreating the race." She stopped and shook her head sadly, "God, Vinnie, everything is so confusing."

I walked over to her and placed my hands on her shoulders and squeezed her head against my stomach. "I know," I said warmly.

"Vinnie, I love you," she whispered, looking up at me.

I pushed her down onto the bed and laid on top of her. Our closed mouths pressed hard on each other; she didn't like to kiss with an open mouth because she thought it was too sloppy. But surprisingly tonight she opened her mouth wide and free, our tongues twisted around each other, stirring up the long overdue passions in our souls. Then suddenly she broke the kiss, keeping her hot face flush against mine, she whispered, "Vinnie, what about the time, please, it's not a good time."

"Never mind the time," I said, with authority, "for once let's forget about that shit. Our bodies are crying for each other."

She said no more, as I started to lightly lick her teeth, the outside of her lips, and her ears where I stayed for a while sticking my tongue in and out. We stopped for a moment to get undressed. When our hot bodies were together again, I licked and sucked her breasts until they were hard. This was beautiful, truly beautiful. She groaned, "Oh, Vinnie, oh, Vinnie." I felt her hands gently stroking my hair. I started rubbing her as she rhythmically moved it up and down against my hand. I then brought my mouth down on her. I felt bristle-like hairs rubbing against my face. She was like a big wave, and I was riding her, riding her, forever. I felt strange. My body was vanishing. I was liquid. I was one with Chris. "Oh, God," I moaned. "I'm free." This was heaven, I thought.

Then together we moved, first me against her. Then her against me; we syncopated ourselves beautifully. Musician Dave Brubeck would've been proud of us. It felt so good. Like being swallowed up by thousands of soft pillows. In a little while, she came. Then finally I came. I hoped, after we'd practice more, we could have a simultaneous orgasm. A book I read on orgasm said it was like participating in the explosion that made the universe.

As she nestled her head in the crook of my arm, she slowly started to comb the curling black and gray hairs on my chest. Afterwards, I kissed her lightly on her head, leaned back on the pillows and listened to the sounds downstairs. I could hear dishes clinking together, cupboards clanging shut, the hollow thuds of the refrigerator door closing, and the old toaster straining to pop up. I thought it was good for the kids to start doing things on their own, especially Paulie.

The shadows of the white morning light cast a crisscross-pattern on the white sheer curtains that hung in our bedroom windows.

Chris turned her head toward me and said, with some concern in her voice, "Vinnie, I just remembered, Paulie needs to have his shot before he goes to school. You know how his eyes get when he doesn't have it."

"Don't worry, dear, he'll be okay," I said confidently. "I think for once in our lives we deserve to stay in bed and enjoy our love for each other without worrying about Paulie's eyes, his shots, having a baby, the right time... It sounds like they're doing okay without us. Just relax, my love."

"Okay, Hon," she said lovingly, "you're the boss." She kissed me on the lips, again with an opened mouth. *Oh, she likes to French-kiss now.* I ran my hand over her smooth body. Our syncopation was even more beautiful than before. I thought about how her skin was not as tightly knitted together as Angie's. Instead, hers moved about as if my body could've wrapped itself inside of her.

I laughed. "One good thing about rhythm and sexual abstinence, is the time you finally do it."

She giggled. "Oh, yes."

I thought how glad I was to have Chris back as my wife again.

Suddenly the loud sound of sirens cut short my tantalizing dreams. When I opened my eyes, I saw red lights flickering in bursts on our bedroom walls. I looked over to the alarm clock on the dresser. It was still early, only eight.

Someone was now ringing our musical doorbell. I closed my eyes, hoping it would stop. But it didn't. The melodious ding-dong kept on and on. If it's that damn Frank, I thought, I'll kill the son of a bitch. Then I wondered why those red lights were still bursting on our bedroom wall.

I felt Chris's warm flesh snuggled close to me. She whispered, "Vinnie, it might be one of the kids. They could've forgotten something and are locked out."

I prayed that it was as I jumped out of bed, picked up my pants from the floor, and quickly slid them on.

"Vinnie, do you think everything is okay?" Chris asked, worried now. "Could it be a fire?"

"I don't know," I said, without looking back and hurrying to the bedroom door. "It's probably like you said. One of the damn kids forgot something. I'll see."

"How come the..."

I didn't hear her finish the question as I opened the door and ran down the stairs. Scared, I opened the front door.

A young policeman stood there. He nodded politely and asked in a respectful tone of voice. "Sir, are you Paulie Serrano's father?"

"Yes, why?"

"I wonder if you..."

"Oh God, no!" I screamed, as I saw a crowd at the end of our street. I pushed by the policeman and ran toward the crowd.

Help me, God, please!

When I got there, I threw myself against the group of onlookers, shoving them away like a wild man. I saw so many faces but didn't recognize any of them. About five feet in front of me, I saw two blue-jacketed men kneeling at the rear of a yellow school bus.

"That's the father," someone said. "Stand back."

Linda ran toward me, crying and screaming.

"Dad, it's Paulie!" She tried to hug me, but someone grabbed her away as I headed for the men in blue. One of them, an older guy with bushy eyebrows, stood up and tried to hold me back. After a moment's hesitation, though, he let me go. There was deep sympathy in his eyes.

Paulie was lying on the asphalt. I fell on my knees beside him. It made a weird splashing sound against the pool of red blood he seemed to be floating in. God there was so much of it. I wished for death more than anything else at this moment. *This wasn't true. It wasn't.*

"Get back," someone yelled, as I felt the crowd pressing around me. I wanted to smash all their faces in.

Most of Paulie's hair was stiffly curled by dried blood. One side of his face, his cheek, and part of his neck were crushed, red and raw, with the cheekbone piercing through it all. *Jesus!* My knees felt wobbly and weak, as I leaned over and gently lifted Paulie's head and pressed it close to my bare chest. Slowly, I rocked back and forth. I could see tiny pieces of his tinted lens sparkling in the puddles of white skin and blood that pooled beneath him. I wondered why the blood didn't smell. I rocked faster and held him tighter to my chest.

Paulie! My Dear Paulie!

His blackened eyes, terrified and alone, now looked up at me. He whimpered, "Daddy, I want to go home."

"Sure, hon," I said. "In just a few minutes. Everything will be all right."

Now some fresh blood started to trickle from the corner of Paulie's mouth. The blue-jacketed man with the bushy eyebrows dabbed at it with a white cloth. Paulie slightly moved his head against my chest and without looking up asked quietly, "Daddy, will Jesus take me?"

"No, never," I said, feeling tears welling in my eyes. "Never, never..."

God, please help me. Please. I need you.

He tried to say something more, but instead coughed and gagged. Some more red blood trickled out from the corner of his mouth. Then his breathing got hard and lower. I could see on the front of his once-clean shirt, from the top of his chest down, wet, glistening blood was seeping through, soaking his navy-blue tie and falling on the silver zipper of his jacket. If I only could find the missing parts to where he's bleeding from, I thought, I would put them back.

Didn't all things go back together again? It was the rule of the universe.

He coughed and gagged some more. Shaking uncontrollably, I started to unbutton his shirt. The blue-jacketed men gripped my hand and tried to stop me. But it was too late. Bleeding flesh and stringy strawberry-like stuff burst out onto my already blood-soaked chest. "Oh, my God," I screamed as I turned my head away, burying it in the crotch of my arm. Then all of a sudden I felt myself vomiting, then coughing, then gagging. It scared me, it came out so fast. It seemed to go on forever, as I prayed that I would be in the next moment when the nightmare would be over. *Then everything went black.*

The next thing I remember, I was listening to the siren of the ambulance as we passed and weaved in and out of the heavy, morning traffic. A shiver passed through me as I now looked down at Paulie, lying on a stretcher between me and the two blue-jacketed men. His sunken chest was wrapped with a large piece of gauze. Here and there, spots of red were beginning to seep through. Pressed against the missing part of his face was a stark-white towel, to staunch the bleeding. What remained of Paulie's face looked chalky-gray, as if the morning's white light was sucking all the warmth out of him.

I felt a blanket on my shoulders, and, mechanically, I pulled it closer around my neck. Then I concentrated on Paulie's partially open mouth and waited for sounds to come out of it. But the only sounds I could hear were the quick rise and fall of the ambulance siren. Trembling, I reached over for Paulie's hand. It felt cold and limp. Another shiver passed through me.

"Life is funny," one of the blue-jacketed men said in a cold, professional tone of voice. "I'm sorry."

"Paulie, wake up please, wake up!" I screamed, as I violently shook Paulie's limp hand between both of mine.

The hands of the blue-jacketed man were on mine now, trying to break the tight grip I had around Paulie's hand. All I could think about was Paulie breathing again *please, breathe, Paulie, please.*

Then suddenly it hit. Paulie was dead. My dear love was dead. The blue-jacketed man took his hands away, as I now buried my head into my Paulie's blood-soaked coat and cried.

22

I looked at the alarm clock on the dresser. It was nearly twelve-thirty. Chris, like me, was unable to sleep. I heard her footsteps passing around our bed, down the stairs, through the hall and into the living room. Next, I heard the muffled creak of her favorite rocking chair. Almost all night, the creaking of the rocker, her footsteps coming back upstairs, her sliding quietly back into bed, her going back down again—these sound patterns repeated themselves over and over.

Linda had cried herself to sleep.

At last, near dawn, back in bed for an hour or so, Chris slept. Only the sounds of an occasional car passing by, and the soft, steady intake of her breath could be heard. And, finally, I fell into a fitful sleep, with images of Paulie's accident and our lovemaking collapsing into one another.

The only time Chris and I really spoke about it was when we came home from the cemetery. It was Wednesday, late morning. Wanda had taken Linda over to her house, while Chris and I were alone now in the kitchen. I was sitting at the kitchen table, chewing on a piece of toast, trying to slow down my burning stomach. Chris had given the undertaker a Pittsburgh Steelers helmet to place inside Paulie's coffin. At the funeral service, Paulie's classmates, dressed in their Catholic uniforms, solemnly walked in two single files behind Paulie's coffin, girls on one side and boys on the other. The coffin was carried down the aisle of the church by six pious-looking men who belonged to Chris's prayer group. I choked, thinking about the stupid-ass eulogy Father Luke gave about Paulie being in the presence of

God and looking at us from a place in the sky that was like a refreshment stand, and that instead of selling Kool-Aid, he was giving away light and peace. Each time I thought about these things, my stomach felt like I had swallowed ten thousand burning matches.

I took another bite of the toast as I stared at Chris who was standing at the sink, watering some plants that were left over from the wake. She looked pallid, almost pasty. However, the soft and loose-fitting black dress she was wearing made me think of her warm flesh underneath. The thoughts sent a thrill through me.

For what seemed like forever, we remained silent. Only my chewing on the piece of toast and her occasionally turning on the faucet relieved the tense silence.

Eventually, she slowly turned around, with a large potted green plant in her hands. Her eyes were red from crying, and her face now looked like that of a stranger's. The pain of the last few days seemed to have compressed itself in the deep wrinkles that now surrounded the corners of her eyes.

"God, Vinnie, was testing us," she said strongly. "That's because we're weak people. And now, because of our selfishness, he has punished us. The devil, Vin, was in control of us that night."

"I just don't know," I said, shaking my head and trying to avoid eye contact.

"Well, I do," she said, with more conviction than before. "I swear, Vinnie, from this moment on, I will never live a moment without Jesus. Never! I will never give in to the animal temptations of the devil." She paused for a second, then began again. "I think if we really have true love, it means more than sex."

"I agree," I said, feeling guilty because I had soiled a saint.

"Last night I prayed to Jesus, to help me to do what is right," she said reverently. "And he did, Vinnie. I made a decision and feel more at peace with myself than ever before."

"That's good," I said, "wish I did."

"You could, Vinnie," she said excitedly, "if you would only give yourself to Jesus."

"I can't," I said, "that's giving up my will."

"But your will is Jesus's will," she said quickly. "Don't you see, Vinnie, that what happened to Paulie was a sign from Jesus, saying that we were straying from him?"

"I can't accept that."

"Well, I have to," she said, "that's the only way I could live from now on. And that's why I feel so much better after making the decision I did."

"What decision?"

"Vinnie, my love," she said gently and too sweetly, "it's like the sacrifices Jesus made for us throughout his life. We too have to make them, no matter how hard they are."

"I don't understand."

"Vinnie," she said in the same gentle tone of voice, "it's sometimes harder to say, than to make up your mind to do it. What I'm trying to say, Vinnie, is that I'll still sleep with you, and in time I'll even kiss you again and play a little, like we used to before we got married. But that's it." "Forever," she emphasized. "You see, Vinnie, I think this is the sacrifice Jesus is asking us to make."

"You're not really serious," I said.

"Yes, Vinnie," she said, "the time has come to be reborn again, both of us."

She was serious. My path to Heaven was being taken away.

"Oh, shit," I said, trembling, "get off that Jesus stuff, Chris."

"No, I won't," she said, with a tone of anger, "I'm not scared to admit my love for Jesus, and I'm not scared to admit it to you."

"You really believe that?" I asked, struggling with my words.

"Yes," she said firmly.

"That's incredible," I said, feeling my stomach explode, "can't you see that Paulie's death was an accident? And not because, for once in our lives, we had beautiful marital sex together? Look at all the people in this world who do the same thing we did that night, and even more, and they're not being punished. Can't you see that?"

"Please, Vinnie," she pleaded, "I don't want to talk about it anymore. It makes me sick to think of what you did to me that night." She turned around and started to water some more plants.

"Oh, God, you make it sound so dirty," I said.

She turned around and stared at me for a second and then said, "It was, Vinnie, I'm sorry." Her voice was tired and dull now.

"Oh, God, I just don't believe this."

"Vinnie, please, I think we've both been through enough."

"I still can't believe this," I said, shaking my head.

"You're making it very difficult," she said, with kindness again. "I think perhaps it would be best if Linda and I went to see my parents in Miami for a couple of weeks. This may help us to put things in perspective."

Such a nice word, perspective.

"Yes, perhaps you're right," I said, calmly.

"Next Tuesday okay for you to take me to Pittsburgh?"

"Fine."

As she turned back to the kitchen sink, I got up, went to the bedroom, put on my sneakers, jeans, sweatshirt, and left. I ran, and I walked. I ran and walked all over Baywood. Then I ran all the way to Wheeling, where I walked all around the downtown area in kind of a daze. Stopping once in front of a jewelry store, I saw it was near five in the afternoon. I decided to head for the university, which was on the other side of town. I ran all the way, not paying attention to the stares people were giving me as I ran past their cars, lined up in rush-hour traffic. When I got to the university, I sat on a cement retaining wall that was in front of a small quad-rangle. There I sat, until I looked up at the clock on one of the university buildings. It was nearly ten. I headed home, thinking I should call my mother and tell her what happened to Paulie; however, I had decided not to call Boston and let her know, because all of them would come and want to take over. Especially Aunt Concetta. *Enough is enough.*

It was midnight when I got home. Chris was in the living room, in her study area, writing thank-you notes. She looked worried. "Where have you been?"

"Nowhere and everywhere."

"What?"

"I just went back to the office to get my mind off myself."

"Oh, you look terrible."

"I'm fine," I said, as I went to my study, took two flurazepams and drank half a gallon of wine. I slept until late the next afternoon. When I woke up, Chris was standing over me, looking concerned. She asked if I needed a doctor.

"No."

After looking at the blisters on my feet, she asked, "How did this happen?"

"Dancing."

"Well, you might be dancing yourself right into the hospital." I closed my eyes and fell asleep again.

It was around ten that night when I woke up. The stench coming from my body was terrible. The jeans and sweatshirt that I wore for my obsessed race the day before were still on me.

Chris came in. "I think, Vinnie, I'd better change my reservations. I can't leave you sick."

"Oh, no," I said, "I'm going to be fine. I feel better already. I just need to take a hot shower and get something to eat and I'll be all right."

"You sure?"

"Yes."

"Also," Chris added, "you better call and let your parents know what happened."

"I will," I lied.

I asked Chris to fix me some hot cereal and also turn on the water in the shower. She nodded obediently. When I stood up, my head felt dizzy and my knees were weak, but eventually I made it to the shower in the upstairs bathroom.

I took off my clothes and stepped into the hot shower. It made me weaker, and I slid down against the tiled wall and sat in the tub. Hot beads of water drummed down on my head. I wondered how much more weight I had lost over the last few days. That on top of what I had lost from the vinegar diet. I had barely eaten since Paulie's death.

After a while Chris came in, turned off the water, and helped me out of the tub. As she slid my arms through my terry-cloth bathrobe, she asked again, with even more concern, "Vinnie, are you sure you're okay?"

"Yes."

She looked at me, uncertain.

"Really, don't worry."

"Is it because of what we talked about yesterday?"

"No," I lied. "In fact, that talk really helped."

Changing the subject now, Chris told me Wanda called and said that she and Frank were going to Puerto Rico, to see if they could resolve some of their differences. Chris also said that Wanda wanted us to come along. Wanda thought it would be therapeutic. Chris had told her she would've loved to but she couldn't, because she already made plans to go to Miami with Linda and see her parents. For a moment I imagined myself going without Chris, and Wanda and I becoming closer than friends. I would tell Wanda about Chris being reborn again and taking the vow of chastity. Then Wanda would fall madly in love with me. But the fantasy quickly ended, as I thought about *that asshole Frank*.

Reality was a bitch.

23

On Friday afternoon I went back to the office. I was still feeling tired and weak, but the previous night had brought me my first deep sleep in a while. Chris had fixed me a breakfast of hot cereal and two soft-boiled eggs with toast. And today's lunch of chicken noodle soup and a tuna sandwich helped me get on the road to recovery. My feet were also feeling better and only stung every once in a while because of the broken blisters. Wanda and Frank were off to Puerto Rico without us. Wanda may still want me when she comes back. Troubled men are always attractive to women.

I picked up the *Star* I had bought on the way to the office, leaned back in my desk chair, and started to read. On the front page, there was a picture of Elvis Presley in a familiar pose, legs spread, head back, and hips ready to gyrate at any moment. I turned to the feature article that was written about him. It said that three former friends of his were writing a book and would tell all. The only part of this piece I found interesting was where Elvis got mad one night and shot a cue stick at a girl who called him a son of a bitch.

After this, I skimmed some other articles, about Starsky and Hutch being surrounded by thirty-five beauties, about a frightened mother describing how a giant bird carried off her ten-year-old son, on and on they went. None of them seemed to interest me now. So I stood up and decided to file some of the shit from the in-basket. I was doing fine for a while, pasting grade-sheets on student folders, filing add- and drop-slips, throwing away publishers advertisements of new math books, then, then, damn it,

I came across a memo from the chairman of the Committee of Committees. Automatically, I started to read it. It seemed that the chairman was deeply concerned about the tasks the committee was involved in. He felt that a new committee should be formed, which would deal with larger issues and decisions, and that the committee that now stands, should deal with smaller issues and decisions. The name he suggested for this new committee was *Committee of the Committee of the Committees*. Angrily, I threw the memo into the wastepaper basket and then threw the in-basket in after it. I slammed the open file drawers shut and yelled out loud, "Assholes!"

The phone rang. Right now I felt so alone and isolated that I even hoped it was my mother. I had finally called her earlier and told her about Paulie. She'd wanted to fly down right away. But I told her about Chris going to see her parents. Anyway, I would be coming to Boston to rest, but not for another couple of weeks. She'd said that Aunt Concetta would make me well again. *I bet.* Sadly, she never knew Paulie, because of my father. There's not too many Italian grandparents who never knew their grandchildren. Perhaps it was a good thing, considering the family craziness in Boston. Paulie and, in a way, Linda are free of them.

The phone rang again and stirred me out of my thoughts. I picked it up quickly. It was Fay, who was calling to tell me that in fifteen minutes there was going to be a staff meeting, and Art's secretary had called her to see if I was there today, because Art wanted me to attend.

"Okay," I said. Art had been kind to me since Paulie's death. He had gotten a substitute to come in and teach my classes, and he had Fay cancel all my appointments. In addition, I figured the meeting would at least waste some time. Now, time seemed to be something to get over with as soon as possible. Somehow, I felt like I was rushing toward something, but that something was far, far away. Heaven, I hoped, on second thought. *Or hell.*

The conference room where the staff meeting was being held reminded me of a lavish corporate office suite I once saw in a movie. The walls were painted mint-green, the floor was a spongy dark-green carpet. Hanging on the walls were scenic photographs of West Virginia, framed in light, wormy wood. One photograph depicted an olive-green lake with a huge boulder rising out of it. Another print showed people standing on a wooden-fenced overlook, gazing at the West Virginia hills that blushed light-green in the distance. The third image was of a steep and narrow waterfall crashing down on the rocks that were already worn smooth.

The majority of the staff members sat around a long, dark, expensive-looking conference table. The matching office chairs were heavily cushioned with some kind of vinyl, the color of maple syrup but speckled with white.

When I walked in, Art was sitting and talking from one end of the long table. He looked over at me, as he continued with his opening remarks and smiled.

I smiled back, as I took a seat in a far corner of the room, outside the circle of faculty and staff that sat around the table. Three or four others were scattered on the outside, hoping, I guessed, to sneak out early, or to be among the first ones out when the meeting ended.

Jarvis was there, sitting at the other end of the table. He looked over and winked. I couldn't remember whether or not I had seen him at Paulie's funeral.

It didn't matter.

I smiled at Jarvis and then turned my attention to Art. He was somewhere in his mid-forties and in excellent shape. His skin always looked tan, like that of a devoted tennis player; his hair was graying near the sides, and near his high forehead there was a slight suggestion of thinning. I thought, except for a mouth that twisted to one side when he talked, Art was fairly handsome and distinguished looking. Today, he was immaculately dressed in a blue and white checkered leisure suit. Underneath he wore an open-collared powder blue shirt.

"This department may truly make it," he said, looking down at his notes, "it really depends on our willingness to anticipate and deal with the services we can provide, apart from, and in addition to, our meaningful ongoing campus activities. That is,

I have worked hard this year to convince many people that this department is not like traditional mathematics departments. It is interested in and concerned with developing interfaces, quote, unquote, throughout the state. Of course, you know that effect has been initiated in terms of the state itself." He looked up now, as if to make sure he didn't lose his audience, and also to give the staff a feeling he was well-prepared. He went on without looking at his notes.

I thought Art talked like many politicians and news commentators. They all give you the impression that you have heard something of importance, when, in reality, all you have heard is shit.

"Over the last couple of years I've had this idea about getting some monies from the federal government and from perhaps a large private foundation. The idea is really very simple. I know it would help with public relations and also would give us a new building which we so desperately need. What I want to do is to erect a National Mathematical Hall of Fame, quote, unquote. Of course," he smiled deviously, "the majority of space in this new building would be used to take care of our overloaded freshmen math classes."

Two older female faculty ladies, sitting to one side of him, started to clap. They had been teaching freshmen math for years. At least that's what I was told. Their jerking clapping embarrassed everyone. It was like when one or two people prematurely clap before a concert piece is finished.

"Thank you," he nodded in their direction. "I wrote to Senator Haley, and after not expecting any answer, he wrote back last week saying he liked the idea. I also wrote to the president of the university concerning this. He hasn't responded yet but that's because he's probably getting ready to steal the idea and claim the glory for himself," he said, half laughing.

"If it's approved," he went on, "and we get the funds, I think I know who will head up the project for the Hall of Fame." His dark eyes fell on me, and so did everyone else's.

I nodded and slowly stood up.

"Yes. Vinnie, go ahead," he said kindly. "Please do."

He, faculty, and staff always expected me to say something great and intellectual. I imagined it was not only because I had published more than anyone else in the department, but because here and there I dropped a clue that I had gone to Harvard for a while.

"Thank you," I smiled ever so gratefully. "Art?"

"Yes," he said excitedly.

"Go fuck yourself, I would really appreciate that. And please take that Hall of Fame shit and stick it up your asshole where it belongs."

He looked at me, stunned and open-mouthed.

"Thank you."

Slowly I walked toward the door, opened it, and left.

Back in the office, I noticed someone, probably Fay, had taken the in-basket out of the wastepaper basket and placed it back on my desk. A letter with my name and address, written in beautiful longhand, caught my attention. I picked it up, sat in my chair, and saw that it was from Candy.

As I laid Candy's letter back down on the desk, I felt disappointed. I hoped it would be from someone like Tatum or Angie. Soon, thoughts of Tatum's body trembling with passion for me took over. I knew she would help me forget all the shit that was going down.

Pushing everything else to the back of my mind, I quickly picked up the phone, dialed information in Boston, and asked for Tatum's phone number. I hoped she was home. I looked at my watch. It was nearly four in the afternoon.

After getting her phone number, I started to dial but couldn't finish. I was trembling. What would I say, I thought.

I dialed again and completed it. It was ringing. I wanted to hang up after the first ring, but it was too late; a female voice was on the other end.

"Hello."

"Hi, Tatum, do you know who this is?" I asked in a quivering voice. The question was so stupid. So uncool.

"No." She said and then paused. "Vinnie, oh my God, you son of a bitch."

"I was thinking about you," I said more calmly, "it's one of those lonely Friday afternoons. How have you been?"

"Fine."

"How's your job going?" I tried hard to remember what she did.

"Oh, I quit the secretary job. I couldn't stand my boss anymore. A real shithead. I'm into something now that I've always wanted to do. I'm teaching art at night and learning about running a gallery during the day. Two friends of mine are starting a gallery, and they asked me to be their buyer. I'm really excited about it."

"Great. Well, I just thought I would call you and just see how you're doing."

"I see," she said. The excitement in her voice a minute ago was gone. She seemed cool now.

"How's Boston?" I asked with my voice quivering again.

"I still like it," she said. "I'm meeting some very important people in the field of art."

See you are external like I said in the airport.

"The same old Tatum."

"What?"

"Nothing. Well, I told you I would call."

"Yes, you did."

What's wrong? It's not going as I expected it to go. She really seems pissed off.

I could hear someone laughing in the background. It sounded like a man's laugh. There was music too.

"Well, Tat, I got to run, I just wanted to say hello and see how you're doing."

"All right," she sounded confused and sad.

I wondered if that voice belonged to a guy who was taking care of her nympho needs.

I thought about Angie now. Her mature lovemaking, her smooth and warm skin. She really seemed to have her head together. I needed someone stable, someone who would mother me and care for me. *That was Angie. I wish I had kept her number.*

So, nervous, but not that nervous, I dialed information in Pittsburgh and got the phone number for Angie's home and for Carnegie Mellon. First, I tried her home. No one answered. Then, just as I was beginning to dial Carnegie Mellon, I heard someone knocking at my door. I sat there frozen, with the receiver in one hand, and with the forefinger of the other hand inserted in slot three of the phone dial.

The knocks continued. "Vinnie, are you there?" It was Jarvis. He knocked some more.

A few minutes later, he gave up. I heard his footsteps walking away from my door. Thank God, I started to breathe more easily.

On the second ring, the Carnegie Mellon operator connected me with Angie's office.

"Angie?"

"Yes."

"This is Vinnie Serrano, how you doing?"

"Good. I was thinking about you the other day." Her voice sounded friendly and sexy.

"Hey, look, I'm coming to Pittsburgh next Tuesday. I'm driving my wife up to the airport. How about meeting me at the Hilton in the South Plaza? I want you to get a room there."

I was scared she was going to reject me, as she hesitated for a second. "Okay, what time?"

"About five."

I knew from Chris's previous trips to Miami that she liked to take the mid-afternoon flight out of Pittsburgh.

"Please use the name Sandy Brown, just in case."

"Look, Ang, I got to run so I can't talk. We'll have a lot of time next Tuesday. I'll call you at the Hilton when I get there in order to find out what room you're in."

"Okay, I look forward to seeing you," she said, sounding like she really meant it.

"Bye," I said, as I hung up and thought, this time, Jacqueline Kennedy, you'll go bananas before I get finished with you.

I picked up Candy's letter from the desk, sat down and opened it. It was written in pencil on three-hole notebook paper.

It looked terribly long, as I unfolded the pages. I decided, physically and mentally, I wasn't ready to deal with any more of her shit and Jimmy's murder.

Quickly I folded up the pages, slid them back in the envelope and, without further thought, I threw Candy's letter into the wastepaper basket. I picked up my jacket and left.

A lonely woman is a dangerous woman. Sometimes a lonely woman is a bored woman. Bored women act on impulse. I think I read that in a novel by Jill Essbaum.

24

I walked down University Drive, as I thought about Angie and what we would do next Tuesday. I headed up Lowe Street, over to Seymour and Cottage, and down Wall until I was standing in front of Dom's. I stood outside, smiling and nodding at some of my students as they walked in. I hoped they didn't think I was queer or something, standing there. I looked impatiently at my watch, hoping they would think that I was waiting for someone. It was six in the evening.

Finally, I decided to go in. The noise and people might be comforting.

I saw Jarvis, Karen, and Julie sitting at a table at the far end of the room. I wanted to turn around and leave. But it was too late. Jarvis had already spotted me and was now waving to me to join them.

With a fake smile on my face, I walked over to their table. I thought I'll have a quick beer and then say that I'm sorry, I've got a headache, and then I'll leave.

When I got there, Jarvis stood up and motioned for me to take his seat between Julie and Karen. Then he grabbed an empty chair from another table and sat on the other side of Karen, facing me.

Julie smiled warmly at me, as I took my seat and said hello to her and Karen. She looked beautiful with her long, dark braids gently resting on her breasts. Like knotted silk.

"Vinnie, I was just telling them how great you were today," Jarvis said, with excitement in his voice. "God, Vinnie, you should've seen Art's face: it was as pale as the foam on my beer here. Shit, I still don't think he really believes what you said to him. It was too beautiful."

As Jarvis went on to describe how Art stumbled his way through the rest of the meeting, Julie got up and, without asking me, brought back a beer for me. It felt good. It cooled the burning in my stomach.

Jarvis continued to revel in what happened at the meeting.

"Hey, Vinnie, that son of a bitch had it coming, him and his content-free sentences. Everyone knows how scared he is of getting into conflict situations."

"Yeah," I said.

Julie seemed to be moving closer to me, as I felt her arm touch mine. I wished she would take me in her arms and hug me tight. I wanted her. Jarvis's rehash of today's meeting was really not what I needed.

"I think, my old buddy," he went on, "we're ready for a change. You have struck the mighty first blow. And now are you ready to join us in battle?"

"I don't know," I said dully. "I really don't think I give a shit anymore."

"Hey, what do you mean?" he asked quickly.

"I don't know," I said.

"Well, if you're really worried about the system doing something to you, because of what you got started, forget it. Nothing will happen to you. Hell, you know why?"

"Why?" I asked, not really caring about the why.

"Because, man, the system needs people like you in order to look good. You see, they'll go to the Board of Regents and say their procedure at the university is to listen to all sides of an issue before a decision is made. That's what a good liberal university is supposed to do. Hell, Vinnie, those shits will say they're meeting the criteria for making viable and open decisions, which was spelled out last year in a Board of Regents Policy Bulletin. They want to protect their asses just as much as we do. Don't you think, Vin?"

I nodded, knowing he wanted to continue.

"After the faculty and staff meeting today, Vinnie, some of us got together and decided to have a meeting tomorrow night at my place. We want to develop some strategies that will help keep the pressure on Art and the administration. The damn 'up there' decisions have to stop." His thumbs jerked vertically and wildly toward the ceiling.

Karen laughed out loud, while Julie only laughed politely. That made me feel better. At least Julie was as bored as I was with Jarvis's talk about changing the system. It was so useless. That fad went out with the Sixties. I wondered, what was Jarvis's real motive? There must be something behind all of this. Oh, shit, yes. Once I remembered Jarvis telling me how he tried to get Marilyn Peters in bed but couldn't, because she thought he was too insensitive to the oppression of women that went on in universities. Now it all made sense.

"Is Marilyn Peters going to be there?" I asked.

"Yes."

"Good," I said. "She's a fine person.

He knew that I knew.

"A lot of other fine people are also going to be there," he emphasized, "John Griffin, Russ Patrick, Tom Lodi, Paul Martin, all of them are fed up with Art's shit. And we want you to be there too. Your courage to stand up to him got it all started. Will you come?"

"I don't know," I said. "Really..."

"Shit, man," he said, shaking his head and acting mad at himself. "What an ass I am. Here I'm pushing you to think about other people's problems, when you've already been through enough shit to drive one to immediate suicide. Jesus, I'm sorry, Vin."

"That's okay," I said, feeling my eyes getting watery. "Don't worry about it."

"Could I help, Vin?"

"No, I'll be fine," I said.

"Jesus, what an ass I am," Jarvis repeated, as I stood up.

"Hey, I said don't worry about it. See I'm doing fine. Really, I just need to get some air." Then I turned to Julie and asked, "Let's take a walk, okay?"

"Sure," she said, as if she had been ready since I walked in. *Good.*

Julie's apartment looked the same. The sleeping bag with the quilt in the middle of the floor, the old sofa, the plants, the stereo, the bookcase.

This time she didn't ask me if I wanted a joint; she just lit one and handed it to me. It was great, just what I needed, as I started to immediately feel relaxed. She asked me to take off my shirt so she could massage my back. I did. She said she learned about the powers of massage from her friend Sonja.

It felt good as she sat on my rear and gently rubbed and pounded my back. I could've fallen asleep, but, a few minutes later, her pulling down my pants and shorts, taking off my shoes and socks, brought me back to complete alertness. She started to kiss, one by one, from the top down, the vertebrae that knitted my spinal cord together. Or my Kundalini. Julie said that this is where all my sexual energy got started. Wonderful. I wanted to turn over but I was scared it would ruin the mood.

Her lips and tongue were warm and wet. We got into the sleeping bag. She pulled the quilt over us. The zipper teeth were pressing into my back. But it didn't seem to matter. She was warm. Tender. A great teacher. Also, it really didn't seem to matter that the heaven experience I'd felt with Chris wasn't there. It was okay. I was drifting. Gently drifting. Then the dark clouds descended. Then sleep.

After what seemed like hours, I heard her ask, "Do you want something to eat?" She was gently stroking my hair.

"What time is it?" I asked thickly and forcing my eyes open.

The pleasant feeling of making love still lingered. I didn't want to wake up. So cuddly here. So nice.

"About three in the afternoon."

"You're kidding," I exclaimed, while I tried to wipe the sleep out of my eyes with my fingertips.

"No."

"Oh, my God, I haven't slept like that for years."

"Good," she smiled warmly. She had on a black Indian-looking robe with gold trim.

I thought about Chris and wondered if she was worried. I had never stayed away all night.

Julie understood when I told her that I had to go. "No problem," she said sweetly.

After dressing, she walked me to the door.

"It was wonderful," I said, as I reached for the doorknob.

I opened the door and turned. She pulled me toward her and gave me a big hug. Then we kissed. I could've done it again, I thought, if it wasn't for Chris.

25

When I reached home, I figured I would tell Chris that I had stayed at the office and worked on my book all night. Then, I would tell her, I passed out in my desk chair, exhausted, and didn't wake up until a little while ago.

This lie wasn't needed. I found Chris in the living room, still writing thank-you notes. I couldn't believe how peaceful she looked. Hell, look at her, she's almost smiling to herself. She looked beautiful again. Her life was in God's hands.

"Did you have a good sleep at Jarvis's?" she now asked, smiling at me.

"Huh, oh, yes, just fine, fine," I said, wondering what the hell she was talking about.

"He had called here last night and said that you had fallen asleep on the sofa. He thought it was just what you needed. I agreed. You know, sometimes I think I could really get to like Jarvis."

"Good."

Thanks, Jarvis. You're really a good friend. I would've never thought of doing that for you. That's really being sensitive to one's needs.

She then started to talk about how many more thank-you notes she had to write. She wondered if I wanted to help. I said no.

I told her I was going upstairs to take a shower and clean up. I wondered if I smelled of sex. Thus, I kept my distance from Chris.

Matter of factly, Chris said that my mother had called and asked how we were. Chris said she told her everything was fine.

I asked when she planned to tell her family about Paulie. In time, in time, she repeated. There was nothing they could do, anyway, she said. She would tell her family when she got to Miami.

Fine, I said. I was feeling too good to really care one way or the other. Julie was still on my mind.

The sun was breaking through the car's windshield, giving a bright peach glow to everything inside. I glanced at the digital clock on the dashboard. It was close to two in the afternoon. Outside, it was early spring. Warm and breezy. Now and then, I could see the strong breeze whip up the backs of leaves, which looked like hundreds of starlings being scared off into a bright blue sky.

As Chris talked to me about the meals she had prepared for me, how they were marked, and where I could find them in the freezer, I thought about Angie, and if I would be any good with her in bed, especially after that wonderful night with Julie.

Stop, Vinnie. I tried to concentrate on what Chris was now saying about spending Christmas vacation with her parents. She said it would be good for all of us as a family.

I agreed. Some of the best times we had as family were on the beach near her parents' home.

Chris then went on to say that we would have real fun, and we would not think about anything.

I agreed again. No problems. No pain. Her parents never got upset about anything. Their lives seemed to be perfectly ordered. The mother, who could've passed for Chris's sister, had her golf, tennis, and bridge. The father played tennis, too, and he had his semi-retired interest in stocks. It was easy to fall into their routine when we were visiting.

8:00 a.m., wake up; 8:30, breakfast and read New York Times; *9:30, Chris's mother leaves for golf, father leaves for friend's stock broker office, we leave for the beach; noon, Chris and her mother fix lunch, and we eat while watching "Hollywood Squares" and then listen to the 12:30 news; 1:00 p.m., nap time; 3:00, more beach time; 6:00, usually eat out; 9:00, parents babysit for us and go to bed, Chris and I walk the beach; 11:00, bedtime. The next day and the next, the schedule never changed. It was like the order and routine I had in graduate school. I loved it.*

I remembered how Paulie loved the ocean, except for one day when a large wave picked him up, turned him over, and threw him up on the beach. He got terribly frightened. It took me two days to get him back on the beach again. That frightened look on his face was the same that was on his face the morning of the accident.

Anyway, those times in Miami were great relaxing times. Chris was right. Taking Linda down to see Grandma and Grandpa now, and a family vacation there later, would do us all good.

When we got to the airport, I dropped Chris and Linda off at the terminal, so they could pick up their tickets while I parked the car.

Afterwards, I met them at the gate, where their flight was to board for Miami. As we sat and waited, Linda talked to a dark-skinned boy.

Then Chris started to give me a list of things I should do. *Check with Father Luke about the masses that were supposed to be said for Paulie; check with the funeral director to see if we owe him any more money; check to see if the stone we ordered for Paulie's grave was in; check, check, check. She went on and on, but I didn't listen anymore.*

Finally, thank God, Chris's flight was called to start boarding. I stood up, leaned over and gave Linda a kiss on the cheeks.

"Bye, Dad."

"Bye, sweetie."

Then I turned to Chris, kissed her closed lips (never to be opened again), and started to say bye, but she interrupted.

"Vinnie, I hope God will help you, as he helped me."

"He will," I lied.

"I'll pray for you," she said, crying now. Her mood had completely changed. The peace-with-herself-look was gone, replaced by worry.

"For Linda's sake, we must get everything back to normal," she urged me.

Normal, normal, sure.

"I know, dear," I lied. "Last night I really did pray to God for help."

"You mean it?" she asked, surprised. Her crying stopped.

"Yes."

"Oh, thank you, God," she said with a sense of relief, looking straight into my eyes. "I knew my prayers would be answered. Oh, I love you, Vinnie."

"I love you too," I said.

The last boarding-call for their flight sounded over the loud-speaker.

"Listen, call when you get there," I said. *Oh, God, no, why did I ask that. I won't be home.*

"And, look, hon, if I don't answer, it's because I'm sleeping soundly, like I did last night at Jarvis's."

"Okay."

"Bye!"

"Bye," she said, as she turned and gently pushed Linda ahead of her on the ramp. She seemed nervous now, as she wrapped her bone-colored sweater around her.

At the top of the ramp, she turned around and stared at me. Tears were in her eyes again. It was as if she wanted to say something to me, but nothing came out. She waved quickly, turned, and walked into the gangway.

Once the plane started to pull away, I turned and made my way toward the exit. I felt my pace quicken, faster, faster, and faster. Hell, I couldn't believe it. I was now running at full speed.

She was gone! She was gone!

People turned their heads and stared, as I zigzagged and pushed my way through the crowd. I didn't care about them. About anything. I was feeling too free and too reckless to care.

Outside, the warm breeze seemed to sweep me off my feet, as I started to run even faster. I inhaled the sweet-smelling air, which had a trace of airplane exhaust in it. I took long, deep sniffs with my nose, and then exhaled quickly through my mouth. My feet were no longer touching the ground. I felt like I was flying.

"Hell, I'm free!" I yelled out loud. "I'm free. Son of a bitch, I'm free." *Finally.*

I unbuttoned my shirt, slid off my light-brown corduroy jacket, rolled it into a ball, and stuck it underneath my arm like a football. I ran harder.

For once, the intense burning in my stomach seemed to be gone, completely vanished.

"I'm going to be screwed in the nude, I'm going to be screwed in the nude," I sang and laughed to myself, as I ran to my car. I couldn't wait to meet Angie.

26

I stopped in front of a gas station directly across from the Hilton. I got out and walked over to a pay phone that was on the curb of a busy, exhaust-filled highway. Loud, roaring trucks vibrated the booth's glass, as I stepped in and closed the folding door behind me.

After looking up the Hilton number, I dialed, and prayed that Angie would be there. As the phone rang, I spotted the phone number scrawled on the aluminum phone directory holder, followed by the name "Jean." I wondered how many other men had done the same thing.

A low, crackling female voice answered, "Hilton."

"Sandy Brown, please."

There was a disgusted sigh on the other end of the line, then a long pause. I wondered what she suspected.

"She just checked in, I'll ring," she said, in a bothered tone of voice.

Fuck you lady, I thought. I really wish we could be honest with each other. Then I would ask, "Is Sandy Brown, my fuck, in?" And you, lady, would say, "Sir, I'll check to see if your fuck is in." Then I would say, "Thank you ma'm, for ringing my fuck." And you would say, "You're welcome, sir. Have a good fuck, you hear"

Angie picked up the phone on the other end, "Hello."

"Hi," I said, "I'm here."

"Okay," she replied. She didn't sound as excited as I thought she would be. Was something wrong, I asked myself. The hotel operator, and now her.

"What room are you in?"

239

"101."

"Okay, I'll be there in a few minutes."

"Okay," she said.

"Bye."

"Bye."

I hung up, opened the folding door of the phone booth, got back to the car, and drove to the Hilton parking lot. As I pulled into an empty space, I noticed that the parking lot was nearly full. I wondered how many of these cars were involved in affairs. I locked the car and made my way down one of the passageways where a sign read "Rooms 100–126."

Out of the corner of my eye, I saw three, white-and-green state police cars parked directly across from the office. That's all I need, I thought, to be caught in some kind of raid or something. Now I knew why the hotel operator was so snotty to me. She's probably the one who called them. I wondered why the police were here, though. Perhaps they found out I know about Jimmy and his murder. No. How could that be?

Come on, Vinnie, stop it. Everyone does this.

I opened a heavy door and walked down the long, wide corridor until I came to Room 101.

I knocked.

The door quickly opened, as if Angie was standing there waiting for my knock. The euphoria I was feeling not too long ago at the airport was gone. Instead, I was scared.

"Hi," she said. She seemed nervous, too. The room was hot and stuffy.

"Hi," I said, as I turned, closed the door behind me, and fumbled with the chain latch. I didn't know what to do. Should I kiss her now or wait? Hell, I didn't want her to think that I was an animal.

She now turned and walked ahead of me. She was as beautiful as that time in Rochester. Even more so. Her silky black hair seemed to be even silkier and fuller than I remembered. It was longer, too, as it fell below her shoulders now. I still couldn't get over how she looked like Jacqueline Kennedy. She was wearing a denim-skirt and matching vest with a yellow blouse. She had taken her shoes off.

There she stood, in the middle of the room, and looked at me. Suddenly, a series of images flashed across my mind. I imagined two broad-shouldered, crew-cut state policemen breaking down the door. I saw them grabbing me. I saw them beating me. Then I saw them throwing me in jail with only my underwear on. I saw a *Star* headline: "University Professor Caught in Hotel with Pants Down: Sex Maniacs Teaching in Today's Universities" and, below, in a smaller font, "(See Page 41 for details.)"

Come on, Vinnie, Cool it.

"God, it's hot in here," I said.

"I know," she said, "I don't know how to adjust the air conditioner."

Hurriedly, I walked past her toward the large picture window. Its brown drapes were tightly closed. Underneath was the conditioning unit. I bent over, opened a small compartment, and turned it on. Right away, a swift cool breeze was hitting my perspiring face. It felt good.

I turned around and thought. Don't worry, baby, you'll get it, give me a chance.

Now she sat gingerly on the edge of the bed facing me. I sat down on the chair in front of the air conditioner. The cold air started to fan my back and unglue the shirt from my hot, sticky skin.

Please, God, help me. Don't let me screw up.

"Jesus, Vinnie," she said worriedly. "I had a heck of a time getting in here using that name, Sandy Brown."

"No," I said.

"Yes," she said sharply. "For some reason, they asked for my identification. It was unreal."

The three state police cars parked side by side flashed across my mind.

"Shit," I said. "Hotels never ask for identification."

"I know," she said, nervously, "but they did. I tell you, I'll never do that again. They really hassled me. Finally, I just told them that

I was from Maryland and had left my ID at home. I don't think they believed me, but they let me register anyway."

Hey, great, Angie, just great. The damn he-men will be breaking down the door any minute now. They'll see you have Pennsylvania license places on your car instead of Maryland plates. Jesus, why the hell didn't you just leave? You could've waited outside for me, and then we could've found another hotel. I don't believe it, Ang, I just don't. Asshole. Come on, Vinnie, you got something to take care of. Jarvis would laugh his ass off now, if he could see how scared you are. You did it in Rochester. Come on.

"Don't worry about it," I said, looking at her as calm as I could. "I heard on the radio coming over that last night someone held up a McDonald's in Pittsburgh last night, and they've been searching all around the area." This was true; I had heard it on the radio.

"Oh," she said, somewhat relieved, "that's why they are checking so closely."

"Right."

Smart thinking, Vinnie.

Now she leaned over, pulled the pillow from underneath the covers, and nonchalantly threw them against the headboard. Then she leaned her back against the pillows to make herself comfortable and brought her knees close up, clasping her hands around her ankles. The burnt-gold shag carpeting that covered the floor looked dirty.

I thought, hell, she was close enough to me now that with one good heave I could be on her. The silence that existed between us while she was getting comfortable was still there.

Mechanically, I reached over and picked up a magazine from a small, round coffee table near me. I flipped through the pages, wondering what to do, what to talk about, how to move to the bed.

Finally, without looking up from a picture I was staring at, I asked, "Did you ever hear about Big Foot?" I turned the magazine around, so she could see a picture of an ape-like man disappearing into a thick forest.

"No," she said, squinting her eyes to better see the picture.

"It's interesting," I said, wondering what the hell she must be thinking. "If you get a chance read about it."

"I will," she said.

I knew she was waiting for me to make the first move.

"Look Angie," I began, with great seriousness as I placed the magazine back on the coffee table and straightened up my back against the chair. "You know, every time I think about Rochester, I can't figure out how I was able to let myself go with you. It seemed so easy and natural. Not like now."

"I noticed," she said with a smile.

"Ang," I said, "let's be completely honest with each other. Why did you accept the date to meet me here?" *I got to get her to do some exposing of feelings.*

In a relaxed tone of voice, she said, "I find you interesting, and to be perfectly honest, sexually fascinating. You see, now that I've worked through my divorce, I want to get to know people like you. Before, my husband controlled all my interactions with men."

Sexually fascinating, Sexually fascinating, Great. Another woman hot for my body.

"How's your husband doing?" I asked, too embarrassed to deal with the sexually fascinating thing.

"Well, I guess he's having some problems," she said, with a sense of satisfaction. "He wanted to come back to me since I saw you. But I wouldn't take him. I did that once before, and it was a mistake. Also, for once in my life, I have found someone whom I'm really happy with." Her face was beaming. "I met him after I came back from Boston. He's the kinda guy a girl dreams about in high school but never gets asked out by him. Well, this guy did, and I'm having the greatest time of my life with him. I wouldn't do anything to violate his trust."

Violate his trust. A guy. What the hell is going on here? I don't understand.

"Hey, how about you, Vinnie, does your wife have a name, an identity?" she asked, in a tone suggesting she wanted me to do some revealing.

"Chris," I answered slowly. "Oh, yes, good ole Chris." *Shit, I don't want to talk about her. I want to find out more about this violate-his-trust business.* "I guess you would say that she's a very good strict Catholic type and an outstanding dedicated mother. All she lives for is her Jesus and her family. Perfectly good. A saint. Sometimes, I've thought of leaving her because of this. But my kids were too important. I just lost one child, Paulie. A beautiful child. I only have one now, Linda. Also beautiful, but spoiled. Anyway, with one remaining, I still believe a child needs a strong anchor to get through this screwed-up world."

"I'm sorry to hear about your son," she said sympathetically. Then she shifted to a stronger tone of voice, "but I think you're kidding yourself by using your kids as an excuse to remain married."

"Perhaps," I said, shrugging my shoulders, "I just don't know."

I had the feeling she was trying to rationalize her divorce, which I really didn't care about. My concern was whether she wanted to go to bed with me or whether she didn't, because of that "violating trust." Was I wasting my time?

"Does your wife have other men in her life?"

"Hell, no," I laughed. Then I mumbled something about her worshiping me.

"I don't believe that."

"Well, it's true," I argued.

Shit, I couldn't believe I was defending Chris.

"Do you love her?" she asked, with persistence in her voice.

"Yes, I think so," I hesitated, "but I also love a lot of other people. I think there are different types of loves." I had to let her know that I was open to going to bed with other women.

Then, with sudden ease, I got off the chair and slid onto the bed. She was still grasping her ankles. I wanted her. Right now. I wouldn't know what to do if she rejected me now.

"I don't know... it's difficult sometimes..." I said aimlessly, searching for something to say, while I tried to figure out what to do next. Finally, with a great deal of concentration I was able to put some sentences together.

"Look, Ang. I don't want you to think I came here just to get you in bed." *That's it, Vinnie. Good start.* "I really enjoy being with you. If I had some other thoughts in my mind, I would've been dishonest with you about loving my wife. I could've given you a lot of shit about having all sorts of problems with her, and about not loving her, and about getting a divorce. But I didn't give you any of that shit, Ang, because of the way I feel about you. I have some very warm feelings for you, especially now."

Her eyes and body silently moved closer to mine.

Shit, God, it's working. She believes me. She believes me.

"So do I, Vinnie," she said. "That's why I gave you the clue about my friend."

"That's what I thought," I said, wondering if this still meant she wouldn't do it. "I'm not out to violate anyone's rights. All I like to do is to reach out to people, to touch them and feel their souls."

Attaboy, Vinnie, that sounds like some good shit.

"I'm not against that," she said, "I also like to reach out and touch. I have no problem with that."

A light color of red now crossed her face. I was confused. The business about her friend just didn't go together with her wanting to be touched. Then, I thought, maybe she said that so I wouldn't think she was easy. I moved closer to her, lifting and resting one of my legs on her now outstretched legs. The soft flesh underneath was challenging.

"I really thought," she said, "you would have a problem with me not wanting to violate my friend's trust but..."

Before she could finish, my opened lips were pressed hard against hers. Hers opened, too. Lovely. Her small, tight breasts moved closer against my chest. Like two hills pushing themselves out of a valley. Soon she was playing with the long hair in back of my neck. Then, I couldn't believe it, one of her elbows was now rubbing my thing. I made it even harder.

"Oh, Angie," I said, as I moved my hand underneath her blouse and delicately circled her breasts, around, around, and around. Her elbow was also going around, around, and around. I pushed my knees closer, so it would be easier for Angie to do what she wanted to do with her elbow.

I brought my lips down to the curve of her neck. I gently sucked on it. At first, the perfumed skin tasted tart, but soon it was lost in my watery mouth, and only the scent of her remained. I loved it. I truly loved it. The scent of a woman.

Now, resting my head for a moment against her breasts, I said, "Ang, you know what you give me? It's your sense of maturity. I appreciate that."

Then somehow, I think with her help, one of her breasts popped free of her bra-cup. That was her response. Thank you, thank you, I said to myself, as I unbuttoned her blouse and started to suck on her. My head started to warmly spin. *No. No.* I grabbed her tightly. *No. Damn it. I've got to go. I've got to go. Play it cool, Vinnie.*

I lifted my head up, shook it, and said, "I'll stop now before it gets more difficult. I promised you I wouldn't violate your friend's trust." Then I kissed her lightly on the forehead and stood up.

She looked up at me in stunned disbelief.

I know, I got you all hot and bothered, and now I'm leaving. It was unfair, I know, but I have to.

"Maybe that's a good idea," she said, in a distant voice.

You must think I'm nuts. I can't help it. I must go.

I headed toward the door and turned when I got there. She was now standing up and slowly walking toward me. She still looked like she was in some sort of hypnotic trance. When she reached me, I put my arms around her slim waist, pulled her close to me and kissed her, but without the intensity of before.

"I'll see you again sometime, somewhere," I said, being the first to break off our kiss. "It's been fun."

Jesus, Serrano, couldn't you think of anything better. You're really bad.

"Okay," she said, as I turned, opened the door, and hurried out.

I didn't have the courage to look back to see that stunned face again. *Jesus, you blew it again, Vinnie. A perfect setup, and you blew it. What the hell. Maybe it's a good thing. I bet those state policemen had checked on Angie's license plates and were just getting ready to break down the door and ask me about Jimmy. I do love you, Chris.*

As I walked toward my car, I thought about Angie becoming so pissed off at me for frustrating her that she might call the university and report me. She could be a very spiteful person, I suspected. You never know with divorced women like her. Well, if she did that, I would just tell the university people that she was an older student whom I had been counseling in a personal and friendly way. And that the only reason I met her here at the hotel was because she called me and told me she was contemplating suicide. So I came to help her out. Then, when I got here, she tried to seduce me, but I only played kissy-face, thinking that would help. I never went any further. I swear.

Then I also thought about what I said to Angie about Chris. It was true. I really loved her. *I really did.* Leaving Angie frustrated was the proof. Chris was the only one for me. *Great.* Now I had something to believe in again, just like when I used to go to communion. We all need something to believe in. *Thank you, God. Thank you. You are really up there watching over people.* No more guilt, no more pain because I don't need an affair like other husbands. I have Chris now.

When I reached my car, I turned my head in the direction of the hotel office. The three green-and-white state police cars were gone. Above, the sky looked like red-hot coals smoldering under a layer of gray ashes. The night was just beginning, just like my life.

As I pulled up into my driveway, I decided that tomorrow I would go to Art and apologize. Yesterday I had found a note in my in-basket saying he wanted to see me. I'll tell him that Paulie's death was hard to get over. He'll understand. I'll even consider heading up his Mathematical Hall of Fame.

I turned off the ignition, got out of the car, and walked toward the front door. On the way, I brought up my wrist to catch some of the streetlight's grayish glow. It was ten fifteen.

I unlocked the front door, walked in, turned the hall light on and closed the door behind me. Almost at the same moment, the phone started to ring. I thought it's probably Chris calling to tell me that she arrived safely. I decided I would tell her how much I loved her, and that she was right about God watching over us.

Happily, I walked over to the desk in the living room, turned on the desk lamp, and picked up the receiver.

"Chris?"

"Mr. Vincent Serrano?"

"Speaking."

"Sir, this is Dave Falter, Regional Director for Trans Florida Airlines. Your wife and daughter who were on Flight 331 to Miami were involved in a crash. And, sir..."

"What?"

"We have evidence," he said grimly, "sir, that your wife and daughter were killed in the Everglades, just outside the airport. If you like, we can make arrangements with..."

Suddenly my body started to tremble. The penetrating words were being repeated over and over. Shit, no. Oh, God, no. *Your wife and daughter... in the Everglades... killed... Your wife and daughter..."*

I felt shaky and sick to my stomach, as I dropped the receiver and held on to the desk for support. The words were now loudly screeching in my ears. I had to get out. I had to.

"Mr. Serrano, Mr. Serrano, are you still there, Mr. Serrano...," a nervous voice kept repeating in the receiver from below.

Then, with my head down and with my arms crossed over my face, I ran and threw myself against the large, plate-glass door. Everything suddenly caved in, the glass-door, me, my skin, my arms... everything. *God, I love you, Chris, Chris. Bring back the moments before you left...please.*

I stumbled off the narrow porch into the bushes in front. Something was dripping from my lips that tasted like bitter cherries. Quickly, I pushed myself out of the bushes and ran. My face stung and burned, as if I'd cut myself shaving. However, now I welcomed the pain. *All the pain. I wanted more. More. More.*

I ran and ran and ran.

Finally, I felt my feet slapping hard against the blacktop surface of the high school track. I ran harder as sharp, stabbing pains came and went in my stomach. Then, there came a pain so intense and so painful, that I gasped for air and doubled over. I swayed on the track like a first-time jogger nearing the end of his first mile. Now I felt like I had to take a shit. I tried to hold it in, by tightly crisscrossing my arms around my stomach. But soon, warm watery stuff dripped down the insides of my legs. I stopped running. The pains in my stomach subsided, but I felt terribly weak.

When I finally started to walk again, my feet wobbled and eventually caved in under me. Suddenly, the cold hard pavement was scraping against my stinging face. It got completely dark. *I saw Paulie coming toward me. He was walking on white sand. Chris, dressed in white, followed. I heard the ocean roar. They couldn't reach me. They were dancing. They seemed happy. Laughing. Oh, Chris, Oh, Chris.*

I saw myself getting up and running toward Chris. Her hands were reaching for mine; mine stretched out for hers, but still we couldn't touch.

After a while, I could feel salty tears coming out of my eyes. They burned my face. Then I could hear the roar of the ocean again, while images of Chris and Paulie kept fading in and out.

There were voices in the background. Confused and whispering. They got louder. I tried to move away from them. But I felt arms getting wrapped around me. Huge arms. Then strong fingers were forcing my eyelids open. A bright light pierced the black clouds. Like a midnight sun. Which was a title of a poster I remembered. Then I heard someone scream from inside of me. *Chris don't leave me.*

27

My body felt numb.

I heard the clanging of a pail and two loud voices talking with heavy West Virginia accents. I kept my eyes tightly closed, pretending that I was asleep.

Now I heard a man talking. "The supervisor said the corners needed to be cleaned."

"When did you find out about this?" a female voice asked.

"This morning," the man answered. "He said that some doctor reported that the corners in this wing were filthy. Now we have to do this whole damn floor."

There was a long pause; the female voice didn't respond, so the man continued. "He told me I've got to finish all these rooms on this side before lunch."

Then I heard a toilet flushing, a swishing mop, whispering, a door slamming shut, trays being rolled, and a Doctor Hubert or something like that being paged.

I opened my eyes. Everything seemed hazy for a while. Then things became sharper. I made out a metal stand at the foot of my bed with a large portable color TV on top. The picture was on, but the sound was off. I watched a short, overstuffed, middle-aged woman, who was dressed up like an ostrich, clap her hands rapidly together in a prayer-like position. Now she was jumping up and down around the host of the show, who smiled embarrassed at her antics. The next image was of a large red, white, and blue box. Then the picture switched back to the clapping and jumping overstuffed woman, then back to the box, then back to her, and then to a shapely frosted-haired model who was standing in front of a shiny red, compact car. That blew the woman's mind, as she now tried to hug and kiss the host who kept backing away.

At this point, I lost interest and started to look over the room. The walls were painted a cheerful light green color while the linoleum floor contrasted in a darker shade of green. It was not the kind of room that one expected to find in a hospital. But the Lysol, which I now got a whiff of, didn't surprise me. I hated it. The pervasive smell of all hospitals. I always thought that underneath that supposedly clean and sterile smell was the smell of death.

As I moved my hand, I felt some pinching and pain. There was one tube penetrating my wrist and another near my elbow. Plastic bags were hanging over the tubes, dripping yellow liquid into them.

I blinked at the bright sunlight that came through a large picture window. The brilliant sun made the small, white, frame houses stand out in the distance. Behind the houses were the beautiful West Virginia hills. In the foreground, to the right, stood a large-humped hill, covered with yellowish-brown grass, as if it were still winter. On top was a short, gnarled tree trunk with bare branches, twisted and bent out of shape.

I kept staring at the tree for a long time, as it stood alone against the clear blue sky. I thought its soul had left it a long time ago, while its body stayed behind to decay like everything else in this world. Then I thought how great a photo of this scene would be on the front cover of my book.

These thoughts were comforting me when suddenly the door to the room swung open. The good-looking doctor, whom I'd seen about my stomach problems, walked in, with a slim blond-haired, sad-faced nurse not far behind.

"How you feeling?" she asked strongly.

"Okay, I guess," I said sluggishly. "It seems like I've been sleeping for days."

"You have," she smiled confidently, "four to be exact. I do realize you've had more than your share of troubles lately."

I wondered what a normal share of troubles was. I imagined scientists trying to measure troubles in a test tube.

She continued, "You lost a lot of blood from the cut on your left forearm and from a nasty bleeding stomach ulcer. We gave you six transfusions. The other cuts on your face and legs were superficial and are healing nicely. But that ulceration inside of you worries me. I think we've stopped it, but I want to make sure. We're going to keep you on your IVs for another couple of days."

Then she looked at the neat string of tiny stitches on my left forearm. "We'll take these out in a few days. It looks super."

I nodded.

"Again, let me say this," she said, full of professional authority, "we'll watch that thing inside to see if it heals or not. If it doesn't, I'm afraid we're going to have to operate."

I tried to look concerned, even though the idea of someone slicing open my gut made very little difference to me now. In fact, in a way, the thought excited me.

"Also, I told Nurse Frances, no visitors for at least two days until we see what happens. For now we'll keep you fairly well sedated to help you with your pain. Be sure to let her know if the pain gets worse."

With a sad demeanor, Nurse Frances wrote something on the clipboard she was carrying. I would find out that Nurse Frances did everything with a sad demeanor.

I noticed that her breasts were awfully large for such a slim body. And the crow's feet at the corners of her eyes and lips indicated to me that she must have gone through a great deal of suffering in her life. I hope, I thought, we'll get a chance to talk.

Nurse Frances was very efficient, as she now skillfully changed one of the IV bags that the good-looking doctor felt was not quite right.

Afterwards, I wondered if the good-looking doctor ever got sick. *She looked so damn healthy. Probably not. She probably gets stronger by watching people cringe in pain and die. Sure, the sicker her patients become, the stronger she becomes. A modern-day vampire. Yes.*

I thought, like Longo, the Boston funeral director, our good-looking doctor is outside the play, while also inside, directing the melodramatics of their players in today's hospitals. And what makes it even more attractive for her is that she has the right to flirt with the divine and supernatural. Lucky bitch. I wondered if I would ever get a chance to flirt with the divine and supernatural.

Another nurse entered and told me that I needed to save my urine when I went to the bathroom.

"Save it," I repeated.

"Yes," she laughed, as she nervously straightened out the sheets on my bed.

"I'll pick it up in the morning," she said. Then she left.

I was repulsed by the thought.

Later in the day, Jarvis came by. He had told Nurse Frances that he was a friend of mine and had come all the way from Europe to visit me. He said she wasn't impressed. I knew she wouldn't be. But, he said, she finally relented.

"I can only stay for a few minutes," he said. "I promised her. She looks mean and bitchy."

"S... She is," I stuttered. Damn pills, I thought.

I could tell from the look on Jarvis's face that I looked terrible. I needed to have a look at myself in the mirror.

"I wanted to see you," he said. "I thought what I had to tell you will cheer you up. It's about a memo that a group of us wrote to the whole department."

"Fine," I said, trying to speak clearly. I hated stuttering.

"Marilyn and I wrote most of it."

Of course, I was right about them hooking up.

"I'll tell you, Vinnie, we spelled it out in very clear terms, how upset we were with the decision-making process in the university. And we also indicated how inconsistent Art has been over the years. I especially pointed out how some professors only teach six hours, while others like myself have to teach fifteen. And I wrote that if we're going to be a democratic faculty, like Art says we are, we should be involved in making these kinds of decisions. I heard the dean is really pissed off and is in the process of writing a lengthy response to our charges. And this makes me happy as shit. We got them on the defensive now. And that's what we want."

I really don't give a shit, please go, go!

"Good, Jar," I said.

Then Jarvis went on to tell me how close he and Marilyn had become since writing the memo. By the way, he inserted, Karen and Julie were asking about you. Then he shifted back and talked about how the majority of the faculty in the college of arts and sciences were behind him. "They're ready to meet the challenge too. In a few more days, you'll be out of here, and you'll be able to give us more direction. Your courage to stand up to him was the major trigger. By the way, we are all sorry about Chris and Linda."

"Thanks." *I wish he would go away. It hurts to talk.*

Sad-faced Nurse Frances came in and fussed with my pillows, until he got the hint to leave.

"I'd better go," he said. "I'll see you tomorrow."

"Okay," I said, as he went out the door.

As Nurse Frances changed my IVs, she said, "People are like vultures."

"Yes."

I tried to remember when I thought the same thing, but I was too tired to think now. The pain in my stomach was back. She gave me a shot. I asked her what it was. She said morphine. Soon, the warm liquid that was spreading through my blood brought the swirling black clouds. *Thank you, Nurse Frances.*

I slept. I slept without dreaming.

On the seventh day, I started to feel a little bit stronger. The pain in my stomach was still there, but it had been dulled by the daily shots of morphine.

Jarvis was still stopping by each day, to report on the progress of his efforts "to make the university more responsive to its faculty members." *I just wish he'd leave me alone. I don't care anymore about the university and all that shit.*

Even Fay, my secretary, started to drop in, once in the morning and once in the afternoon. She was very concerned. She brought student registration forms that needed to be signed, dissertations and comprehensive exams that needed to be read, letters from publishers that needed to be answered, surveys from university committees that needed to be filled out. On and on it went. She told me that I was feeling too sorry for myself, and if I kept occupied with the business of the university, it would get my mind off myself, and then I would get better quicker. She said she had received many calls from students and faculty asking about me.

Shit, I thought, in no time there will be thousands of vultures descending upon me. There was no escaping them.

I did get a small chuckle out of a memo Art wrote concerning the switching from cups to cans in the Coke machine. He wrote, "if ecologically there are problems, cups will be my only choice." I was glad, I told Fay, that Art was still making important departmental decisions.

She laughed. Then she started to read to me a ten-page memo the dean wrote in response to Jarvis's memo. Terrible. Really bad. Not one sentence made any sense. Worse than Art's writing. I stopped her somewhere in the middle of it and told her to go through the rest of the stuff and take back to the office with her anything that dealt with the university. That included the dissertations and comprehensive exams that I was supposed to read.

She did it quickly and efficiently. She placed the stuff I didn't want in a large shopping bag she had brought with her, leaving me on the bedside table cards from well-wishers, bills from bookstores, an invitation to present a paper in Dallas, and a letter from Tatum.

However, afterwards, she went on to give me another lecture on brooding over things. She said she didn't think it was a good idea to bring all these things back to the university but she would. I assured her that I was doing fine without them.

At that point she got up and started to admire some of the flowers people had sent. I hated them. They reminded me of Uncle Louie's funeral. Fay was just beginning to read who they were from when Nurse Frances came in.

"He needs to have his bed changed," Nurse Frances said in an icy tone.

"Oh, yes," Fay was flustered, "I've stayed too long already."

"I believe so," Nurse Frances added quickly. "Thank you."

Fay squeezed my hand, shot Nurse Frances an angry glance, and left. Someone else was competing with Fay's overprotectiveness, and she didn't like it. Not one bit.

After Nurse Frances changed my bed, she flashed a half smile just before she went out the door. I thought she understood. She understood about Fay. We had something in common now.

Then I picked up the letter from Tatum, opened it and slid out two typewritten pages on stationery that had "Logan's Art Gallery" on the letterhead. It read,

Dear Vinnie,

I'm writing this two hours after you called. I just had to. First of all I want to apologize for not being more friendly on the phone. There were too many people around. You should understand that. Next, let me say that there are no words to explain how I feel after leaving my job and taking on my new responsibilities. No more being hassled by turkey lawyers who think because you're a woman all you're good for is to go to bed. No more kissing their asses just to get a "20 cents raise." No more "running" to get their coffee. No more any of that shit. I'm through with that. Finally, Vinnie, I have won my freedom, my independence and there are no words to describe my feelings within. A week ago, I broke down in tears of happiness for the first time in my life, and my friend was totally taken aback because he had never seen me like that before, he had only seen it in the movies.

At last, Vinnie, I'm being respected as a Human Being. Nick Logan, who runs the gallery, has been just great to me. He's willing to teach me all the insides of the business. Although I really love my teaching in night school and my students, I also knew I wasn't truly satisfied. That's when a parent of one of my students introduced me to Nick Logan and his friend Peter Markson, who's his partner. The business world, Vinnie, is an exciting place. The challenges for a woman are unlimited. I think my qualifications are just as good as any man's. That's why I could not just teach all my life. I need to do more. Power, ego, influence, money, or whatever are all involved, and I love it.

Vinnie, you don't know how happy I am and I would very much like to see you and share my happiness with you, but if and when I do, I would be very nervous, even thinking about it makes me nervous. I guess it's because I made such an ass out of myself at the airport that time. Every time I think about it, it gets me depressed.

Vinnie, I do love you very much and always will and I hope that doesn't offend you or scare you. You will always have the upper hand in that. I can honestly say I need to see you. But that has to be your decision. But let me also say this, that when I needed to have you, you left me. But I can understand it better now than I could then. If you want to see me, I'll be waiting with open arms.

I am so sorry about Chris and your daughter. They are in my thoughts and prayers.

I hope to see you soon.

I love you,

Tatum

I wondered about Chris and Linda's funeral. I can't think about it now. But her words, "you will always have the upper hand," ran through my mind, as I reached over to the bedside table, picked up the phone, and called Tatum.

A man answered. He said she was in New Orleans on business. He asked who I was. A friend, I said. Oh, he answered in an unfriendly tone of voice.

After I hung up, I decided I couldn't blame him for being so unfriendly. If I was in the same position and knew that someone was trying to move in on my hot nympho, I would act the same way.

Chris and Linda are dead, and I feel nothing. What's wrong with me? All I can think of is getting another fuck.

The next day, as I was walking out of the bathroom feeling sick because of the smell and the look of the watery yellowish stuff I just flushed away, Frank came in.

I could see that the smell and the way I looked made him nervous. Slowly, I got back into bed. He looked great. Healthy and alive. I wondered how things were going between him and

Wanda. Then I wondered, why she hadn't come to see me. Perhaps she had, and I just couldn't remember.

"Holy shit, Vinnie," he said, "I thought you were dead. All I was able to say to Wanda was that poor son of a bitch. And when the ambulance drove off with you to the hospital, I thought we would never see you alive again." He looked at me with eyes full of pity. I hated him.

"Next time, I'll make it," I said coldly.

He didn't hear my response. He went on talking about a new coal mine he was buying near Elkins, and how he was getting involved in coal gasification. "The energy savior of the future," he said.

I prayed that he would leave, as he now talked about being forced by the federal government to give blacks a break on the coal miners test. Then he talked about his son being selected captain of his Little League team. Then he talked about the deplorable potholes in our streets. On and on he went.

"That's good," I interrupted him in the middle of a sentence, hoping he would stop.

But he didn't; he just changed the subject. "Hey, I met your mother and father the other day at your house, and also that good-looking aunt of yours. They said they're going to be taking care of you when you come home."

"Tell them to fuck off," I snapped angrily, fighting the memories that were trying to move into my mind.

"Jesus, Vinnie, they're just trying to be nice," he said, shocked. "They took care of all those things that were not so nice."

"What things?" I asked, raising myself up and leaning on my elbows.

"Well, things that are not so good to talk about," he said, glancing left and then right, and avoiding contact with my eyes.

"I'm a big boy now, Frank, you can tell me," I said, not really wanting to know, as the muscles in my face tightened.

"Look, Vinnie," he said sternly, "one of the reasons why your parents and aunt haven't come to see you is because the doctor told them you weren't ready for the family. She thought friends would be easier to handle. But God, Vinnie, you're making it awful tough."

"I'll try to do better, Daddy," I laughed, leaning back against the pillows.

"For Christ's sake," Frank exploded, "you shithead, we've all been trying to make it easier for you. How could you make a joke out of this?"

"Hey, Frank, you fuck off."

"You're unbelievable," he said with disgust. "Here I am trying to be a helpful friend, and you..." He stopped suddenly, as if he didn't want to finish the thought. He began again. Very mad. "I know it hasn't been easy, man, but maybe it might help to think of someone else."

"I will when I decide who I am, and where I am," I said.

"What?" he asked, with a blank look.

"Oh, nothing, Frank, just leave me alone, I'm tired."

I closed my eyes, turned over and buried my head in the pillow.

Frank muttered something. Then, after a few minutes, I opened my eyes, turned over, and he was gone. Now Nurse Frances was standing there with my Valium.

Sometime during the night, I woke up perspiring. The hospital gown was sticking to my skin. The covers were on the floor. I was shivering. I looked to my right for Chris. For a moment I thought I was home. I remembered our lovemaking that night. Soon after my head started to ache, and the pain in my stomach was back. I rang for the night nurse. She gave me a shot of morphine. The world became hazy again, and in five minutes all was black.

The following afternoon, Art, dressed in a loud green leisure suit, came to visit. He looked like he was approaching my coffin.

"I just knew something was wrong, Vinnie," he said, as his mouth jerked over to the right. "Oh, and I'm so sorry about Chris, Linda, and everything. How much can a guy take?"

"I don't know." *Another asshole... leave, please, please.*

"The nurse out at the station told me I could only stay for a few minutes. She said you had a bad night."

"Sort of," I said.

"Well, I just wanted to see how you were doing," he said. "I won't stay long. I thought it might make you feel better if I told you that both the dean and the president agree with me, that you're the best one to head up the Mathematical Hall of Fame Project." He paused, flashed a benevolent smile, and went on. "We want you to get us a slice of all that federal money that's floating around."

"Sure," I lied. Thoughts of the last faculty and staff meeting flickered on and off in my mind.

"Think of what it will do for tourism in the state." He was excited.

"Yes." *Please leave.*

"That's why the Board of Regents is really interested in it."

"Right," I said.

"Hey, Vinnie," he said, with a smirk on his face, "can't you see those little old ladies who go on all the tours, staring in awe when they come to a room and find a man dressed up and looking exactly like Archimedes studying the stars?"

"Yes."

"I do too," he said, smiling confidently. And to make it even more real, just like they do in Williamsburg, we'll have Archimedes talk to them and demonstrate the formulas, the books, the maps, the measuring devices he's using in his works, et cetera. The Drama Department said they would develop a historic role-playing module. They're going to have their graduate students, along with ours, do research on the personalities of mathematicians like Archimedes. Of course, they want part of the grant. The arts are really hurting in the university."

"Of course," I said.

"Do you want me to send you a draft of the original proposal?"

"Not now," I said weakly.

"I won't bother you anymore," he said, looking sad because he knew he had. "I promised the nurse. Don't forget to tell Fay if you need anything from the office."

"I will," I said.

"Take care."

He left.

That night, they decided to operate. While a male nurse with red hair was shaving my chest, the good-looking doctor came in.

"I don't understand," she said, shaking her lovely head, "You seemed to be coming along so well."

"I don't either," I said.

"The human body is a perplexing organism. One never fully understands it. But you've had a lot going on. Almost too much."

"True."

"Well, don't worry," she said, in a more confident tone, "I haven't lost anyone yet in this type of operation. Not that it's as easy as taking out your appendix, you understand."

"Yes."

She then went on to describe the procedure and the reasons for operating on my stomach ulcer, but I didn't hear very much of it. My preoperative morphine shot was soon bringing sleep.

For days, it seemed that faces and voices were moving in and out of a thick fog. Fay looking distracted; Jarvis whispering in my ear that what I needed was a good screw; Nurse Frances grimly asking me to cough, cough; good-looking doctor saying it went fine. Then I thought I saw my mother, crying; Aunt Concetta, smiling warmly; and my father, brooding.

The nights were the worst. The stabbing pains in my stomach always got worse then. Also, I started to have hammering headaches. However, I tried not to complain. I didn't want the nurses to think I was weak and uncourageous, especially Nurse Frances.

During this foggy period, I remembered one night shivering with cold, and dreaming that I was teaching. I saw the students sitting there, like always, some with faded jeans on, some with T-shirts hanging loosely on their pale, skinny bodies. They looked bored, like always. I saw a small bony hand being raised like a wave. I recognized the wave. "I don't understand it, Dr. Serrano," said the voice that belonged to the wave, "could you connect it with something you said yesterday." "Sure," I said. Then I saw myself, like a nimble gymnast, jumping on the table where my lecture notes were. Next, I saw myself dropping my pants, turning around so my back was facing the students, pulling down my powder-blue jockey shorts until they were underneath my cheeks, and then laughing wildly. I saw myself repeatedly pointing to my ass and shouting, with my head twisted to one side, "Assholes, this is what the connections are about, study it good and hard." The faces of my students looked still bored. Afterwards I saw myself pulling up my powder-blue jockey shorts, kicking off my pants into their bored faces and jumping off the table onto the floor. When I came down, I assumed the crouched position of a karate fighter. My arms were stiff, forming right angles, and my hands were wide open in a chopping position. Then I saw myself slice the air with short, quick strokes and yell, "Ya, ya, this is the lecture for today, ya, ya... you jerks!" Then I saw myself straighten up and assume my normal calm lecture position, stroking my chin with one hand. I started to talk about how watery stuff felt, as it dripped down the insides of your legs. Then, as if someone had taken hold of my body, I jumped up in the air, and when I came back down, I was in the karate position again. "Ya, ya, you fucks, I dare you to question my shit." Then I got to laughing so hard, I couldn't breathe. *I was choking. Why can't I breathe?* Everything started to get stuffy. *I felt hot now. Terribly hot. Help.*

I opened my eyes. A tall nurse with thick glasses was trying to force a white plastic tube into my mouth, as she demanded, "Please breathe in, breathe in!" I refused, and bit deep into the tube. *I was sure she was working for Jimmy.* Around me, I could see white-uniformed people, working silently and nervously. Then one of them started to stick a tube up my penis; another one started to stick a tube in my wrist; another one with the strength of Hercules shoved a tube the size of a peashooter up my nose. *They all worked for Jimmy.* I gagged. Now I waited for the tiny piece of meat to come quickly flying through. But nothing happened, except for wanting to tickle an itch that seemed to be buried deep in my stomach. In a few minutes, I saw the tube in my nose filling up with puss and phlegm.

"Breathe in, breathe in," the nurse still pleaded with me.

Mechanical and docile now, I opened my mouth and swallowed a cool mist that felt like an ice-cold drink going down my throat.

"Thank God," someone said, a thousand miles away.

I had pneumonia.

The good-looking doctor said one of my lungs had collapsed. She also said that any major operation like I had traumatizes the body and because of this we just don't know how all patients will react. Some have no problems, she said, while others, like you, run into all sorts of problems. It all deals with the body chemistry. She went on to say that we know very little of it, but hopefully, in the future we'll have a better understanding of it. *Wonderful, I thought sarcastically. I hated the word* hopefully. *What does it really mean?*

Then she said that my temperature for three straight nights got up to 105, but was now leveling off between 101 and 102, which was still not good.

"Absolutely no visitors," she emphasized, "you must have complete rest and quiet. I can't believe you had so many people come in and out of here. People are part of your problem. Can't they see you're a sick man? Hell, we've got to get you on your feet again. I want you to concentrate on getting yourself better, and nothing else. Forget the people, the job, the problems, everything except yourself."

"I'll try." *How can I forget Chris, Paulie, my little Paulie, and beautiful Linda?*

In the afternoon, during the period when I was sequestered from the vultures, I especially liked watching the TV soap operas with the sound off. Even though I was in a constant state of grogginess, I would concentrate really hard on the TV picture when some guy was making it with a girl. I would dream that I was the guy and the girl was Nurse Frances. I needed to be laid so bad. I could tell Nurse Frances was the type that I could lay without ever worrying about making a commitment to her. And that's what I needed now. I needed to forget everything.

Finally, I started to feel stronger, after my temperature had been normal for a few days. That afternoon, I even decided to shave. Of course, Nurse Frances stood by. She was now working the three-to-eleven shift.

"The crazy shift," she said grimly. "Everyone seems to get worse during those hours."

When I looked into the mirror and saw the dark, dark circles under my blood-shot eyes and the brown scabs on my face, I winced and turned away. I was skinny, skinnier than before, and really old looking.

After a few minutes, I got the courage to look in the mirror again and finish shaving. I remarked to Nurse Frances about the large amount of gray hair dominating my head.

She replied, "I heard, for every gray hair that falls out a new hair grows in stronger and with its original color."

"Is that right?"

"Yes."

The next day, the tall nurse with the thick glasses told me that I was allowed to have visitors again, but they couldn't stay very long. She added, "We can't afford another attack of pneumonia, could we now?"

"No," I said. I hated being treated like a little child.

After she left, I decided I would sit up in the heavy, padded lounge chair beside the window. Once the vultures start coming, I thought, I won't have a chance.

Outside, the day looked hot and humid. The blacktop of a road in the distance shimmered with heat waves. I looked down at the hospital parking lot underneath my window. I could see a nurse unlocking her car door. From the back, she looked pretty. Her honey-colored hair spilled loosely over her shoulders, and her ass was tight and firm. I wanted to see her face; sometimes good-looking asses have ugly faces. The girl now got into her shiny green car, backed out, and drove off. I thought about working out a deal with her, so I could escape from here. I envied her freedom.

Later, streaks of yellow sunlight and the heat penetrating the windowpane crept over to my chair, making it very uncomfortable to sit there. So I stood up, walked over and lay down on the bed again. The TV was on. A freckle-faced girl with glinting eyes was giving the news. I wanted to meet her and tell her how beautiful her eyes were. I thought she was probably so busy that she doesn't have anyone around to tell her that. I started to drift off to sleep, with images of her interviewing me, and then afterwards saying, "God, why are you so damn handsome?" Then I was being kissed on the cheek by a woman. The lips were cold. I opened my eyes and saw my mother standing over me. She was dressed in the same black dress she wore at Uncle Louie's funeral, with tears in her eyes. *Fuck. No...*

"How are you feeling, Vinnie?" my mother asked with concern.

"Okay, getting there."

Aunt Concetta, who was on the other side of the bed now, leaned over, smiled, and kissed my other cheek. Her smile was fake. She was dressed in a bright-blue pants suit, and she was still as elegant-looking as ever. A feeling of lust suddenly crept into my mind.

"Hi, dear," Aunt Concetta said.

"Hi," I said.

"Are you eating?" my mother asked.

"Yes."

"Well, you'd better," she said, in a demanding motherly voice, "I'm so worried about you."

"Don't be."

"Are they feeding you good here?"

Questions, Questions, Questions, the wonderful method to keep your distance. She was so damn good at it. Why didn't you ever tell me 'I love you'? I always felt like a piece of furniture that needed to be polished and cleaned. Why couldn't you love me?

"I'm on a bland diet, Mom," I said, wishing she would stop. "Eggs, cereal, baby food, and stuff like that."

"What will I cook for you when you come home?"

Oh, shit.

"Anna," Aunt Concetta interrupted, in a reassuring manner, "don't worry about those things. There's a hospital dietitian who will help you plan his meals. Isn't that right, Vinnie?"

I nodded, yes. *Chris, I love you.*

"I don't know what I'll do," my mother said, as if she hadn't heard what Aunt Concetta had said.

"I don't know what..." Now my mother stopped in the middle of her sentence.

"Vinnie, do you want me to get someone from the Harvard Medical School to examine you?" Aunt Concetta broke in with authority, as if she was waiting for my mother to falter. "I know a couple of doctors over there. I'll even fly them in."

"No thanks, Aunt Concetta," I said. "They're treating me fine."

"Now it's no trouble, I'll be glad to get one of them to come," she insisted.

"I know you would," I said, trying to sound grateful, "and I really appreciate it, but I'm really satisfied with the care they're giving me here."

My mother sat down in a chair next to the bed. She was crying. "Look at him, Concetta, he looks so pale, my God. We had the funeral. Chris's parents insisted. They felt we would have a large memorial mass when you came home." She was crying uncontrollably now.

Quickly Aunt Concetta went over to her, patted her on the shoulders, and handed her one of her infamous black silk handkerchiefs. "Don't worry, Tree," she said softly, "once we get him home, we'll put some color back into him."

After consoling my mother, Aunt Concetta came back to the side of my bed, reached over and patted my hand warmly. "Please understand, Vinnie, your mother has been under a great deal of strain of late, and your father, I don't know. He's just getting like Uncle Louie was, talking stupid and saying hateful things all the time." There was a mocking tone in her voice. "He said we're destroying him. And that we'll do the same thing to you. Listen to such foolishness." She shook her head suddenly. "You know, he's waiting in the lobby for us to go before he'll come up to see you. A sad, sad man. I just can't believe how he has changed since Uncle Louie's death. It's like he sees his role now to become as miserable as Uncle Louie was, and to make everyone else around him just as miserable."

I wondered why she always called her husband "Uncle Louie."
Was it easier to deal with him as if he were a family problem, and
not her own individual problem?

"These are not the kinds of things we should be talking to you
about with you lying here in the hospital," she said, trying to be
apologetic.

"That's okay," I said.

"These are difficult times for all of us," she said, patting my
hand again.

"Yes," I said.

"You know, Vinnie," she said, resting herself against the bed,
and looking straight into my eyes, "I just don't know why you didn't
tell us all about Paulie until weeks later. When your mother told
me about Chris and Linda, I took right off from work. My boss was
very nice about it. Of course, like any other businessman, there
was an ulterior motive behind his compassion." Now she hit her
stride: "Anyway, he thought it may be a good opportunity for me
to check out the possibilities for opening up a major office around
here in West Virginia. He said that futurologists predict that the
state will became a haven for creative writers. Sort of like one huge
national park, except the park in this case would be a place where
writers could live and write, and not worry about being mugged,
murdered, raped, or whatever. Another thing he said, which was
very interesting, is that the federal government may decide to do
what Ireland does, subsidize the country's writers if they live in a
place like West Virginia. It can be what Paris was for the artists in
the Twenties and Thirties."

Go away, please...

"Sounds good," I said, wishing her boss had come instead of
her. "Where do you think you'll locate your office?"

"I don't know yet," she said. "There are some ideas that I have
about making West Virginia a new kind of model for the publishing
world. For instance, let's say we make Wheeling the major office,
then I could see certain small towns in the state having branch
offices where writers could come in with their manuscripts and get
immediate feedback from an editor. Also, I could see all the edi-

tors at Apollo being required to do a so-called tour of duty in one of these branch offices. It would be a great change and learning experience for all of us. I talked with Jimmy about this before I left, and he said he liked it. He said he wished there was something like that available for actors. Oh, I almost forgot," she said, slapping her forehead with the palm of her hand and looking up at the ceiling, "Jimmy told me to tell you he's planning to come and see you in a week or so. I guess he wants to stay with us, while he's trying out for a movie they're making nearby in Pittsburgh. He said Robert De Niro is acting in it. I hope Rose and Patsy also come. I miss them. You know, they all love you like a brother, Vinnie."

"I know," I said, feeling a slight trace of guilt coming over me as I thought about Jimmy killing his father. But really I was surprised how little it was. *Almost indifferent now.*

"Candy also asked about you," she said. "That poor girl, I feel so sorry for her. I don't know why she needs so many men."

Now, resting half on and half off the bed, she leaned over and whispered, "I hope, Vinnie, you can be of some help if we move down here from Boston."

"How?" I asked.

"I want you to be one of our consulting editors."

"I don't know," I said wearily.

"Oh, I don't need an answer now," she said quickly, "but Jimmy did it for a while and he loved it. He told me he learned more from that job than from any of those schools he went to. I think if you help me out, we'll be able to publish your book that you talked to me about without any trouble. You see, once you're considered to be working for us, it's kinda difficult to reject one of your own people's manuscripts," she smiled slyly and then winked.

"Okay," I said.

"Good," she said, pushing herself up and sitting on the bed. "But before we talk about these kinds of things, we must talk about something else."

"What?"

"About your mother," she said. Then with one hand on either side of my stomach, she leaned over to get closer to my face.

I looked over to my mother; her head was still lowered and she sniffled quietly now, looking out the window.

"Yes?" I asked, meaning for her to go on.

"Vinnie, my dear," she said, firmly but softly, "you must do what you have to do. Jimmy had to do it. I won't have your mother go through what I did. I love her too much."

She wants me to murder my father, shit...

"My God, I can't..."

"Shhh," she said, bringing her forefinger up to her closed lips and quickly looking back at my mother. "I even think, he'll be happier. Really."

"I just don't know, I don't know," I said, in a scared whisper. "I can't."

She winked again and flashed an unbelievably genuine, warm smile. "Don't worry, my dear nephew, you got a lot of time to think about it. You'll see when you come home, how bad he really is."

They can't expect me to do that. They can't.

Now Aunt Concetta slid off the bed, stuck her hand into a dark leather purse, pulled out a large, somewhat wrinkled, brown envelope, and placed it on the bed near my hand.

"We'll see how good you are on your first job as our consulting editor," she said, in a friendly-like voice. "The writer is Matt Ziegler, the one I told you Jimmy liked. He just sent this new manuscript to us."

The devil has many faces.

"We'd better go," she said, smiling and patting my hand. "I don't want you to get more sick."

After they left, I had to go to the bathroom. The stabbing pains in my stomach were back. When finished, I looked down. No blood. I flushed it away. Fuck it, there was very little I could do about my life, and where it was going. I would let it run its course. My mind had other important things to grapple with, especially now that I had a chance to publish my book on Heaven. Hell, somehow I just knew, things inside my mind were part of the expanding consciousness that would help men all over the world to find Heaven. And what happens in this world makes little difference. I knew this for so long, but now I was going to actually practice it. *Here I come, Heaven. Chris, be happy for me.*

Feeling tremendously light, I got back into bed and thought how I would combine ideas of cosmic energy with God-Energy and us being one, and that's the heaven I will write about. We're connected to everything, and once we fully realize this, we transcend to a higher consciousness of heaven.

Then the door opened, and nutsy Father Luke walked in.

"Hi, Vinnie," he said. His voice was full, bouncy, like a child's. "The nurse said I could visit you for a few minutes. Okay?"

"Okay," I lied.

He stood at the foot of the bed and looked at me with that fucking pious smile on his face. He wore his Roman collar over a bright-yellow frilled shirt. And over that he wore a golf jacket, with the words "Wheeling College" written on the left breast.

"God, what a difference," he said. "I saw you right after you came out of the operation, and you looked terrible then. Thank God you're getting better. I couldn't stand to see you that way. Do you need anything, Vinnie?" he asked.

"No," I said. *Please go.*

"The nurse told me that they're thinking of sending you home in a week," he said. "But I guess, according to her, you're going to need a lot of rest. I wonder if you would like to come to our parish house for a while and rest. It's quiet and peaceful there."

"No, thanks," I said. "Listening to people singing and greeting each other with Hallelujahs and Praise the Lords, wouldn't be my idea of resting."

"You'd get used to it," he said smiling, "and perhaps, who knows, you might even join in."

"Sure," I said sarcastically.

"Why not?" he demanded. "I think, after staying with us for a couple of days, you might see, like Chris understood, that once you have Jesus, you want to share it with the people around you. The joy of Jesus is wonderful. I think Chris is here with us." He was excited.

"Chris?" I asked angrily.

"Yes," he said, "only through Jesus can you be saved. Only through his teachings and love can we be reborn again. And you can find Chris again!"

"I can't believe this," I said. "Get the fuck out of here."

He blushed, frowned a bit, and continued. "And I believe that people who haven't taken Jesus cannot live without him. I don't know about others. Jesus Christ will unite all religions in the end. He's ecumenical. The Charismatic movement just had a meeting in Rome where Episcopalians, Baptists, Methodists, Roman Catholics, and Presbyterians from all over the world joined together under the banner of Jesus Christ. I was there, and one day when we were on our knees, I could feel the spirit of Jesus Christ uniting us. Praise the Lord! I can't describe it, just that Jesus was there saying 'I love you, I love you, my people.'"

"Please go," I said weakly.

Just go. Asshole. Just go.

"Peace be with you," he said. He patted my leg and left.

Later, Nurse Frances was taking my temperature when the door slowly opened and my father came in. It was almost evening. The room was gray. The light made him look pale and old, as he walked over to the bed and nodded sadly. I mumbled hello.

Nurse Frances took the thermometer out of my mouth and noted the temperature on the chart at the foot of the bed.

He smiled politely and shook her hand. Then she came over to me again and handed me a Valium and a tiny paper cup of Maalox to wash it down with.

Afterwards, she whispered, "Do you want a back rub tonight?"

"Yes."

The time has come. Unbelievable. See, Dad, just like you, I have my whores.

She went to the door, opened it, turned, and looked at him. "Mr. Serrano, don't be long now."

"No, madam," he answered, in a soft tone of voice.

Then the door closed behind her.

Silence.

He seemed scared, as he stood away from the bed. His powerful built and confident soldier-like stature had vanished, and he seemed more bent over than the last time I had seen him. So he, too, was suffering. Welcome to the club. His tan sports jacket and the white shirt looked as if he had slept in them for days. His hair was grayer, thinner, and uncombed. He hadn't shaved in days, it seemed. I thought about the drunks who slept in the Boston Commons.

Finally he spoke, "I'm sorry, Vinnie," he said in a trembling voice. "It hurts my heart to see you like this." His eyes brimmed with tears. "I really loved Chris and the kids."

He started to move closer to the head of the bed, as if he was getting ready to physically touch me, but then suddenly he jerked back and said, "I tried to do everything that was right in this country. I worked hard, saved money, and put you through school. And people say, 'Mario Serrano is a good person.' I don't owe anyone any money. I pay all my bills. I try to be a good person, Vinnie." He was sobbing.

Stop it, Dad, I can't bear to see you cry, please, God, don't cry.

He wiped his tears away with one of his huge knuckles. "All morning and afternoon, I waited downstairs, trying to get up the courage to come up and tell you how sorry I am. I love you."

Tears also came to my eyes. *I do love you, too, Dad.*

I thought I don't know if it's love. I don't know if I can feel love... my life is too complicated with the obsessing with sex. Did I feel love for anyone? Did Chris and the kids love me? I think I was a good father and husband at times. Still, a lonely and sad life could be very dangerous.

"People think Mario Serrano looks healthy on the outside," he was saying. "A good, strong man. Sure, but, my son, inside they don't see the animal chewing away at his soul. Killing him. It's so hard," he said. "My life would've been nothing, except for you and my brother Louie. You'll never know the hate your mother has for me. A woman everyone thought was so wonderful treated me like dirt, especially after you went to college. As soon as you left for college I hardly saw her. She was always over to Concetta's, helping her or going someplace with her. Of course, when you came home on vacations, she stayed around to show you how much suffering she was going through. She's a great actor, you know."

"I wish I could've talked to you then, Dad," I said. "I have so many thoughts and dreams about those days. My whole life seemed to be split between the time before that night I saw you with that woman, and the time after. I often wondered about you and Mom. I really felt she was being very brave about everything."

"Brave, my ass. Listen, she rejected me when I came to her time after time. She said she didn't want to get started again then be rejected by me. I told her I was ready to come back. It was over with other women. She didn't believe me. That's why I went back to the other women. I had no one but them."

His eyes brimmed with tears again. He tightened his lips, the upper over the lower. "You look so sick. How I wish it could be me instead of you."

"Dad..."

"Vinnie, I'd better go now."

He leaned over, kissed me on the forehead, and rushed out.

I stared at the door as it closed behind him. I rolled over onto my side, facing the window, with my hands under my head, my knees pulled close to my chest. I stared at the dark outside. I'm like you, Dad.

"Turn over, please." I heard a voice in the background as if it was on the other side of a thick wall. "Please..."

I opened my eyes and slowly turned around in bed. Nurse Frances was standing over me. She smiled, sadly of course, and motioned for me to roll over onto my stomach.

I obeyed.

"Your father seems like a nice man?"

"Yes," I lied, "He is."

I was surprised how calm I was when I answered her. My thoughts of him were gentle again. I was starting to realize that there was nothing I could do about his women. We were both the same. I was always thinking about other women even when I was with Chris and the kids. Maybe that's why God took them away from me. Everything seemed to go away, the worries, the despair... the more preoccupied with sex and its pleasure the less I had to think about how sad I was. Suddenly, I began to cry as I remembered this and the love and devotion she had for me. She was a saint, and now I understood why people thought that. Then there is Linda, with her deep, penetrating blue eyes, She loved me but wouldn't take any shit from me. I pity the guy that falls in love with her. Crying more, I thought about Paulie, who just wanted my love and just wanted to be my buddy—for life. I now realized I had an unconditional love for my family. I didn't care what I might get for myself with them. Still crying, I tried to catch my breath.

"Are you feeling okay?" Nurse Frances asked, as she started to massage my back with long, soothing strokes. Her hands felt warm and strong.

"Yes," I said.

Concentrate on her, Vinnie, concentrate...

"Now relax and enjoy it. Forget everything else."

I remembered what Ouspensky once said—that the being dies and separates from this world to a higher consciousness. There everything is certain. Here in this world everything is doubt and insecurity until... In love we find other worlds....

Now she turned me over and cuddled in my arms. As I drew her closer, I thought about later. I would call the Boston Police and tell them about Aunt Concetta and Jimmy murdering Uncle Louie. But Jimmy was fucking family, so I don't know.

I kissed Nurse Frances on the forehead and smiled to myself.

Everything was good now, thank you, God.